DATE			

CONFLICT
OF
INTEREST

NANCY TAYLOR
ROSENBERG

CONFLICT
OF
INTEREST

HYPERION

New York

Library of Congress Cataloging-in-Publication Data

Rosenberg, Nancy Taylor
    Conflict of interest / Nancy Taylor Rosenberg.—1st ed.
      p.   cm.
    ISBN 0-7868-6620-9
    1. California, Southern—Fiction.   2. Public prosecutors—Fiction.   3. Women
lawyers—Fiction. I. Title.

    PS3568.O7876 C66   2002
    813'.54—dc21

                          2001039923

FIRST EDITION

10 9 8 7 6 5 4 3 2 1

This book is dedicated to Thomas Villani.

PROLOGUE

ELI CONNORS gazed up at the morning sky, watching as a flock of seagulls soared over his head. At forty-eight, he was a quiet, introspective man. With the exception of those who paid for his services, he didn't have much use for people.

The *Nightwatch* was anchored a short distance offshore, midway between the California cities of Ventura and Santa Barbara. Clasping a steaming mug of hot coffee in one hand, Eli took a sip, then lowered his head to the telescope mounted on the bow of the seventy-two-foot fishing vessel. The ship thrashed about in the choppy water, the waves pounding against the hull. A strong easterly wind had developed during the night, the primary reason the fog had lifted. The telescope was bobbing up and down, yet Eli had no trouble maintaining his balance. He stood six-foot-six and weighed three hundred pounds. Dressed in a white cotton T-shirt and drawstring flannel shorts, his feet encased in size seventeen deck shoes, his ebony skin glistened in the morning sunlight. The cold air didn't bother him. Eli had always been oblivious to temperature. Weather, however, was something he couldn't afford to ignore. For the past seven years, the sea had been his home.

Seacliff Point, the enclave where his subject resided, presented extensive surveillance problems as the houses were nestled among mature trees. With the Celestron Nexstar 8, an automated positioning telescope with pinpoint computer control and high-speed photo capability, he could track and record the movements of just about anything. He could not, however, track something the telescope could not see.

Eli's adrenaline surged as he caught a glimpse of the woman. She was frantically darting from one house to the other. A young girl he recognized as her daughter was standing next to a white Lexus, shouting and flailing her arms around. As he attempted to zoom in on the woman's face, she disappeared behind a large tree. "Damn," he said, knocking over his coffee mug as he spun the telescope around and started snapping pictures of the girl.

Had it not been for corrupt politicians, Eli Connors would be a high-ranking agent within the CIA. But that was the past, and the past couldn't be changed. To some degree, he relished the fact that he was no longer with the agency. Before he'd joined the CIA, he'd been a captain in the navy. He'd grown tired of taking orders, having people look over his shoulder, dealing with the inherent problems of government bureaucracies. His only regret was not bailing out sooner. In the private sector, Eli's skills were highly marketable.

With one hand resting on the telescope, he used his free hand to depress a button on what had once housed a refrigerated storage container, the type commercial fishermen used to store their bait and catch. Just as the storage container was not what it appeared to be, the *Nightwatch* was not really a fishing vessel. On the main deck, the boat was outfitted as a commercial ship, allowing movement from port to port without drawing unwanted attention. Below was enough sophisticated equipment to run a small country.

Even though he wasn't certain what was unfolding, Eli prepared to take action. In his line of work, there was no margin for error.

The electronic mechanism moved the fake cover on the storage container to one side. A metallic cranking sound was emitted as the Mk 45, a lightweight .54 caliber automatic weapon, rose and locked into place.

ONE

FOR TWO years Joanne Kuhlman had gone to bed each night not knowing whether her children were dead or alive. That morning, Leah, her fifteen-year-old daughter, had made her so angry that Joanne had felt like shipping her back to her father. Even if she'd been serious, the man was currently in jail and would more than likely be sentenced to prison.

Exiting her white Lexus, Joanne jogged toward the main entrance to the Ventura County courthouse. She wondered how many people in her office knew about the situation with her ex-husband. Worrying about gossip, she told herself, should be the least of her concerns. Her prayers had been answered—Leah and Mike had been located and returned. The fact that Doug's first trial would be held in Los Angeles was another reason she should be grateful. At least the divorce was final now. The papers had come through the previous month. Joanne had filed over a year ago, yet with Doug's whereabouts unknown, the proceedings could not be finalized.

At thirty-nine, Joanne was a petite and youthful-looking woman, with shoulder-length chestnut-brown hair, pronounced cheekbones, and large hazel eyes. Naturally slender, she self-consciously tugged on the hem of her jacket. In less than three months, she had gained ten pounds. People said she looked great. She didn't mind having a curvaceous body, but she couldn't afford to buy a new wardrobe.

Pushing her way through the heavy oak doors, Joanne leaned against the back wall to catch her breath. Leah was shifting from one behavioral problem to the next. The night before, she'd decided to go joyriding, then failed to turn the headlights off once she returned home. The battery on the Lexus had been dead that morning. With the help of their neighbor, Emily, Joanne had scrounged up a pair of jumper cables in the cluttered garage and managed to get the car started. The court hearing had been scheduled for nine, however, and it was already nine-thirty. Joanne was not only late, but she had a run in her nylons and a grease stain on the front of her turquoise blazer. Thrusting her shoulders back, she shook her hands to release the pent up tension, then strode briskly down the aisle to speak to the bailiff.

"Did Judge Spencer get my message?" Joanne asked, glancing over her shoulder at the defense attorney and his three clients. "My car . . ."

Officer John Shaw was a stone-faced redhead in his late twenties. He tapped his watch with his finger, his voice as flat as his personality. "The longer he waits . . ."

"Right," Joanne answered, feeling idiotic for offering an excuse, particularly to a bailiff. Unless something unexpected occurred, Shaw's job consisted of saying a few words and then standing around like a statue.

Shaw plucked a piece of chewing gum out of his mouth, wrapped it in a scrap of paper, then tossed it across the room into the trash can. "Are we ready?"

Joanne was leaning over, yanking her paperwork out of her green nylon backpack. Her co-workers made fun of her, telling her she looked more like a camper than an attorney. Compartmentalized to hold file folders as well as her laptop computer, the backpack had been a birthday present from her father. For years, she had lugged around heavy litigation cases or costly briefcases. Next month would mark her ten-year anniversary as a prosecutor. Image no longer mattered. All she cared about was distributing the weight evenly on her back. "No, John," she said facetiously. "I thought we'd just sit around and shoot the breeze for the next hour."

The bailiff's jaw dropped, but he knew to keep his mouth shut. Joanne Kuhlman might be slightly frazzled today, but she was a major player in the Ventura County judicial system. Although she'd declined for personal reasons, she'd been offered a judgeship the previous year. Everyone knew she was renting Judge Spencer's beach house, and had even become friends with the presiding judge's wife who lived next door.

Anne McKenzie, the court clerk, was a pretty blonde with dove-gray eyes and a pleasant disposition. Dressed neatly in a white shirt and black sweater, she took over for the bailiff. "Are you serious, Ms. Kuhlman? Should I buzz Judge Spencer or do you want us to wait for you to get organized? I've already called the jury room."

Picking up her pen and jotting down a few notes to herself, Joanne answered without raising her head. "I assumed you notified Spencer as soon as I got here." When she discovered her pen had run out of ink, she threw it aside and grabbed another one.

"I just thought . . ."

A muscle in Joanne's face twitched. She stared at the clock mounted on the wall over the clerk's console, the minutes clicking off inside her head. "I appreciate your consideration, Anne," she said, attempting to smile. "We should begin immediately, though, don't you think?"

Her neighbor had lectured her over the hood of her car that morning. "A human being can only take so much stress," Emily Merritt had told her. "You need to take yoga classes, meditate, book yourself a nice vacation."

Emily was married to the presiding judge, Kenneth Merritt, a man twenty years her senior and extremely wealthy. She knew Joanne's predicament. When you lived at Seacliff Point, everyone knew your business. The community consisted of only thirty-three homes, the lots so narrow, they could hear each other's toilets flushing.

Judge Kenneth Merritt had inherited the fifty-acre parcel of prime coastal real estate from an ancestor, then later sold lots to handpicked individuals, most of them friends or family members. Unlike Joanne, Emily spent her days shopping, sunbathing, or playing bridge at the only commercial establishment Merritt had allowed behind the gates at Seacliff Point, a spectacular structure he had named the Cove.

Perched on a cliff above the water, the Cove was shaped in the form of a star, with the rooms branching out in five different directions. The building was supported by enormous steel poles embedded deep in the core of the rock's surface. Merritt boasted that the Cove was sturdy enough to withstand a major earthquake.

For the residents of Seacliff Point, the Cove was their exclusive club. With the availability of on-line shopping, investing, and other computer-related technology, the residents never had to physically venture beyond the gates to the outside world. The Cove was their kitchen, their recreation room, their meeting place, their local pub, their ballroom. The way it was designed, a person could enjoy a sunset and watch the waves breaking on the shore directly below from all but two of the five public rooms.

Emily's intentions had been good when she spoke to Joanne that morning. Regardless of the differences in their lifestyles, Joanne liked the woman and enjoyed having her as a neighbor. But Joanne couldn't walk off her job or leave her kids to go on a vacation. Her ex-husband was facing child-stealing charges for abducting her children, along with a multitude of other crimes. Her children were home now, but the emotional damage Doug had inflicted would take years to overcome. Taking yoga classes wouldn't replenish her bank account. A second job might help. There weren't enough hours in the day, though, let alone enough energy.

The lovely home Joanne had owned in Ventura had been sold the previous year, the profits used to trace her children's whereabouts. Judge Spencer, the man she had kept waiting this morning, had been kind enough to let her use his beach house until she managed to get back on her feet financially. The clock was ticking there as well. In three months, she would have to find another place to live. While she was struggling to pay off her debts and become financially stable, her despicable ex-husband had a pile of money, more than likely stashed in an offshore bank account. The problem was finding it.

"Division 23 of the Ventura County Superior Court is now in session," the bailiff announced, his deep voice echoing in the courtroom. "Judge Richard Spencer presiding."

Spencer was a brilliant and well-respected judge. Joanne watched as he climbed the stairs to the bench, his black robes swirling around him. With his white hair and bushy beard, he resembled a good-natured grandfather. She heard two of the three defendants snickering across the room. They probably thought drawing Spencer as their trial judge meant they were in for an easy ride. They were in for a big surprise, Joanne smirked, feeling some of her earlier anxiety slipping away. Of all the Ventura County judges, Spencer was by far the most punitive. People swore he would send his own son to prison if he was certain he'd broken the law.

"The State of California versus Ian Decker, Thomas Rubinsky, and Gary Rubinsky," Spencer spoke into the microphone. "Case number A987243."

Joanne glanced over at the three defense attorneys. Arnold Dreiser, who was representing Ian Decker, was a tall, handsome man in his forties. Dreiser's area of expertise centered around medical malpractice. Rumor had it that his fees were astronomical. Not only did Dreiser hold a law degree from Harvard, he'd also served a year on the Los Angeles bench.

Gary Rubinsky was represented by Joseph Watkins, a public defender. At five-eight, Watkins had thinning blond hair, blue eyes, and a round face. Marilyn Cobb, Tom Rubinsky's attorney, was also a public defender. At twenty-seven, she had curly red hair, freckles, and was toothpick thin. Whereas Watkins had been a public defender for seventeen years and was a supervisor over his unit, Marilyn Cobb had only been with the agency for a year.

The case involved the December 16, 2000, armed robbery of a Quick-Mart convenience store. Since none of the defendants possessed criminal records as adults, the court had released them on bail. Ian Decker had never received so much as a parking ticket. The Rubinskys had committed numerous offenses as juveniles, all fairly minor, the majority having occurred during their early teens.

In the past, juvenile records were inadmissable in adult proceedings. Laws had recently been passed, however, that allowed the court to consider both the adult and juvenile histories of an offender when rendering decisions regarding bail or sentencing. As long as the defendant's juvenile offenses didn't involve acts of violence, or weren't reflective of a specific pattern of criminal behavior, Judge Spencer didn't attach a great deal of weight to them.

Two of the defendants, Ian Decker and Tom Rubinsky, were each twenty-one years old. They had been childhood friends who had only recently renewed their friendship. Tom's brother, Gary Rubinsky, was twenty-five. Neither of the Rubinskys had been employed during the past year, leading Joanne to suspect that they were far more entrenched in criminal activity than their records indicated.

Decker, on the other hand, had been attending welding classes at Franklin Junior College as well as holding down a job as a busboy. From what Joanne had been told, the Rubinskys' parents had disowned them, so they weren't getting money from home. This meant Ian Decker was the only one of the three who had any legitimate income prior to their arrest. The question that kept nagging at Joanne was how Decker had come up with enough money to hire Arnold Dreiser.

Joanne read through the list of witnesses, knowing she needed to focus on the business at hand. At least the trial was not fully under way, which would have made her tardiness even more serious. The present stage of the criminal proceedings was technically referred to as voir dire—the process of selecting a jury.

While a young Hispanic housewife was being questioned by Dreiser, Joanne's gaze drifted over to the three defendants. Ian Decker was a pale, meek young man, with dirty blond hair, a narrow face, and a dull look in his murky brown eyes. In contrast, the Rubinsky brothers stood over six feet, had bulging biceps and crude tattoos, their appearance more or less in line with the crime they were accused of committing.

From Joanne's experience, robbers looked and behaved like robbers. They moved around in their seats with restless energy, laughed inappropriately, and spoke when it was in their best interest to remain silent. Individuals who committed crimes such as homicides or rapes were harder to profile. The crime of robbery required a high degree of boldness. Fast money, she called it, especially when the suspects targeted a convenience store.

Robbery was on Joanne's list of what she called stupid crimes. It wasn't like a murder, where, in the majority of cases, the only witness was dead. When a person confronted their victim face-to-face, it was usually only a matter of time before they were apprehended. The odds grew even greater with convenience stores, gas stations, and establishments that stayed open late at night as most of these places had security cameras. The defendants in this case had lucked out. The videotape from the Quick-Mart had been so severely distorted, Joanne had decided not to introduce it as evidence.

The three scruffy defendants might not be bright, but they had nonetheless grown up in the technological era. According to the clerk at the Quick-Mart, Gary Rubinsky had pointed what appeared to be a cell phone at him, advising him it was actually a firearm. When the poor man decided to call their bluff, one of the Rubinsky brothers had pushed a button on the decoy phone and fired off a round. After several months of research, the ballistics division reported that the weapon the clerk described had first surfaced in Europe. Since it wasn't legal, the authorities knew the gun was being traded in the underground market. The police had not recovered this new deadly device during their search of the defendants' property, which would have made Joanne's job far easier. They had the bullet, though, so they had sufficient evidence to prove that the crime had been committed with the use of a firearm.

Seeing Ian Decker slouched in his seat, Joanne wondered if he was under the influence of narcotics, also a common denominator in most holdups. Decker turned around and stared at her. Joanne felt a chill, but it wasn't menace she saw in his eyes. He seemed to be attempting to communicate with her.

During breaks, the Rubinskys acted as if Decker didn't exist. He stood several feet away from the other men, his arms dangling at his sides. Crime partners were known to stick together for a number of reasons. Something about these men struck Joanne as strange.

Several more jurors were examined before Judge Spencer recessed for lunch. He removed his glasses and rubbed his eyes, a bedraggled look on his face. Voir dire was one of the more tiresome stages of the criminal process, and Arnold Dreiser seemed to have been moving at a snail's pace. "I'd like to accomplish something by the end of the day. We'll reconvene promptly at three," Spencer said, giving Joanne a stern look.

TWO

THE MOST memorable event in all of Ian Decker's twenty-one years had occurred the night before he'd driven Gary and Tom to the Quick-Mart. The most beautiful girl he'd ever seen had appeared on his doorstep.

It was late, almost midnight. Ian had already gone to bed. He was wearing a white cotton T-shirt and the bottoms to his green-and-blue flannel pajamas. His hair was rumpled and his eyes were puffy from sleep.

"My name is Trudy," the girl said, her voice soft and lyrical. "Gary Rubinsky said you might not mind if I spent the night here."

For a long time, Ian left her standing outside, gawking at her as if she were an apparition, certain if he blinked his eyes, she would disappear. She looked young, almost like a teenager. "Ah," he said, letting the word hang in the air, "how do you know Gary?"

"He's not my boyfriend or anything," she said coyly. "I met Tom and Gary years ago at a dance club." She thrust a paper-wrapped bottle with a bow on the top toward him. "Here's a little gift for you."

Ian clutched the bottle to his chest, his eyes feasting on her gorgeous face, her flawless skin, her shoulder-length black hair. She was not only real, she'd brought him a present! Even if it turned out he was dreaming, for once he'd found a dream he never wanted to end.

"My girlfriend dropped me off at this house about five blocks from here," Trudy told him. "The people were supposed to be having this big party. I must have got the date wrong. By the time I realized no one was home, my girlfriend was gone. I called Gary to see if he could give me a ride because I know he and his brother live around here. He said I should crash here tonight, then he'd borrow your car and take me home in the morning. I guess Tom and Gary sold their car."

Ian had picked up only a few words out of the dozens the girl had spewed out. He tried to say something, anything. The words seemed to be stuck in his throat. He felt light-headed, confused, disoriented. "I could drive you now."

"I live all the way down in Los Angeles," Trudy said, lifting one shoulder and tilting her head. "Besides, I might not be able to get into my place. My roommate has the key, and I think she's going straight to her boyfriend's house. Can I come in?" She wrapped her arms around her chest, then moved her body from side to side as if she were shivering. "It's chilly out tonight, isn't it? This coat isn't very warm."

"Oh . . . sure . . . I . . ." Ian stammered, opening the door and stepping aside for her. What was he supposed to do? Why would a girl like this possibly ask to spend the night at his apartment? Wasn't she afraid he might hurt her?

Trudy brushed past him, heading straight to his kitchen. Ian followed behind in a trail of perfume. She smelled like vanilla ice cream. Most girls wore such strong perfume that it made his eyes water.

No wonder she was cold, Ian thought. The fabric of her coat was transparent and he could see the outlines of her shapely body underneath. Ian was so bedazzled, he didn't remember opening the bottle she had handed him. Other than an occasional beer, he didn't drink or use drugs. It was hard enough for him to follow people's conversations without polluting his mind. He realized with surprise that Trudy was flirting with him. The more nervous he got, the more parched his throat became. Each time he emptied his glass, Trudy reached over and refilled it. He asked her why she wasn't drinking.

"I don't like alcohol," she said, running a finger down the side of her neck. "Smoking pot makes me feel sexy. I already smoked a little with my girlfriend in the car. I'm really disappointed about this party. They told me there would be a lot of important people there, like movie producers and agents."

"Are you an actress?" Ian asked, flabbergasted.

"I'm supposed to be," she said, sighing despondently. "Gary tried to convince me he could get me a part in a movie. He was only trying to impress me. Guys pull that stuff on me all the time."

Ian remembered Gary using the same line on another girl. "Have you ever been in a movie?"

"I've gone out on a few auditions," Trudy continued. "No one has ever called me back, though."

"You're gorgeous!"

"Thanks," Trudy said, flashing a little-girl smile. "I have some pot if you're interested."

"Ah . . . no . . ." Ian stammered, holding his glass in the air. "This stuff is fine with me." He purposely coughed so she wouldn't think he was a prude. "I'd smoke some, see, but I just got over a cold." He held up a hand. "I'm fine now. I won't give you a germ or anything."

They talked in the kitchen for awhile, then Trudy removed the long black coat she was wearing and flopped down on his sofa on her stomach. Her rose-colored silk dress looked more like a slip or a nightgown, and the way she was positioned, her breasts spilled over the top. Ian marveled at her body. Her waist was tiny, her hips perfectly rounded. When he realized he had an erection, he switched off the light in the kitchen and stood watching her from the shadows.

He didn't have much furniture, yet he'd lucked out on the apartment. He was paying the same rent as he would for a studio except he had a separate bedroom. In the complex where he lived, the majority of the units were studios. Because he'd been on the waiting list for over a year, his mother had badgered the manager until she'd let him move into the first available apartment.

Trudy giggled as she kicked off her shoes. "Do you mind if I turn on the TV?"

"No . . . yes . . . go ahead." The alcohol was kicking in, and Ian had to brace himself against the counter to maintain his balance. He was also drunk on the girl, swirling in a fog of feminine sexuality.

Trudy picked up the remote, then frowned. "I've never been able to figure these silly things out. Would you mind showing me how it works?"

Ian crossed the room in a trance. As soon as he was standing beside her, she scooted herself forward on the sofa and wrapped her arms around his legs. When he felt her mouth on his penis, he jumped in shock. "I . . . don't . . . stop." He reached down to pull his pajamas back up when she brushed his hand aside.

"Doesn't it feel good?"

"Yes . . . but . . ."

Trudy locked her arms even tighter around his legs. "Then stop fighting me and enjoy it."

Ian thought he was going to melt, as if all the bones had been extracted from his body. He'd never experienced such incredible pleasure. He'd masturbated, but it wasn't the same. The greatest part was that Trudy seemed to like doing these things to him. Most girls just teased him, then pushed him away. My God, he thought, what if she was only a teenager? His mother had warned him repeatedly, telling him that if he ever had sex with an underage girl, they would send him to jail. Elizabeth told him that it didn't matter whether or not the girl was willing. Even if she encouraged him, it would still be a crime. "How old are you?"

"Old enough," Trudy said, her brown eyes gazing up at him. Then she saw the apprehension on his face and snapped, "I'm twenty-three, okay. Do you want to see my driver's license? I look young, that's all. Even my mother looks young for her age."

"I don't want to get in trouble."

"I'd get arrested before you," Trudy said. "You look about fifteen."

Ian's face fell. As usual, he'd ruined everything. He wasn't going to cry, though. He'd made a big enough fool of himself already.

Trudy sat on the sofa, flicking the ends of her fingernails, plotting out what she was going to do next. Standing, she draped her arms around his neck. "It's okay," she said, her tone soft and consoling again. "I'm glad that you asked about my age. That shows you care. Gary was right. You really are a special guy."

Leading him into the bedroom, Trudy nudged Ian onto the bed. Wiggling out of her slip, she climbed under the covers with him. When he didn't move, she took his hand and guided it behind her legs, show-ing him exactly where she wanted him to touch her. "Slow down," she whispered. "We have all night. Girls take longer than guys."

Ian had never touched the intimate part of a woman's body. He knew what it looked like, though, because he'd rented porno movies. He was glad the lights were off in his room. In the movies, the girls weren't young and innocent-looking like Trudy, and the men used dis-gusting language. In addition, everything was bright, noisy, and phony.

Ian was still stroking Trudy when she suddenly arched her body upward, causing his fingers to slide inside her. She tossed her head from side to side. "Go down on me."

"Where?" He thought she meant he should touch her somewhere else.

"Use your tongue," Trudy said, pushing herself up with her arms. "You know, do what I did to you in the living room."

With his feet, Ian kicked the covers off the foot of the bed. Trudy spread her legs apart. He knelt in front of her, but he still wasn't certain exactly what she wanted him to do. His pajama bottoms were in the living room, but he was wearing his T-shirt. Trudy yanked on the edge of his shirt, then placed her hands on his head, moving her hips until she connected with his mouth. "There," she sighed, leaning back against the pillows. "There, right there."

It wasn't bad. Ian liked it. He liked it because she liked it, and the more she liked it, the more he explored and experimented. And she smelled fresh, clean, sweet. He soon experienced something he'd never felt before, a sense of power. She was his, he told himself. She would do anything for him now. When he stopped for even a minute, she laced her fingers through his hair and begged him to do it again. He rubbed his genitals against the mattress.

"Yes, yes, yes," Trudy cried out, her body contracting in a series of spasms.

When they finally had intercourse, Ian soared to another level—beyond sex, pleasure, even above the electrifying sense of power. He no longer felt inferior or alone. For a few fleeting hours, Ian Decker knew what it was like to be normal.

THREE

"WHY DON'T we have lunch together?" Arnold Dreiser asked, stepping up beside Joanne at the counsel table.

"Oh," she exclaimed, surprised by the attorney's invitation. "Thanks. Since my car wouldn't start this morning, I should have it checked and pass on lunch today."

Losing her train of thought, Joanne stared out over the room. How could she punish Leah after all she'd been through? A certain amount of rebellion was to be expected under the circumstances. The biggest problem was that Leah refused to believe her father had done anything wrong. After Doug had taken the children and disappeared, he'd been forced to concoct some kind of story. He'd told Mike and Leah that Telinx, the computer corporation where he was employed, had transferred him to another city and that their mother would join them as soon as she returned from St. Louis. Joanne's father had been hospitalized at the time, and she had flown to his bedside. After weeks passed and their mother never showed up, Doug had told the kids that their mother had fallen in love with another man and abandoned them.

Night after night Joanne had sat wringing her hands by the phone, certain if Mike and Leah were alive, they would find a way to call her. At the same time, her children were repeatedly dialing their mother's number and listening to a recorded voice tell them that her phone was no longer in service. Doug had simply redirected any calls made to her home or the county switchboard to a nonworking number.

Even if Leah was still in denial, Mike no longer believed the lies his father had told him. Joanne's twelve-year-old son was exceptionally mature for his age, far more so than his older sister. Leah loved her mother, but she would never turn against her father.

Dreiser coughed to get Joanne's attention.

She slipped her backpack over her shoulders. "What do you think about this new phone gun?" she asked. "Have you seen the pictures?"

"Outside of the victim's statement," Dreiser replied, "there's no proof my client possessed any type of firearm. I did read an article on the decoy gun about a year ago, though, so I can't contest its existence."

Joanne was concerned about the overall ramifications of such a weapon. "I thought a gun was a complex mechanism," she said. "Now the police are going to panic every time someone pulls out a cell phone. If we don't find the individuals manufacturing the dreadful things and put them out of business, we're going to have a nightmare on our hands."

Although Dreiser was eager to talk to her, he had no desire to discuss the weapon used in the commission of the crime. "I'd help you with your car," he told her, "but I'm not much of a mechanic. Don't you have some kind of road service?"

A tall, middle-aged woman with thinning brown hair and dark circles etched under her eyes rushed over to speak to Ian Decker. Gary

Rubinsky grabbed Decker's arm and steered him down the aisle. His brother, Tom, exchanged words with the woman and then followed the other two men out of the courtroom. The woman placed her hands over her face and began sobbing.

"Excuse me," Dreiser said, wanting to see what had transpired.

The public defenders had already bolted from the room, the clerks and bailiff not far behind. Not only did Joanne need to make certain her car would start that evening, she wanted to stop by Judge Spencer's chambers and apologize for not appearing on time. Thinking her conversation with Dreiser was over, she picked up her backpack and turned to leave. Judge Spencer was a creature of habit. He went to lunch during the first hour of the recess, then spent the remainder of the break either in conferences, or attempting to plow through the mountain of paperwork that made its way to his desk. Rather than try to catch him now, she decided to stop by his chambers before the afternoon session began.

"Wait," Dreiser shouted, scrambling to catch up to her. "It was rude of me not to introduce you. That was Ian's mother, Elizabeth Decker." He ran his hands through his hair, his face flushing in embarrassment. "Ian's my second cousin, in case you haven't heard."

At least one piece of the puzzle had clicked into place, Joanne thought. They were in the corridor now, heading toward the elevator. She opened her mouth to say something, then found her thoughts drifting off again. She had a sentencing scheduled for five o'clock that afternoon, and she had as yet to review the probation report. She also needed to call Leah's psychologist and inform her about the incident with the car.

"I asked you to lunch to discuss the situation with Ian Decker."

Joanne shot him a look of annoyance.

"I know . . . I know," Dreiser stammered. "I should have had my secretary call your office to schedule an appointment instead of tapping into your lunch hour. My firm just lost a class-action suit we've been working for the past six months. To top things off, one of my partners quit last week." He brushed his hand over his chin, dotted with stubble. "I even forgot to shave this morning."

"I wouldn't worry about it," Joanne said, pointing to the grease stain on the front of her jacket. Stepping into the elevator and depressing the button for the third floor where the district attorney's office was located, she felt better knowing she wasn't the only person whose life seemed to be skidding off track. Dreiser may have forgotten to shave, but he smelled good. The scent was fresh, more like soap than cologne. She took in the angular slant of his nose, the shape of his chin, not too prominent yet strong. There was an attractive sprinkling of gray in his dark hair. When he accidentally brushed up against her, she felt a rush, an unexpected burst of energy. Her previous anxiety suddenly vanished, and she found herself staring at his hands. Her father had been a concert pianist and had amazing hands. Dreiser's hands reminded her of her father's—his wrists were slender, and his fingers were long and tapered. Unlike her father, though, this man had done some type of physical work.

The elevator stopped at the third floor. She stepped out, then impulsively turned around, wedging her body between the door to prevent it from closing. "We could have lunch sent up from the cafeteria," Joanne told him. "My car will probably be fine. Emily Merritt and I jumped the car ourselves this morning because I didn't want to wait for AAA."

"Emily Merritt," Dreiser repeated, recognizing the name. "You don't mean Judge Merritt's wife?"

"Yeah," Joanne said. "They live next door to me."

Dreiser laughed, placing a hand over his stomach. "Forgive me," he said. "I can't picture Emily working on a car. The last time I saw her, she was wearing an evening dress and dripping in diamonds."

"Believe it or not," Joanne said, smiling, "Emily knows more about cars than I do. When she was a teenager, she belonged to a car club called the Rocking Angels. The members were all girls. Guess the old adage holds true."

"What's that?"

"You can't judge a book by its cover."

"Interesting," Dreiser remarked. "Do you like Chinese food? Getting out of this place for a few hours would do us both good, don't you think?"

"I'll meet you in the lobby in five minutes?" Joanne answered, unable to resist. "I need to stop by my office and pick up a probation report. It's only a few pages long. I can read it in the car."

Joanne and Dreiser were facing each other across the red linen tablecloth at the Mandarin Inn, a spacious older restaurant near the courthouse. Since she hadn't had breakfast, she consumed an entire plate of cashew chicken and fried rice. Dreiser waited until the waiter removed their plates, then stated, "I might consider letting Ian plead guilty to a misdemeanor."

Joanne jerked her head back. "You've got to be kidding. Robbery is a serious offense. And this new gun makes the crime even more serious."

"That's why I didn't approach you about negotiating this from the onset," Dreiser told her, fiddling with the knot on his tie. "I don't want this kid to have a felony conviction on his record. They'll use it as an enhancement if he gets in trouble again. This is how guys like Ian get caught up in the system."

A good amount of time passed in silence. Around the office, they jokingly referred to Joanne as the queen of the pregnant pause. People often repeated themselves, thinking she hadn't heard them. She tried to explain that her personal database had grown so large that she needed time to sift through the unnecessary clutter. "The state has a strong case," she told him, clasping her hands together. "We have no reason to settle."

"Just hear me out," Dreiser said, sighing in frustration. "Ian Decker is developmentally disabled. The Rubinskys conned him into acting as their wheelman. While they were allegedly committing the robbery, Ian was waiting outside in his car. These two assholes told him they were going into the market to buy beer and cigarettes."

Joanne placed her napkin over her mouth and chuckled. The longer she spent with this man, the more he impressed her. He certainly wasn't afraid to speak his mind. Although he had purposely inserted the word "allegedly" into his comments, for all practical purposes, he had just admitted that his client had been involved in the crime. "You'd better watch your mouth, or you won't get paid."

"Trust me," Dreiser said, grimacing. "I'm not making a dime off this case. I agreed to represent Ian as a favor to Elizabeth."

"If your client is innocent, why do you want him to plead guilty?"

"Put this guy on the witness stand and there's no telling what will come out of his mouth," Dreiser told her. "The Rubinskys completely control him. They won't even let him speak to his mother. Didn't you see that fiasco in the courtroom? Elizabeth is frantic. She doesn't know where Ian is staying. The police impounded his Firebird, and as far as we know, the Rubinskys don't have a vehicle. No one knows what's going on with these men."

"Maybe Ian doesn't want to talk to his mother," Joanne said. "I might not want to talk to my mother either if I'd made a mess of my life. He may be a little slow, but he is an adult."

"About a settlement . . ."

Joanne arched an eyebrow. "A felony, right?"

"You're tough," Dreiser said, mumbling the words under his breath. "I explained why I won't let him plead to a felony. Make it a misdemeanor with a year in the county jail, and three years of supervised probation."

Joanne leaned forward. "Absolutely not."

"Fine," Dreiser snapped. "Let the poor guy go to prison. By the time he gets out, he'll be a hardened criminal. Then he'll kill someone and end up on death row."

"Let's not get carried away here," Joanne said, tossing her napkin on the table. "The only way a person can end up on death row in California is to be convicted of first-degree murder with special circumstances. Even then there are no guarantees. The prisons are filled with killers who will never be executed." She paused and cleared her throat. "Don't try to tell me you actually believe that prison causes a person to go out and start killing people."

"Maybe with a normal person," Dreiser continued, "I'd agree with you. But when you take someone with the mental capabilities of a ten-year-old and warehouse them in an institution of violent offenders, you're on the road to creating a monster."

"I refuse to listen to this," Joanne said, having been down this road too many times in the past. She felt like getting up and walking out of the restaurant, then reminded herself that she had no way to get back to the courthouse. Usually, she made a point of bringing her own car. The attorney's charisma had affected her reasoning.

"People commit crimes, Arnold," Joanne continued. "Without the system, we'd have no way to protect society." She picked up a chopstick, snapping it in half. "There's an easy way to stay out of jail. Don't break the law. I'm sick to death of all these excuses. Everyone has problems. You could lock me up for years for a crime I didn't commit, and it wouldn't cause me to rob or kill someone once I was released."

"Do you have any idea what it's like to be inside the mind of a person with this type of disability?" Dreiser asked, his eyes expanding with intensity. "The frustrations are mind-boggling." He picked up the check for their food, waving it in front of her. "Something as simple as paying this bill, counting money, figuring out how to get to their job every day without getting lost. And what about registering their car, paying their taxes, dealing with the frustrations of HMOs and other huge corporate entities like banks and utility companies. Just using a pay phone these days is complex, for God's sake."

Joanne opened the file she had brought. "Good speech," she said, reading through the first page of the report. "Save your energy for the courtroom."

"Elizabeth is a wonderful woman," Dreiser answered, refusing to back down. "Her husband was killed in a car accident when Ian was a toddler. She's been fighting this kid's battles since the day he was born. You saw how awful she looked today. She'll never be the same if her son goes to prison. Her health is another factor. She had a liver transplant a few years ago."

"Is she an alcoholic?"

"No," he said. "She had chronic liver disease."

"It's not that I don't appreciate your position," Joanne told him, setting the report aside. "Any mother would be devastated. You probably felt obligated to represent this man."

"A person with Ian's disabilities doesn't belong in a prison environment," Dreiser told her, his voice escalating. "He'll be brutalized from the first day he gets off the bus."

"If your client is incompetent to stand trial," Joanne countered, irritated that he'd waited until now to bring such a serious issue to light, "then why didn't you petition the court to send him off for a ninety-day diagnostic before the preliminary hearing?"

"Nothing would have come of it," the attorney explained, tapping a spoon against his water glass. "The state psychologist would have ruled that Ian was competent to stand trial. Most of his IQ tests have come in around seventy, give or take a few points. He's borderline, the worst possible scenario. He looks normal. He can drive, mow a lawn, read and write at around a fifth-grade level, perform simple tasks. As far as the courts are concerned, he's the same as any other defendant."

Joanne still needed to finish reviewing the report on the sentencing hearing, make a few phone calls, and try to scrub the stain off the front of her jacket. The first hour of the recess had already passed, and she was becoming even more anxious. "You've just described 50 percent of all criminal defendants," she told him. "You do realize that, don't you?"

Dreiser's courtroom demeanor began to surface as he attempted to make his point. "Yes, Ian knows right from wrong. Yes, he can cooperate with his defense. He's still a child trapped inside a man's body." He paused, handing the waiter his credit card. "If he'd stabbed someone, then I wouldn't have a problem if he ended up in prison. But this crime doesn't involve violence. The Rubinskys took advantage of him. They needed a car. When they bumped into their old pal from the neighborhood, Ian became the perfect solution to their problem." He paused and then continued. "I've changed my mind about negotiating a settlement. I'll get Ian acquitted."

Joanne crossed her arms over her chest, giving him her undivided attention. He was providing her with information she could utilize during the trial. "I don't see how you'll ever get a jury to acquit Ian Decker when we have an eyewitness who can place him inside his car, parked in front of the Quick-Mart at the time of the robbery. He's not blind, is he? The store has glass windows. How could he sit there and not see what was going on? And what about the gunshot the Rubinskys fired with their disgusting new weapon?"

"The victim is so confused," Dreiser said, "he'd probably identify his own brother. He's contradicted himself five times during the preliminary hearing. And this witness who placed Ian at the market just got out of drug rehab. He's mistaken on the location of the car. Ian says they parked on the north side of the market. He wasn't able to see what was going on inside. There's a concrete wall there. Don't tell me you have an airtight case, because I know better."

Joanne tapped her fingernails on the table. The clerk at the Quick-Mart was one of the weakest links in their case. "Mr. Bhavan got confused during some of the questioning," she told him. "I think he had trouble understanding the interpreter. That's why I asked the court to hire someone else for the trial. Bhavan is here on a six-month visa from India. I have to keep reassuring him that we're not going to deport him."

"Doesn't matter," Dreiser said realistically. "Whatever he says on the stand is his testimony."

"Bhavan picked all three of your clients out of a lineup," Joanne tossed back at him. "He just can't remember which of the two brothers fired the gun. Your memory might be a little fuzzy too if someone opened fire with what you thought was a cell phone."

"Ian was asleep," Dreiser said, not prepared to reveal the rest of what the young man had told him about the night before the robbery.

"Bullshit," Joanne said, shocked that Dreiser would try to use such a lame excuse. "Instead of the Rubinskys conning your client, you're the one who's being conned. Decker was a willing participant. You're wasting your time, Arnold."

"Elizabeth bought him that car for his twenty-first birthday," Dreiser told her, staring at a spot over her head. "Ian had finally managed to move into a subsidized apartment building and was doing fairly well living independently. The Rubinskys knew they could trick him into acting as their wheelman. They also got him to hand over the money he got from his monthly disability checks. When he couldn't pay his portion of the rent, the complex evicted him."

Joanne watched as he scribbled his name on the credit-card slip, then slapped it back down on the table.

"Ian was a lonely guy, okay," Dreiser said. "Individuals like this are exploited every day. Offer them a few hours of companionship, and they'll give you the shirt off their backs."

"We have to leave," Joanne said, standing and smoothing down her skirt. The attorney wasn't as charming as she'd thought. He was cunning and relentless. If nothing else, she would make every attempt to learn from him during the course of the trial.

"I didn't intend to argue the case over lunch," Dreiser said as they walked out of the restaurant into the bright afternoon sunlight. "I just don't want to see this kid take a fall."

He circled around to the passenger side of his black Cadillac Escalade, opening the car door for her. Once Joanne had fastened her seat belt, he headed off in the direction of the courthouse. "I want to confirm something," she asked him. "You're not receiving any compensation for representing Ian Decker?"

"Zilch," Dreiser told her. "Elizabeth doesn't have any money. She mortgaged her house to pay for Ian's bail."

Joanne contemplated their conversation. Recently, there had been a rash of publicity regarding developmentally disabled offenders. In Texas, they had executed a man who wasn't even aware he was going to die. He had asked the guards to save his dessert for when he returned. She wished she'd never accepted Dreiser's offer to go to lunch. "Can you get me copies of Ian's school records, along with any recent psychological evaluations?"

"Elizabeth has boxes of that stuff," Dreiser told her. "You'll have it by tomorrow morning."

Once they had pulled into a parking space at the courthouse, Joanne reached for the door handle, then turned back to the attorney. "I doubt if anything is going to come of this," she said. "You should probably tell his mother that you want to look over his records yourself. Giving her false hope will only make things worse."

"I agree," Dreiser said, remaining in the car with his hands on the steering wheel. "Do you have children?"

"Two," Joanne answered. "What about you?"

"I had a sixteen-year-old son," he said, his eyes misting over. "I lost him five years ago."

Joanne pulled her hand away from the door. "What happened, if you don't mind me asking?"

"Jake committed suicide," Dreiser said, his voice so low she had to strain to hear him. "After all this time, we still don't know why. He didn't use drugs. He had wonderful friends, was active in sports, did well academically."

"Your wife . . ."

"We were divorced at the time," he said, leaning back against the headrest. "The divorce was amicable."

Joanne felt small and helpless. When someone revealed something this tragic, words became meaningless. Listening was the only consolation.

"Not knowing is what eats away at you," Dreiser continued, brushing his hand underneath his nose. "Jake didn't leave a note. In the beginning, I thought someone had killed him and set it up to look like a suicide. The police couldn't find any evidence of a crime, so we had no choice but to accept the truth. It's a bitter pill to swallow, that your son never wanted to see you again, let alone live."

Joanne reached over and touched his hand. "Maybe after the trial is over," Joanne told him, taking a deep breath, "we can have dinner. I've never been through anything close to what you have, but I've had some serious problems related to my children. My ex-husband is awaiting trial in Los Angeles. He embezzled a fortune. Because he thought I was going to report him, he took off with my kids. I didn't know where they were for two years."

"I'm sorry," Dreiser told her. "I don't know what caused me to start talking about Jake. It was around this time of the year that it happened. I try not to think about it, but it always hits me like a tidal wave."

Joanne's eyes darted to the clock on the dashboard. "The hearing begins in seven minutes," she said, quickly jotting down her home number on a scrap of paper. "I can't afford to be late again. Call me tonight. By ten, the kids will be in bed, and we can talk as long as you want." She tried to give him the paper, but he looked away. She placed it on the center console. Why had she mentioned her children? He would never see his son again. Her stomach was churning. She felt as if she had somehow moved inside his mind, and was swimming in a murky pool of grief. Was this what he was referring to when he'd been talking about Ian Decker? She'd never felt this way before. She had trouble focusing her eyes. "Perhaps I should tell Judge Spencer I'm not feeling well, ask for a continuance?"

"I'm fine," Dreiser said curtly. "All I need is a few minutes alone."

Joanne leapt out and hurried toward the front of the building. Leah taking the car the night before no longer seemed important. All she'd done was drive around inside the gated compound. If she'd managed to relieve her tensions without hurting anyone, was it really worth punishing her, putting even more strain on their relationship? She had lost two years out of her children's lives, years that could never be reclaimed. Arnold Dreiser's passion for this particular case was understandable in light of what he had just told her. Obviously, he was trying to save more than just Ian Decker. Having a child commit suicide was a parent's worst nightmare. She could only imagine the demons that assailed the poor man. Was it something he had done, something he'd said? Did he fail to see the warning signs? Could he have somehow prevented it? For the rest of his life, he would be asking himself the same questions.

Joanne glanced over her shoulder, seeing the attorney slowly making his way across the parking lot, moving his feet as if they were encased in concrete. Although she didn't believe that every event that occurred in a person's life was preordained, she did feel people sometimes came together for a reason. It might not have been uplifting, yet she'd needed to hear this man's story. No matter how frustrating her day was, when she got home that evening she would put a smile on her face and make certain to tell Mike and Leah how deeply she loved them.

FOUR

ROOM 734 at the Economy Inn in Ventura was filled with the pungent odor of marijuana, body odor, and stale beer. After the three defendants had been released on bail, they'd taken up residence at the motel.

Gary Rubinsky stepped out of the bathroom with a towel wrapped loosely around his waist. He scooped up his pants off the floor and dug in the pockets for another joint, fired it up, and took a puff. Although the brothers were both good-sized men, Tom was in the best physical shape. He'd played on his high school basketball team, and, whenever he could ditch Gary, he spent Saturday afternoons shooting hoops. Although Tom had failed in his attempts to obtain a basketball scholarship, he'd been accepted at several universities. Their parents were going through some rough times financially, however, and were unable to provide for his tuition. Because Gary had skipped college, he'd convinced his younger brother that it was a waste of time, that he'd end up with a mountain of student loans and drop out before he received his degree. A degree was just a lousy piece of paper, according to Gary. If Tom wanted a degree, Gary told him he could get one of his friends to print one up for him.

Ian Decker was seated in a mauve-colored upholstered chair, coughing and waving his hands in front of his face. "Can't you get Gary to go outside when he smokes that stuff?" he asked. "I can't breathe, Tom."

Gary had muscular arms and broad shoulders but he carried most of his weight in his midsection, causing his stomach to spill over the top of his towel. "You're breathing fine, asshole," he told Ian, trying to hold the drug inside his lungs. "If you weren't breathing, you'd be dead."

Tom was sprawled on the king-size bed, several pillows propped behind his head. They'd requested a room with two queens, but none was available. Gary slept on one side of the bed, while his brother slept on the other. Ian either tossed a pillow and blanket on the floor or dozed off in one of the chairs.

"Give him a break," Tom said. "He used to have asthma when he was a kid, remember? What are you going to do when our stash runs out, huh? No one's seen Willie lately. When we were in the tank, a guy told me he's got a warrant out on him for dealing. I don't think this is the time to start trying to find another drug connection, know what I mean?"

"We've been cooped up all day," his brother said. "I feel like putting my fist through the wall. I don't give a shit how important Ian's attorney is supposed to be. He runs his mouth too much, if you ask me. I thought he was going to ask that one lady what kind of underwear she was wearing."

"You're just jealous because Ian has a better attorney than we do," Tom said, leaning down and pulling a beer out of a foam cooler by the bed.

"Ian's mommy wants to protect her baby boy," Gary responded sarcastically. He spun around and faced Ian. "You stay away from your mother, you hear me? Your mother's nothing but trouble. She'll have you locked up in a nuthouse if you don't let us handle her. No phone calls. Nothing. When she shows up in court, don't even look at her."

Ian shook his head in confusion. "I don't know what you're talking about."

"Your mother will do anything to keep you out of the joint," Gary continued. "I've heard her talking to Dreiser, telling him that you're a retard. You think prison is bad. At least in prison, a man has rights. At a state mental house, they'll pump you full of drugs and lock you in a padded cell. Guys that go in those places sometimes never come out."

"My mother would never do something like that," Ian said, remembering his mother's anguished face.

Gary took another puff of marijuana. "Don't kid yourself," he said. "That's why I don't mind having a public defender. The last thing I want is my mom and dad involved. Parents want to protect their own reputation. They don't want their friends to find out they've got a kid in jail. Tom and me, well, our folks have already washed their hands of us. Elizabeth thinks she's some kind of saint or something."

"My mother's a good person," Ian said. "She loves me, that's all."

"Oh, yeah," Gary said. "She's kept you under her thumb since you were a baby. You're like her little pet. She makes such a big deal about looking after you, always talking about all the sacrifices she's made. Don't you understand? She likes the attention. Everyone feels sorry for her 'cause she's got this son who isn't right in the head."

"Knock it off, Gary," Tom said, wishing he could flush his brother's dope down the toilet. Gary had been smoking marijuana since he was twelve. He thought it was the same as smoking a cigarette.

Gary ignored his brother and continued. "Your mother didn't want you hanging out with us because she didn't want you to have any fun."

"That's enough!" Tom shouted. "You're getting on my nerves."

Ian tuned out the brothers' bickering. They were at each other's throats all the time, particularly since they'd been arrested. Gary's tan sweater was tossed over the back of his chair. Ian hated the way marijuana smelled, but body odor was even more offensive. It smelled disgusting, like sour milk. Gary had worn the same pair of Levi's and the same sweater every day for the past week. Ian was glad that Gary'd finally taken a shower, even though he knew the man would probably put the same stinking clothes back on.

Ian's mother had always drilled him about personal hygiene. Her voice echoed inside his head, *Did you take a shower today, honey? Did you brush your teeth? Don't forget that you have to use deodorant. You're a man now.*

Mr. Dreiser had told the Rubinskys that they should shower and try to dress appropriately when they came to court. Tom was fairly neat in comparison to his brother, but neither one of them had washed their clothes since they'd taken up residence at the Economy Inn. It wasn't as if they had an excuse. The motel had a laundry room.

Tom seldom lost his temper the way Gary did, and sometimes when his brother was passed out from booze or dope, Tom would sit and talk to Ian, reminiscing about people they knew from the neighborhood, telling jokes, or fantasizing about places he wanted to visit someday. Still, when his older brother told him to do something, Tom might bitch about it, but he always ending up doing whatever Gary said.

Overall, nothing much had changed since the days when they lived three houses away from each other on Mercer Street. Ian and Tom had been best friends until the fifth grade. Once Ian had been placed in the special-education program at Elmhurst Elementary, none of his former friends would have anything to do with him. He'd not only been branded a loser, he'd discovered that there were only a few kids in the program with legitimate learning disabilities. The majority of his classmates were bullies, thieves, and thugs—what the teachers classified as behavior problems. An assignment that might take Ian hours, many of his classmates could finish in thirty minutes. They then scribbled nasty words all over their papers or made paper airplanes out of them, almost as if they wanted the school to expel them.

Tom reached for another beer and noticed there were only three remaining out of the two six-packs they had purchased the night before. "Hey, Ian," he said, "go buy some more beer. And while you're out, pick us up some grub. What do you want, Gary?" Tom sat up on the edge of the bed and belched, kicking a pizza box across the floor. "Can you believe the maid left the trash in the room? Place is gonna be crawling with roaches."

Unfurling the towel and whipping it out at his brother, Gary told him, "You left the Do Not Disturb sign on the door. Sometimes I think you're more retarded than your buddy Ian."

Ian dropped his head in shame. He wanted to strike back, tell them how much it hurt when they ridiculed him. The one time he had found the courage to speak out, though, Tom had said they were only joking, that words didn't mean anything between friends.

"I'm not hungry," Ian told them, wondering if the things Gary had said about his mother could possibly be true. A few months after he had renewed his friendship with the Rubinskys, Ian had stopped paying his rent. The manager of his apartment complex had called his mother, asking her to come and pick up his belongings. When Elizabeth had came to post his bail, she'd been furious, telling him he would never be able to live independently again. And it was more than simply an apartment. To qualify for it, a person had to go through a series of tests to make certain they were either mentally or physically disabled. They taught people how to cook and manage money, along with other necessary skills. Once Gary and Tom had taken over his life, Ian had stopped attending any of the programs held in the recreation room. Several times he'd thought of sneaking out of the motel room and calling his mother from the pay phone down by the office. He wanted to tell her that he loved her and appreciated everything she'd done for him, that he was sorry for causing her such heartache.

One of the primary reasons the Rubinskys didn't want Elizabeth snooping around was the credit card. When she'd arranged for Ian to get his own MasterCard, Ian's mother had made him promise that he would only use it in case of an emergency. Opening his wallet, he pulled out a small piece of paper where he'd been attempting to keep track of how much they were spending. He wasn't that good with math, though, and Gary and Tom took his credit card and charged things without even asking.

The most serious problem was the car theft. Ian had nightmares about what he'd done, certain that if the court didn't send him to prison for the robbery, they would put him away for stealing the car. As soon as the attorney had posted their bail, Gary had coerced Ian into stealing the keys to his family's business. Elizabeth and Ian's uncle Carl were partners in a company called ABC Towing and Storage. ABC had a contract with the city to handle their abandoned vehicles in addition to their regular service calls. Everyone had always laughed about the name. When people asked Uncle Carl what he did for a living, he told them he owned ABC, knowing they would think he was referring to the television network. His uncle Carl was a pretty smart man. Using that name had made them a lot of money. When their car broke down on the road, people generally called information for the name of a towing company. Since telephone operators weren't allowed to give recommendations, the caller would ask for the number to any towing company. The letters ABC were the first three letters of the alphabet, the first in the listings, and therefore, his family's company received the majority of the calls.

When the three were arrested, the police impounded the green 1996 Firebird that Ian's mother had given him for his twenty-first birthday. Once they were released on bail, Gary said they couldn't get by without transportation. Gary and Tom claimed to have sold their Jeep Pioneer a few weeks before reconnecting with Ian at the shopping center. Ian's mother had warned him that the brothers would get him into trouble. In the beginning, Ian had been having too much fun to believe her. Gary and Tom had tons of friends, even as far away as San Diego. They took him to bars, parties, sporting events, introduced him to girls. The days sped by in such a flurry of activity, Ian couldn't remember half of the places they'd been to, or the dozens of people he'd met along the way.

Once the police arrested them and impounded Ian's Firebird, Gary came up with the idea of taking a car from the ABC lot. Ian had to admit there were tons of cars on that lot. Some owners never claimed their vehicles because the storage bills ended up being more than the cars were worth. After a certain period of time, the city allowed ABC to sell the cars to satisfy the storage fees. Ian had seen the same cars for as long as a year, most of them rusted out heaps that his family eventually sold to a wrecking yard.

The only good thing about the car situation, Ian told himself, was that Gary and Tom hadn't asked him to steal an expensive car, just anything that ran and had current plates on it. He'd found a 1996 Chrysler Cirrus with the side bashed in, but the car's engine was in perfect condition and the registration was up to date.

Beads of perspiration formed on Ian's forehead. He'd never intentionally stolen anything. What if the police found out and thought his mother was involved? His sister, Pauline, had moved back home to help out when his mother had become ill. With the problems Ian had caused, he was fearful his mother would get sick again. Her face flashed in front of him. Her skin had been yellowish today, the way it had looked before she'd had the liver transplant.

Ian buried his face in his hands. Gary and Tom swore they would return the car as soon as they were cleared on the robbery charges. They were certain Mr. Dreiser would get them off. Then they would take the car back to the ABC lot, and no one would be the wiser. They weren't really stealing anything, they kept telling him. Stealing meant keeping something forever. All they were doing was borrowing.

The Rubinskys had insisted on taking one of the cars from Ian's family's business because they knew it wouldn't show up on the police computer as a stolen vehicle. Ian's mother had never said anything about the missing key, let alone the car. He assumed she had several keys to the storage lot and just thought she had lost it.

The Chrysler was now in the parking lot at Costco, located next to Albertson's supermarket, about three blocks from the Economy Inn. To make certain his mother didn't see them driving the car to court, they left early every day and parked behind the jail where the prisoners were released. Ian had come up with that idea as he knew his mother would never park in a place where she didn't feel safe. Ian doubted if she would recognize the car, anyway, not with everything else that was going on.

"You didn't eat any lunch today," Tom commented. "Are you certain you're not hungry?"

"What are you now?" Gary asked. "Ian's big brother or something? Maybe he needs to toughen up. Who cares if he eats or not? He can starve for all I care. All I want him to do is drive down to the corner and get us some food."

"And pay for it," Ian mumbled under his breath.

Gary spun around, pointing a finger at him. "Did you say what I think you said?"

Tom placed his body between the two men. "Chill out, will you? He doesn't have a lot of money left. Here, Ian," he said, pulling out a twenty. "Go get us a bucket of chicken or something. We can't use his credit card."

"Why not?" Gary asked. "We used it this afternoon and there wasn't a problem."

"All Elizabeth has to do is call MasterCard and check on any recent charges," Tom explained. "You don't want her to know where we are, right?"

"Ian, you stay here," Gary said, a grim look on his face. He scooped up the keys to the Chrysler off the end table. "We've got to run an errand. Just make certain you're here when we get back."

FIVE

JOANNE WASN'T able to pull her car into the garage that evening as it was filled with Judge Spencer's furniture. Since the Spencers had another home, they had graciously offered to remove their own furniture, saving Joanne the expense of storing her own during the six months they had agreed to lease her the house. She pried the key to the Lexus from her ring, then hid it under the floor mat. She doubted if Leah would pull the same stunt two nights in a row, but she didn't want to take a chance.

Judge Spencer's house was a charming two-story, with shuttered windows and a spacious front porch. Most of the lots at Seacliff Point were long and narrow, the houses set a good distance back from the road. Covered with vines, a four-foot white picket fence surrounded the property, more for decoration than privacy. Two enormous sycamore trees stood on either side of the stone path leading to the front door. Through the years their branches had intertwined so that they now formed a canopy, shading the house from the harsh glare of the afternoon sun.

Joanne wished she didn't have to go through the ordeal of uprooting the children. Even if another home were to become available at Seacliff Point, though, the prices were outrageous. Most people would classify the Spencers' house as a beach house. In another location, it would probably sell somewhere in the neighborhood of three hundred thousand dollars. Emily had told her that the last house that had changed hands inside Seacliff Point had sold for over two million, and it was even smaller than the Spencers' home.

Few communities had a private stretch of beach, which was part of the exclusivity of Seacliff Point. Restricting the public was illegal, yet no one could dispute what nature had created. It wasn't just the cliffs, but the ocean currents that swirled around them. People who passed through the front gates felt as if they'd been handed the keys to paradise.

Living in a picturesque area was certainly pleasant, Joanne thought, but individuals who tricked themselves into believing that wealth, privilege, public recognition, or any material possession would lead to genuine happiness were in for a rude awakening. This was a lesson Joanne knew well, for she had learned it the hard way.

Although the ocean wasn't visible from the main floor of the Spencers' house, the master bedroom had a magnificent view, the trees formed a living picture frame around the sparkling water. During the days when she was convinced she would never see Leah or Mike's face again, never hear their voices, never hold them, laugh with them, love them, the ocean had seemed like a cold and desolate place.

Mike was waving at her from the living room through the plate-glass window. She looked toward the north side of the house and saw Leah rummaging around in the kitchen. Her spirits soared as she flung open the front door. She could be happy in a tent as long she knew her children would be waiting for her at the end of the day. In the past, she'd been no different than any other person, dreaming of the day when

Doug would hit it big with one of his computer programs and they could live in luxury. Amazing, she thought, how rapidly a person's values could be realigned.

Mike opened his arms as his mother walked toward him. Her son was not only mature for his age, at five-ten, he towered over both his mother and older sister. And he was a hardy boy. He didn't lift weights or express much of an interest in sports, but he was strong and muscular. She assumed he had inherited his father's genetic makeup. Doug was six-five, so her son was probably a fraction of the size he would be once he reached full maturity. Mike's hair was thick and black like his father's, his olive skin unblemished, and his brown eyes were fringed with long lashes.

"How was school, big guy?" Joanne said, relishing the warmth of her son's embrace.

"Fine," he said, hyped up about something. "They're having a party at the beach Friday night. Can I go?"

"Who's 'they'?" she asked, placing her hands on her hips.

"You know," Mike answered, "some of the kids that live here."

Joanne had heard rumors about the young people's activities. If a kid wanted to party, Seacliff Point was the place to live. Teenagers were known to gather at the beach and get drunk, most of the time on alcohol they swiped from their parents. Since Seacliff Point had incorporated as a private city, no one had to worry about getting arrested. The security guards employed by the homeowners' association manned the front gate but they didn't patrol.

When it came to security, the only comparisons Joanne could think of fell along the lines of the White House, the Pentagon, or the Vatican. The entrance ran parallel to the railroad tracks and the 101 Freeway. An armed guard sat at the gate twenty-four hours a day, and no one was allowed inside unless the resident was notified. Because a number of judges and government officials had homes inside Seacliff Point, their security requirements surpassed that of the average home owner. To enhance their protection, none of the houses had numbers or identifying markings. An intruder who managed to slip past the guards would be hopelessly lost. The area was so densely wooded that many of the individuals who lived there had trouble finding their own homes. They'd have one drink too many at the Cove and find themselves driving around for hours on the narrow, dark roads. There were no streetlights. When people walked to a neighbor's house after dark or took a moonlit stroll on the beach, they carried flashlights.

The cliffs on either side of the entrance were far too high and treacherous to be scaled by anyone other than an expert mountain climber. The land jutted out into the ocean, a triangular-shaped peninsula. Occasionally the body of a swimmer or surfer would wash up on one particular section of the beach. Even when the sea was perfectly calm, the undercurrents anywhere close to the cliffs were deadly. The town's association had placed ropes and buoys around the areas where it was safe to swim. When a body surfaced on the beach, some of the parents took their children to look at it. Insisting that a young person face the consequences of swimming past the roped-off areas wasn't all that cruel in light of the alternative.

"Please, Mom," Mike pleaded, "don't say I can't go. This party means a lot to me. All we're going to do is build a bonfire, roast some hotdogs, maybe tell scary stories. You know, the kind of stuff you do at Boy Scout camp."

Removing her backpack, Joanne let it fall to the floor with a *thud*. "Boy Scout camp, huh?" she said, eyeing him warily. "I was your age once, remember? I don't doubt that you're planning to cook some hotdogs or even tell a few stories. I'd bet my right arm, though, that someone's trying to figure out a way to sneak in a keg of beer. I've heard about the kind of parties that go on around here."

"You're impossible," Mike said, flopping down on the sofa and staring at the TV screen. "Leah took the car last night, I didn't. Now I'm the one who's being punished. That's not fair."

"You're not being punished."

"Yeah, right," the boy said. "Dad let us do whatever we wanted. You treat us like we're in kindergarten."

His mother started to remind him that his father was in jail, then stopped herself. As Joanne headed toward the kitchen to speak with Leah and figure out what she was going to prepare for dinner, Mike started up again.

"There's nothing to do around here," he said, depressing a button on the remote control. "We don't even have cable TV. All the other people who live here have satellites with zillions of channels. But not us. We have to live like the Flintstones."

Joanne massaged her forehead. Her head was throbbing, and her son was using the same tactics that Arnold Dreiser had applied to wear her down that afternoon. Now that she thought about it, Arnold and Mike had similar personalities. Arnold Dreiser was similarly shrewd and relentless, yet underneath, she sensed a kind and sensitive individual. Mike would argue for hours, then break down and cry if he saw a dead dog on the road or watched a sad movie. Joanne's son was a determined, intelligent young man. She wondered if he might follow in her footsteps one day and become a litigator. Compassion and sensitivity were character traits that didn't spring forth strictly due to adversity. Many people who found themselves faced with tragedy became bitter and hard. Arnold Dreiser wasn't bitter, just devastated as any parent would be over the loss of their child.

"Cable isn't available here," Joanne told him. "And I can't have a satellite dish installed in Judge Spencer's home. We're going to be moving in three months."

"Where?" he asked. "I'm just beginning to make friends here. Our lives have been messed up for years. Man, when is it ever going to stop?"

"I told you from the start that we couldn't live here forever," Joanne said, dropping down in a brown leather chair adjacent to the sofa. "You're the one who's not being fair." She pointed at her chest. "Don't tell me you blame me for the things that have happened?"

"I don't want to talk about Dad," Mike said, frowning.

"Neither do I," Joanne told him. "I could have bought another house when you and Leah came back, maybe not in an area like this, but at least we would have owned our own home. We've discussed all this before. It seemed more important to spend the money on you and your sister's education. Waldorf is an expensive school, but they have small classes and excellent teachers. We tried to enroll you in the public school, remember? But, because your father had you tutored at home for the two years you were with him to prevent me from finding you, the public school refused to allow you and Leah to attend classes at your grade level. Waldorf was willing to bend the rules based on your scores on their enrollment tests. When you start applying to colleges, you'll thank me."

Mike sneered. "I'm only twelve, Mom."

"What might not seem important to you now could change the course of your life," Joanne answered, picking up a glass off the end table to carry to the kitchen. "Just because things are tough right now doesn't mean they're going to remain this way forever. Give me a chance, Mike."

They both remained silent. Mike fiddled with the remote, then placed it on the sofa beside him.

With the exception of summers and holidays, there were only about twenty young people who lived at Seacliff Point. The majority of the home owners dispatched their offspring to boarding schools. The remaining kids attended public school in Camarillo, a city located between Ventura and Seacliff Point.

"About this party," Joanne continued. "Who invited you?"

"Susan Goldstein."

"I see," his mother said. "Isn't Susan almost eighteen? This must be a party for the high school crowd. Why would they invite you? You're still in junior high."

"They don't know," Mike answered, excited at the possibility that his mother was weakening.

"You've lost me," Joanne said, confused. "What don't they know?"

Mike leaned forward over his knees. "No one here knows how old I am, see. They think I'm sixteen because I'm so big. Please, Mom, if you let me go to this party, I promise I won't drink or do anything wrong. I just want to have some fun. With all this stuff with Dad going on . . ."

Joanne narrowed her eyes. "I thought you didn't want to talk about your father."

"I don't," Mike said sharply. "That's why I don't want to sit around the house all the time and stare at the walls. How can I not think about him, huh? He called from jail only a few minutes before you got home."

Joanne felt her temper flare. "Didn't I tell you not to accept any collect calls from him? How did he get the Spencers' number?" Her husband must have people working for him outside the jail, a friend with similar technical skills and no ethics.

Mike looked down at the floor. "Talk to Leah," he said. "I didn't give him our number. And he's not calling collect, Mom. I guess he has a calling card or something." He lowered his voice, glancing toward the kitchen. "Don't tell Leah I told you, but Dad calls here almost every day, usually around the time we get home from school."

"You have my permission to go to the party," Joanne said, deciding honesty deserved some type of reward. "I expect you to be home no later than ten o'clock. I'll be waiting up for you. One hint of alcohol or anything else and you can kiss your bike good-bye. Are we clear?"

"Thank you, God!" Mike threw his arms in the air in a sign of victory. "I can't believe I get to go! You're the greatest Mom in the whole wide world. I won't let you down, I promise."

Joanne's shoulders rolled forward. At least her son had something to look forward to that weekend. She hadn't been to a party in years. When she wasn't working, she was taking care of the children or cycling through the chain of events that had caused what had once been a loving family to end up in shambles. During the time her children had lived with their father, the man had let them run wild. Resurrecting innocence and instilling discipline was a trying task.

Terrified his children might figure out that he'd wrecked their lives to protect himself, Doug had decided to make certain that neither of the children developed even an iota of resentment toward him. Not only had he homeschooled them, he hadn't set curfews. A housekeeper had cleaned their rooms and cooked their meals. Doug had squandered enormous amounts of money on them, buying them the best clothes, handing them wads of cash, setting up the latest computer and video games in their rooms so that they became the envy of all their friends. The money her former husband had used to buy their love had been embezzled from not one but dozens of companies. With all the wrongs Doug had committed, the one thing Joanne could never forgive was the fact that he had convinced Mike and Leah that their own mother had abandoned them. To ease their pain, Leah had once told her, she and her brother told everyone that their mother was dead.

Joanne tried to muster up the energy to prepare dinner. She felt herself sinking back into the chair. Right now, they should be sitting down together as a family. Instead, the father of her children was in jail, and she was still attempting to break down the barriers he had created.

The situation was both ironic and tragic. Doug was a genius in his own field. While Joanne had been battling criminals in the courtroom, her husband had been developing the future, designing programs that were now mainstays in almost every home and office. Greed and ambition had played a primary role in his downfall, along with the fact that it wasn't uncommon for people with his energy and ingenuity to become bored in a corporate environment. The same qualities that caused Joanne to fall in love with him had ultimately destroyed him— his adventurous and reckless spirit.

Night after night, Joanne had cooked the meals, helped the children with their schoolwork, cleaned the house, and handled the other household chores while her husband sequestered himself in a spare bedroom filled with computer terminals. He seldom made love to her. They didn't have anything even vaguely resembling a social life. Many times they went weeks without having more than five-minute conversations. He'd started coming to bed later and later, until she would wake up to go to work and find her husband still locked inside his room.

As the situation worsened, Joanne had asked herself if he was having an affair, began to believe she was no longer appealing, even suggested they go for marriage counseling. When Doug had gone from a keylock to a dead bolt on the door to his home office, she'd started to question his sanity. Her concern turned into suspicion when she opened her mail one day and saw a seven-hundred-dollar phone bill.

Since Telinx provided their top-level employees with a phone line by which they could remotely access their office computers, her husband's claim that he was working on company projects no longer appeared valid.

The next day Joanne stayed home from work and called a locksmith to open the door to her husband's office. After eight hours of effort, she still couldn't bypass the myriad of passwords Doug had installed to protect anyone from accessing his computer systems. Before things had spun out of control, Joanne had used one of the computers to catch up on some of her own work. Now none of their regular passwords worked.

To make certain her husband didn't suspect anything, Joanne put everything back in the same order, even touching up the paint on the door where the dead bolt was located. She now had a key, however, and the following day, she contacted a computer consulting firm. The technician who came to the house advised that the way her husband had his computers configured, even the most sophisticated hacker wouldn't be able to open his files. Refusing to give up, Joanne had asked Gene Stone to do her a favor and take a look. Stone was in charge of the technicians who maintained the computer systems at the courthouse. Since these systems were linked to the Department of Justice, the FBI, the CIA, Interpol, and every law enforcement agency in the country, she was certain Gene could get the job done.

Joanne had recently attended an emergency security conference in Washington where Gene Stone had given a seminar. The conference had been called after the DNA and Forensic database had been hacked into, and the entire criminal justice system had panicked. An isolated incident had alerted an entire nation to the perils of advanced technology. A man with ties to organized crime had been falsely cleared in the rape and murder of a young woman. Hiring a brilliant but embittered former government employee with insider knowledge and skills, the killer's DNA records had been successfully altered a few weeks before his case was brought up on appeal, causing the appellate court to rule in his favor and overturn his previous conviction. A hardened killer had been released. As far as Joanne knew, he had not yet been reapprehended.

"The only way to disable the BIOS password," Gene Stone told her, "is to open the metal case on your husband's computers and remove the batteries from the motherboards. The battery is basically a memory chip where information is stored. Once we do this, though, the original factory defaults will be restored. When your husband boots up his computer, he'll know instantly that someone has tampered with it because all his passwords will be gone."

"This technology stuff is over my head," Joanne said, releasing a long sigh. "What's a BIOS password?"

"Here," he said, "I'll show you."

Gene Stone sat down at her husband's desk, booted up what appeared to be his main computer, then almost immediately hit the delete key. This caused another screen to appear where a person could enable or disable various passwords and internal settings. When the computer asked for the password, Gene typed in all the passwords Joanne and her husband had previously used as well as several permutations without having any luck. "There's an ethical issue to be considered," he told her. "Correct me if I'm wrong, but isn't breaking into a person's computer similar to burglarizing their house? I mean, you're the legal expert so I'll let you make that determination."

This question was certainly valid. Joanne paused to give it some thought. "Everything in this room is community property."

"Are you and your husband in the process of getting a divorce?" He glanced down at the floor, then looked back up at her, fearing he had overstepped his limits. "You don't have to answer, Joanne," he said. "I'm just trying to help you."

"No," Joanne said, her eyes misting over. "At least, not to my knowledge."

"Call the numbers."

"What numbers?"

"Didn't you tell me that this first came to light because of your phone bill?" Gene asked. "Then call the numbers."

"I tried that already," Joanne said, holding up the phone bill with checkmarks next to each number. "Most of the numbers are on-line access numbers." She was angry that her husband had placed her in such an embarrassing position. When someone came to your home, though, a degree of intimacy developed. She'd also known Gene Stone for ten years, and due to the type of work he did, she felt assured that whatever she told him wouldn't be repeated. She tossed the thick stack of papers back on her husband's desk.

"Some of these numbers aren't even in the country."

"Outside of taking a baseball bat to him," Gene told her, speaking bluntly, "disabling the BIOS password is the only way you're going to find out what's inside these machines."

"Do it," Joanne told him. "Either that, or I'm going to crack the damn thing open with a hammer."

Gene was intrigued. He'd never been asked to come to a prosecutor's home to check out a personal computer. Judging from the amount of equipment he saw, Joanne Kuhlman's husband was doing more than surfing the Web and playing the stock market. The first thing that came to mind was some type of trafficking in pornographic material. Joanne was too sophisticated, however, not to have already considered this possibility.

After removing the battery on all five computers, Gene stood and dusted off his clothing. It had been a long time since he'd done what he referred to as grunt work, actually getting down on the floor and disassembling a machine. He had a contract with the county, but his employees did the work. Gene spent almost every waking hour of his day either lecturing, or locked in a room writing programs in an attempt to keep up with the galloping speed of technology.

Gene Stone brushed his hair off his sweaty brow. "I'm sorry I suggested this," he told her, glancing at the nuts, bolts, and motherboards strewn all over the floor. "You'll never be able to recover the data inside these computers without the precise code sequences your husband used to safeguard his intellectual properties."

"But I thought you said this would work," Joanne said, wondering if Stone was as knowledgeable as she had thought.

"We got into his computers," Gene explained. "The problem is we can't open any of the files. Every one of them is encrypted."

The next day, Joanne's father suffered a heart attack and she'd taken a plane to St. Louis. When she returned, her children, her husband, and all his computer equipment were gone. The police had finally uncovered the secret Doug had so desperately tried to keep hidden. Her husband had become a compulsive gambler. At the time, Joanne wasn't even aware that such a thing as Internet gambling existed. A person could now sell their soul over the Internet.

The chain of events was fairly simple.

Doug had first begun his downward spiral when he started day trading in the stock market. With insider knowledge in the technology field, he'd quickly amassed a considerable amount of money. Being a risk taker, however, he'd gone on to suffer heavy losses. Soured on the stock market, he turned to on-line gambling casinos. Without Joanne's knowledge, he'd mortgaged the house and taken out loans from all kinds of lending institutions. Prying open a safe hidden under the floor with a crowbar, the police had discovered stacks of computer-generated birth certificates, driver's licenses, documents for phony corporations— a virtual labyrinth of deceit.

Caught up in an endless cycle of wins and losses, Doug Kuhlman had created a program sophisticated enough to embezzle from his employer, Telinx, a giant in the industry. Each day he'd electronically transferred thousands of dollars from the company to accounts set up under the various corporate entities he had fabricated.

"I'm starving, Mom," Mike yelled, startling his mother out of her thoughts. "When are we going to have dinner?"

Joanne headed to the kitchen in a daze. When she opened the door, she saw pots and pans scattered all over the counters and sniffed the distinctive odor of smoke.

"I wanted to surprise you," Leah said, placing her hands behind her back. "I was going to have dinner on the table when you got here. I must have set the oven too high." She looked away, tears streaming down her cheeks. "The casserole not only burned up, I thought I was going to have to call the fire department." She tilted her head toward a stack of soggy dish towels in the sink. "When I tried to take the pan out of the oven, the pot holder caught on fire."

"What a mess." Joanne stared at the walls, covered with soot. "I'll have to paint the whole room."

"I'm sorry," Leah said, blowing her nose on a paper towel. "I wanted to do something nice, to make up for taking the car. Now I've made you even more mad at me."

"The fact that you tried is what matters," her mother told her, deciding a bucket of paint was the least of her worries. She walked over and embraced her. "It's okay, sweetheart," she said. "I was planning on repainting before we moved anyway."

"I know I was wrong to take the car, Mom," Leah said, her voice cracking. "I was upset last night. I couldn't sleep. Dad used to let me drive his car. Lots of the kids who don't have a license drive their parents' cars. Rita told me it was okay because Seacliff Point is private property."

"It's an incorporated city," Joanne told her. "That doesn't mean the state laws don't apply." She walked over and opened the refrigerator, then let her arms fall limp at her sides. Every day she learned another appalling fact about her husband's irresponsibility. "Alone?" she exclaimed. "Your father let you drive the car alone? Or did he take you out in the car to teach you how to drive?"

"Sometimes Dad didn't come home until late at night. The tutor left at three, and the housekeeper left at four. We needed things, you know. Mike got sick once, and I couldn't reach Dad on his cell phone. After that, Dad gave me the keys to the Range Rover in case of an emergency."

"Get your brother," Joanne said, closing the door to the refrigerator. "We'll have dinner at the Cove tonight."

"Really?" Leah said, beaming as she ripped off the apron.

"When we get back," her mother added, "I expect you to clean the kitchen. And you're going to be responsible for preparing the meals for the rest of the week. That way, you'll think twice before you take my car. You don't live with your father anymore. I love you with all my heart, but in my house, there are rules."

Leah tossed her long blond hair to one side, shuffling her feet on the parquet flooring. "If you make me cook, I'll probably burn the house down."

Joanne reached into the cabinet and pulled out a cookbook, slapping it down on the kitchen table. Her daughter was a lovely girl. Her skin was darker than Joanne's, more in the olive tones like her brother. Her caramel-colored eyes were large and expressive. Of all her features, however, Joanne thought her perfectly shaped mouth and glowing smile were the most spectacular. "You can read, right? The freezer and refrigerator are well stocked. Of course, if you prefer, I could take away your computer."

"I'll cook," Leah said, rushing out of the room to get dressed.

SIX

TRUDY WAS curled into a ball on one corner of the bed. For awhile, Ian stared at the ceiling, afraid to move for fear of waking her. Then he quietly got out of the bed and circled to the other side, kneeling down on the floor beside her. He couldn't believe that she was still here, that the night before had actually happened. With her face bathed in sunlight, she was even more beautiful than he remembered. He traced the outline of her face with his fingers. He smiled when she flicked his hand away, then pulled the covers up to her chin.

Closing the door to the bedroom, Ian left a note on the coffee table in the living room, then drove the Firebird to Vons where he purchased two chocolate chip muffins and a pint of orange juice. Trudy was waiting for him on the sofa when he returned, her hair wet from the shower. She was wearing one of his white T-shirts, and a pair of his jeans. To keep the pants from falling off, she'd rolled them over several times at the waist.

"I hope it was okay for me to borrow some of your clothes," Trudy told him, motioning toward the black coat and slip that she'd worn the night before, now folded neatly beside her.

The phone rang. When Ian reached for it on the coffee table, Trudy grabbed his arm. "Don't answer it," she told him. "It might be Gary."

Ian was confused. "Why don't you want to talk to Gary?"

"I'm tired," Trudy said, standing. "I want to go home."

"Last night . . . we . . . I . . ." Ian stammered. "Are you mad at me?"

"Last night was great," Trudy said, collecting her belongings. "That's the problem. You're one of the sweetest guys I've ever met. Look"—she pointed at the sack he was carrying—"you even went out and bought me breakfast."

"I . . ." Ian was shattered. Her words sounded wonderful, but they were just words. People had said nice things to him all his life, things they didn't mean. He could tell if they were sincere by the tone of their voice. It reminded him of how people talked to their pets. He wondered if Trudy was going to pat him on the head. "I'll drive you home now."

"I don't have to leave right this minute," Trudy told him, sorry she'd upset him. "I'm not mad at you. I just wanted you to understand that I can't stay here all day. That doesn't mean we can't have our breakfast."

"Here," Ian said, handing her the sack. "You can eat in the car."

Ian dropped Trudy off in Los Angeles, then returned to his apartment around one o'clock. He saw Gary and Tom in the parking lot. They must have gone out to score dope, he thought, and Willie had given them a ride to his apartment. "I've been calling you for hours," Gary said, hitching his pants up. "Where's Trudy?"

Ian wasn't in the mood to talk. "I drove her home."

"We told her we'd get her back to L.A. this morning," Tom said, leaning against a tree. "Did something happen? You know, was there some kind of a problem? Trudy's a good-looking chick."

"She got sick," Ian told them, locking his car. "She threw up in the bathroom."

The two men took up a position on either side of him. Gary jabbed Ian in the ribs with his elbow. "You ain't that ugly," he told him. "Why didn't you call us last night at our folks' place? Tom and I would have fixed Trudy up." He cut his eyes to his brother. "I guarantee she wouldn't have puked if I had been here."

"I thought your parents wouldn't let you stay at their place any-more?" Ian said. "Isn't that what you told me last week? Every day you tell me something different."

"They're out of town," Gary said, puffing his chest out. "What they don't know won't hurt them. They're supposed to come back this morning. When you didn't answer the phone this morning, we had to call Willie to come and get us."

"We can't stay with him," Tom explained. "That apartment building he lives in is a pit."

The brothers had practically moved into Ian's apartment. "You guys can stay here every once in a while," he said, throwing the paper sack from the supermarket in one of the trash containers, "but I'll get thrown out if the manager finds out. The rules are strict here. I can't have anyone live with me. The state pays part of my rent. I keep telling you. My mom doesn't want you staying here at all. She's mad at me be-cause I've been spending so much time with you."

Tom draped his arm around Ian. "Your mom just wants to control you. Remember, we've talked about this before. Haven't we been hav-ing fun together? Just like old times, right?"

Ian saw a man and woman walking together and holding hands. Couples could live together, as long as they were approved by the board. The excitement of the previous night passed through his mind, and he felt his body swaying from side to side. Was there a chance he could find someone to share his life with? He'd always dreamed about getting married and having a family. After repeated rejections, though, he'd decided no girl would ever want him. His eyes darted from Gary to Tom. Gary's shirt was stained, his pants filthy, his hair shaggy and uncombed. Tom wasn't that bad, but he never went anywhere without Gary. Trudy had said all those nice things to him. Yeah, he thought, smiling. Trudy liked him. It was Tom and Gary that she didn't want to see. They were the jerks, not him.

Ian thrust his shoulders back with pride, remembering the things Trudy had said when he was making love to her, the sense of power and gratification he'd felt when she'd cried out with pleasure. He knew the girls in the dirty movies were actresses, but he'd felt Trudy's body responding to him. No, he told himself, she hadn't been faking. He started to ask Tom for her phone number, then decided he'd try to ditch the two of them somehow and drive back to her apartment. If she wasn't there, he'd leave a note on her door. He'd offer to take her to a movie, maybe take her out to eat. Girls liked those kind of things.

Once they were inside his apartment, Gary and Tom flopped down on the sofa and turned on the television. Ian told them he wanted to take a nap and went to his room. He could still smell Trudy's perfume on the sheets. He would introduce her to his mother and sister. Pauline would help him pick out a new shirt to wear on their first real date.

Gary threw open the door to his room. "Get up," he said. "You gotta drive us to the Quick-Mart."

Ian sat up in the bed. For the first time, he understood what Elizabeth had been trying to tell him. He shouldn't be hanging out with guys like Gary and Tom. "Why?"

"You know," Gary said, smacking a wad of gum. "We need some

smokes and beer. I ran out about an hour ago. We want to be back before the football game comes on at two. It's already past one, so we need to leave now."

"The Quick-Mart is on the other side of town," Ian protested, standing up and stepping into his tennis shoes. "I just drove to L.A. and back. Why can't you get the stuff at Vons? Vons is cheaper than the Quick-Mart."

"I smoke a certain brand of cigarettes," Gary told him. "They don't sell them at Vons. I don't want to miss the game."

"Whatever," Ian said, deciding he couldn't just throw them out. He'd have to think it through, figure out what he was going to say. All he could think of right now was Trudy. He noticed that Gary was staring at something on the floor by the bed. Ian walked over and picked up a white clip that must have fallen out of Trudy's hair. Holding it in his hand was magical. He opened the dresser and placed it in the top drawer.

"When did Trudy get sick?" Gary asked, looking sharply at Ian. "Last night or this morning?"

"What difference does it make?"

"Just curious," Gary said, although his lips had compressed into a thin line.

Ian took a deep breath. He couldn't let them know what had happened. He had to be smart now. He had to lie, something he'd never really learned how to do. If they knew the truth, they would find a way to take Trudy away from him. "She started throwing up this morning," he said. "She got sick right after she got here, though. The only reason she spent the night was her roommate took the key to her apartment." They were in the living room now, and Tom was waiting for them by the door. "You know why she stayed," Ian said, pulling the door closed behind him. "She called you before she came over here. You're the one who told her to come to my place."

"If we're going, Gary," Tom said firmly, "we need to go now."

When they reached the Quick-Mart, Gary told Ian to park on the left side of the building. "Back in a flash," he said, shoving his hands inside the pockets of his leather jacket. "Keep the engine running."

Ian leaned out the window. Neither of the men ever gave him money for gas. "It costs money to run the engine."

"Damn thing stalled out the other day," Tom said, thumping the side panel of the car as he followed his brother into the store.

Ian dozed off, exhausted from the night before and the conflicting thoughts spinning inside his mind. He bolted upright when he heard the trunk of the Firebird slam shut, then Gary shouting at him as he jumped into the passenger seat. "Move it, Ian! Fast!"

"What's going on?"

"I'll tell you later," Gary said, his eyes trained on the front of the store. "Turn right out of the parking lot, then head south on the freeway."

Ian knew something was terribly wrong. He had never seen Gary this nervous. Mad, yes, but never nervous. Gary's hands were trembling as he fumbled inside his jacket for a cigarette. Gunning the big engine on the Firebird, Ian skidded out of the parking lot, then roared up the ramp to the 101 Freeway. As soon as they passed the city-limit marker for Ventura, Gary said, "Take the next exit."

"Over there," Tom said, pointing to the State Farm Insurance building, which was still under construction. "Pull around to the back."

Ian turned the engine off. "Now, will someone tell me what's going on?"

"Didn't you see those two guys in the store?" Tom asked. "They must have come in right after we did."

Still drowsy, Ian rubbed his eyes. "What guys?"

Reaching over from the backseat, Tom placed his hand on Ian's shoulder. He was wearing a navy-blue long-sleeve shirt, his leather jacket now crammed under the front seat. "The two men," he said. "You must have seen them. They were tall. One guy was wearing a leather jacket almost like mine."

"Yeah," Gary's brother said, nodding in agreement. "This big goon was standing by the cash register while Tom was paying for our stuff. His buddy was lurking around in the back of the store. That's when I told Tom we needed to haul ass, that these guys were up to no good."

Gary fiddled with the cigarette lighter mounted in the dashboard. "Happens all the time," he said, his speech rapid-fire. "People get their heads blown off. An off-duty cop walked in on a holdup last year and got himself killed."

"I fell asleep," Ian told them. "I didn't see anything after you and Tom got out of the car. I must have drunk too much wine last night. My stomach's upset."

"That wasn't wine, idiot," Gary snapped, yanking the cigarette lighter out after he couldn't get it to work and hurling it at the dashboard. "This car is a piece of crap. Who took my lighter?"

Tom retrieved a book of matches off the floorboard and handed it to his brother. Once the nicotine kicked in, Gary seemed to relax. No one spoke for awhile, then Ian started coughing from the smoke.

"You got toasted on sloe gin," Gary told him. "Girls like it because it's sweet. How much did you drink?"

Ian's eyes expanded. "I think I drank the whole bottle."

"This isn't the time to talk," Tom said. "It's like a sardine can back here. Even I can't breathe with your cigarettes, Gary."

How did they know that Trudy had given him a bottle of sloe gin? Ian asked himself. He might not remember everything that happened the night before, but he'd been sober when she'd handed him the paper-wrapped bottle. "You paid her, didn't you?" he said, his fantasies flying out the window. "Trudy's a prostitute."

"At least you're not a virgin anymore," Tom told him, chuckling nervously. "Besides, just because a girl has sex with you doesn't mean she's a prostitute. Trudy's a nice girl. She wouldn't have had sex with you if she didn't like you."

Ian's jaw locked into place, certain Tom was only trying to placate him. "Get out of my car."

Gary stubbed his cigarette out in the ashtray. "What would your momma think if she heard about last night, huh? Would she give you a spanking? She'd probably have you locked up in the funny farm if she knew you'd messed around with a woman. She wants to keep you a baby forever."

"Whoever those men were at the Quick-Mart," Ian told him, "why would they follow us? I'm not as stupid as you think. You're lying to me. What am I? Just someone to drive you around and give you money?"

Gary suddenly exploded, balling up his fist and punching Ian in the face. Tom tried to pull Gary back, but Gary slugged him as well. Seizing Ian around the neck, Gary smashed his head through the glass window, knocking him unconscious. Then he reached over and opened the car door, shoving him out onto the pavement.

"What the hell . . . ?" Tom shouted, looking down at the shards of broken glass in his lap. "You could have cut my arm off."

Tom craned his head out of the narrow rear window, trying to determine how severely Ian was injured. He was relieved when he spotted only a few cuts on his face. "I can't tell if he's breathing," he said. "Jesus Christ, Gary, you may have killed him."

Sweat was pouring off Gary's face. He used the edge of his shirt to blot it off. "Get the gun and the money out of the trunk. Ian knows too much now. He's starting to put things together."

"Ian's my friend," Tom said, his voice shaking. "We played together when we were kids. He said those things because he was hurt, Gary.

We shouldn't have sent Trudy over there last night. You heard what he said. He knows we've been using him."

"Using him," Gary repeated. "Maybe we wouldn't have had to hit the Quick-Mart today if you hadn't given Trudy a lid of Willie's best weed."

"You're the one who wanted Ian out of the way," Tom protested. "We planned on hitting the Quick-Mart last night, remember? Trudy was supposed to occupy Ian while we used the spare set of keys and took his Firebird. Then you smoked five joints and passed out. Only a fool would pull off a robbery in broad daylight."

"Shut up and get the stuff," Gary snarled. "I'm the one who makes the decisions."

Tom felt as if he were standing in front of a speeding train. He knew it was coming, yet he was powerless to stop it. "Ian doesn't listen to the news, Gary. More than likely, he'll never know there was even a robbery. He has a short attention span, remember? That's part of his disability. I bet he won't even remember driving us to the Quick-Mart. Since you knocked him out, Ian will be lucky to remember his name."

"There's a skating rink not too far from here," Gary told him, acting as if he hadn't heard anything his brother had said. "They have lockers."

"A skating rink!" Tom exclaimed, slapping back in the seat. "Don't tell me we're going to put the take from the robbery in a locker at a skating rink? That's the most ridiculous thing I've ever heard. And what about Ian? Are we going to cut him up and put him into a locker too?"

"Using this jerk was your idea." Gary found some leftover napkins in the glove box and pressed them against a cut on his left forearm. "The skating rink will work fine. As soon as we stash the gun and cash at the rink, we'll come back and pick up Ian. Then we can dump him at his apartment and steal a clean car. With any luck, it shouldn't take us more than an hour. His mom's storage lot is right around the corner from his apartment. We have to go to his apartment anyway to pick up the key to the lot."

"No way," Tom said, shaking his head. "We should take Ian with us now. What's the purpose of driving to the skating rink, then all the way back to his apartment?"

Gary pounded his right fist against the steering wheel. "Keep talking like a moron," he said, "and I'll smash your head through the window." He stopped speaking, gulping air. When Gary lost control, the reaction was as physical as it was emotional. He sweated buckets, his nose ran, his eyes watered. "What if someone saw us driving away from the Quick-Mart and copied down the license plate? What about that, little brother? As soon as we get another set of wheels, this rattletrap of Ian's is history."

"No one saw us," Tom pleaded. "I kept my eyes on the street while the clerk was handing over the money. We fired off a round, remember? If anyone saw us, the cops would have busted us before we made it out of the parking lot."

"You wouldn't see a cop if he was parked right next to us," Gary told him. "You're only a few notches above your pal, Ian. You never pay attention. The clerk could have easily got a make on the car. Follow my plan and everything will be fine. Maybe we'll jump on a plane and leave town. I'm sick of Ventura anyway."

"The police might find Ian before we get back," Tom said. "He could come to and start talking."

"It's Sunday afternoon," Gary told him. "The playoffs are on right now. The cop assigned to cover this area is probably holed up somewhere watching the game. None of these buildings are even finished. What reason would the police have to waste their time coming around here?"

Gary stared at the figure on the ground. Ian's legs were twisted to one side, his arms spread out at his sides. "He probably won't wake up for hours. Get the sack out of the trunk like I told you. I want to have the gun on me in case we have a problem."

Tom followed his brother's instructions, opening the trunk of the Firebird and removing the brown sack containing the rumpled bills and the decoy gun. He cursed the day they'd bought that awful thing. Gary liked gadgets, though. Before they'd been thrown out of their parents' house, his brother had been addicted to an interactive war game on the Internet. The gun in the game was said to be identical to a high-powered weapon used by real terrorists.

Willie Crenshaw, their drug connection, had been the one to show them the new gun. Several of his friends had stolen a storage container off a loading dock in Long Beach. Willie and his friends had expected to find appliances, clothes, antiques—things they could sell on the street or hock at a pawnshop.

After they pried open the container and discovered that what appeared to be a shipment of cell phones were actually guns, Willie and his friends had known instantly that they'd struck gold. On the street, a firearm was one of the hottest commodities. And a gun that resembled a cell phone! Never had anyone seen anything even remotely similar.

Gary had been certain Willie was trying to pull a fast one. To prove the gun worked, their friend took them to a field and let them test fire it, setting up a row of tin cans. Not only did it work, the gun was accurate, although the shooter had to be able to site a target without the use of a scope. At the time, Gary and Tom had already pulled off four robberies. The last place they'd hit, however, had been a disaster. The owner of the market had whipped out his own gun and started shooting at them.

Gary had been so hot on the new gun, he'd traded Willie their Jeep Pioneer on the spot, believing the uniqueness of the gun would allow them to move up to businesses with more cash. The crucial point in a robbery occurred the moment the robber pulled out their weapon. Many of the clerks or business owners were also armed, which made robbery a dangerous business. With the cell-phone gun, the victim didn't know what was happening until it was too late.

The Quick-Mart was the first time Gary and Tom had used the new gun. The drawback was that they had to fire off a round to prove the gun was an actual firearm, a situation they had not anticipated. Due to the manner in which the decoy gun was constructed, it couldn't be outfitted with a silencer. As soon as they opened fire, they had to flee the scene immediately.

Willie wasn't just their drug connection. He was another kid from the neighborhood. Willie had been transferred into special-education classes around the same time as Ian. Unlike Ian, however, he'd dropped out of school in the tenth grade. He'd been bumming around ever since, working at menial jobs and dealing. His primary occupation was growing and distributing marijuana. Willie was proud of the fact that he'd never resorted to selling hard drugs. His primary problem was he'd been selling dope in the same town for far too long. Even the cops knew he was a dealer. At the moment, he had several outstanding warrants for possession with intent to distribute.

Once Willie sold whatever guns he had on hand, he'd be out of business. Gary had thought of even greater possibilities. He had befriended a man in San Diego several years back who was a gunsmith. Having served a five-year sentence in prison, this individual claimed to have connections with organized crime. Gary was thinking ahead, considering the possibility that their friend in San Diego might be able to duplicate the new gun. Then they'd never have to worry about money again.

Gary's voice rang out. "What's taking you so long?"

"The key got stuck in the trunk," Tom lied, walking over and bending down next to Ian. He placed his ear against Ian's chest to make certain his heart was beating. He also probed his scalp, wanting to see if there were any deep wounds from the broken glass.

"Leave him alone," Gary yelled at him. "If you mess with him, he might come around. That's the last thing we need right now."

Tom climbed into the passenger seat. "At least you didn't kill him," he said, removing the gun from the sack and handing it to his brother. "After we take him to his apartment, we should call an ambulance. We don't have to tell them our names. All we have to do is give them Ian's address and say he's unconscious."

Gary stared at the gun in the palm of his hand, a look of pleasure spreading across his face. "You may be right," he said. "Ian could wake up and call the police."

Extending his arm out the window, Gary pointed the decoy gun at Ian, his thumb floating an inch above the keypad that served as a numerical trigger mechanism. Tom couldn't believe this was happening. He knew Gary possessed an explosive temper, yet he'd never thought he was capable of killing someone, particularly a person they'd known all their life. Was this really his brother—the man sitting next to him salivating at the thought of depressing one of those buttons?

"The more I think about it," Gary said, his voice eerily calm, "Ian has had a really tough time. No matter what happens with us and the holdups, things are only going to get worse for him as he gets older. We might be doing him a favor if we just killed him."

SEVEN

Thursday, February 8, 2001, 8:45 P.M.

DOUGLAS KUHLMAN was speaking to his attorney from a pay phone at the Los Angeles County jail. After graduating from MIT, he had spent most of his adult life working in air-conditioned, nicely appointed offices where the only sounds were the tapping of computer keys, a few words spoken by a co-worker, or an occasional telephone call. The noise level inside the jail was maddening. Doug placed a hand over his ear, trying to hear what his attorney was saying. He wondered if half the inmates were deaf or if they just liked to shout. Then there were the other sounds—the electronic whine of the cell doors, heavy footsteps on the tiled floors, the blasting television sets in the common areas.

"Are you saying there's no possibility of me getting out of this place?" Doug yelled. "How can the judge deny me bail? I didn't kill or shoot anyone. My cell mate was released on bail the other day, and he's on trial for rape. What the hell is going on here?"

"It's not just the nature of the crimes," Jack Cozzens answered, carefully enunciating his words, "as I've been attempting to explain. The problem is the multiple jurisdictions involved. The child-stealing charges occurred in Ventura County, therefore, they placed a hold on you. LAPD was the first agency to arrest and arraign you. This means they get to keep you until you've been sentenced."

"You're supposed to get me cleared, not sentenced."

"We'll use the word adjudicated, then," Cozzens said, even though he thought Kuhlman was out of his mind if he thought he was going to get out of this mess without serving time. "May I continue?"

"Tell me where we stand now," Doug said, anxiously looking up at the clock on the wall. "And make it fast before my time runs out. We have to report for lockdown in fifteen minutes."

"The DA in Los Angeles has placed a hold on you for forty-two counts of felony embezzlement." At sixty-eight, Jack Cozzens had been a practicing attorney for forty years. Most of his colleagues spent their days on golf or tennis courts. Cozzens had advanced osteoporosis, and now had to use a wheelchair. Renowned in the legal field, representing men like Doug Kuhlman was his hobby. From his experience, men like Kuhlman assumed because they were educated, intelligent, and highly successful individuals, the system should afford them special treatment. "Every time you zapped a penny from Telinx's accounts, you committed a felony. You're lucky the DA didn't file even more counts. Usually they hit you with the full boat, thinking they can pressure you into entering into a plea agreement. I've already spoken to Elaine O'Connor, the supervisor in the Crimes Against Property unit. The DA prosecutes the case, but O'Connor makes the decisions, understand?"

A woman, Doug thought, clenching his teeth. Just what he needed. Facing criminal charges of this magnitude when your ex-wife was a prosecutor was bad enough. Now another woman was involved in deciding his fate. "When did you meet with her?"

"Yesterday," the attorney told him. "O'Connor is willing to negotiate but only if you plead guilty to all forty-two counts, as well as the aggravated white-collar crime enhancement, which could tack on an additional five years to your sentence."

"To each count?"

"No," Cozzens explained. "The enhancement can be applied only once during each criminal proceeding. It can, however, be applied to the other companies you victimized as these cases will be tried separately. That's why the number of jurisdictions involved poses such a problem. In addition, subsection (c) of the same code allows the court to impose a fine double the sum of what was taken."

"This is a nightmare," Doug said, incredulous. "You're telling me that if they determine that I took five hundred grand, they can fine me a million bucks as well as add five years to my prison sentence."

"The cap is five hundred thousand per criminal proceeding," Cozzens told him. "Let's focus on the crimes committed against Telinx, which is what we're dealing with at present."

"Fine," Doug said, biting his lip.

"L.A. essentially wants to clear their cases, so they can hand you over to the authorities in Ventura. That's the only reason they'd even consider offering you a deal."

"What kind of deal is that?" Doug said. "According to what you just said, they want me to plead guilty to all forty-two counts, plus this enhancement."

"I'd personally try to settle if I were you," Cozzens said thoughtfully. "I'm not certain if the DA was unable to get the proper documentation from Telinx to file on every offense you committed, or if they simply decided it wasn't worth tying the court up since so many other law enforcement entities have placed holds on you. There's nothing to preclude them from filing more counts, you realize."

"Great," Doug said, feeling as if his head were about to explode. "You're basically telling me that I could have raped someone and had a better chance of seeing daylight. Am I right?"

"I wouldn't phrase it precisely that way," Cozzens told him, chuckling under his breath. This was the part he enjoyed, explaining the ambiguities and absurdities in the criminal justice system to people like Kuhlman, who thought they would never have to face the consequences of their actions. "The judge has the option of sentencing you concurrently or consecutively, so that's a major consideration."

"How much time are we talking about?"

"Approximately nine years," Cozzens answered. "That's a concurrent sentence. You hear the word consecutive fall out of the judge's mouth and you can multiple that figure by forty-two."

"You can't be serious?" Doug said, in such a frenzy he couldn't do the math. "I might as well have killed someone. The way you're making it sound, I could spend the rest of my life in prison."

Doug had been upset even before he'd spoken to Cozzens. Leah had cried again today. Neither Mike nor Leah had visited him once since his incarceration. Joanne claimed she couldn't take the time off from work to drive them to Los Angeles, and by the time the weekend rolled around, she was too exhausted. He knew she was punishing him, wanting him to know what it felt like to be deprived of his children. Keeping Leah away from him, however, was hurting their daughter more than him. Leah had told him she'd been planning to run away when she'd taken Joanne's car, then decided she couldn't survive on the small amount of money her mother gave her as an allowance. He'd reassured her that he could get her whatever money she needed, but he didn't want to encourage her to take off on her own. Although he hadn't said anything to his daughter, for obvious reasons, he had given thought to hiring someone to take the children again and care for them until he was free. Before he did anything drastic, however, he had to figure out where he stood in the legal arena.

The situation with Mike was another cause for concern. Over the past month, his son had barely said two words to him. If Joanne had only been reasonable, Doug told himself, he wouldn't be in this predicament. His ex-wife had tracked him down at the worst possible time, just after he had worked out the remaining problems on a series of revolutionary new operating systems.

"The Denver authorities have also placed a hold on you," Jack Cozzens told him, thumbing through the papers on his desk. "Let's see, the pleading they sent me today lists ten felony counts. I also received some documents in the mail from Switzerland and Italy the other day. I haven't had time to look them over yet."

"I've got more money than you could ever imagine," Kuhlman said, his heart doing a tap dance inside his chest. "I could put my hands on fifty million if you can get me a ticket out of here. I didn't say fifty thousand, Cozzens. I said fifty million!"

Cozzens let out a long sigh. "Under the circumstances, I'm going to pretend I didn't hear that statement."

"The money will come in clean," Doug told him, cupping his hand around the phone. "Remember the company I told you about, Computer Innovations International, the one I sold a software security system to just before my arrest?" This is what really chapped him. He'd seen an entire universe of opportunity unfolding in the area of Internet gambling. In order to study how they were operating the on-line gambling sites, Doug had started betting sporting events and horse races. Working at Telinx had grown stale, and Joanne had been immersed in her work as a district attorney or busy taking care of the children. Before he knew it, he had forgotten about developing the security software to protect such enterprises and found himself sucked into the emotional roller-coaster ride of chance.

"Let me give you some advice," Cozzens told him. "We're talking off the record here. Man to man, so to speak. I won't even bill you for the time. All I want is for you to listen carefully to what I'm about to tell you."

Doug glanced over his shoulder, waiting until one of the guards had walked past. "Go ahead," he mumbled. "I'm listening."

"I've already done some checking on this company," Cozzens said, his tone sharper now. "People always tell guys like you that you can get away with this stuff. Then when the shit hits the fan, they bail out so fast it makes your head spin. They've got nothing to lose, and in some situations, everything to gain."

Doug braced himself against the wall, his stomach rolling over like a beach ball.

"You own Computer Innovations," Cozzens said, his voice laced with conviction. "Just because you've got other people fronting for you doesn't mean anything. There's a paper trail a mile long and it leads directly to your doorstep. You're a smart fellow. It's hard for me to understand this type of deal, even though I see it all the time."

The money amounted to years of mind-boggling and tedious work. This was Doug's bailout, his only hope, the one thing that kept him from going insane inside this filthy, stinking institution. Admittedly, he'd made serious mistakes, both in the financial and personal arena. What he'd told Cozzens, however, was the truth. Before Joanne had tracked him down, he'd successfully sold his new software program to Forrest Hoyt Technologies for fifty million dollars. Forrest Hoyt Technologies was now the largest manufacturer of computer software in the universe. After a legal battle between the established titans in the industry had ended in a stalemate, the three major players had merged under the Forrest Hoyt Technologies umbrella. Doug's timing had been impeccable. As people all over the world grew weary of using telephone lines for Internet access, and converted to cable or high-speed DSL connections, the risks involved became apparent. Doug's program, Lockout, was revolutionary in the industry as it not only blocked all attempts to hack into computer systems, it provided documentation that could be presented in a court of law.

Due to the money he'd embezzled from Telinx and dozens of other computer firms over the years, Doug was forced into funneling his profits through from the sale of Lockout by means of an offshore corporation. The law firm who'd negotiated the deal with Forrest Hoyt Technologies had suggested he set up an offshore corporation, and one of the attorneys had even taught tax law. Of course, the lawyers had no knowledge of Doug's true identity or any reason to suspect that he was involved in criminal activities. As soon as he'd taken the children and fled, he'd legally changed his name to Walter Evans Breymore. He'd needed a cover anyway to keep Joanne from tracing his whereabouts. The children had even grown accustomed to using the Breymore name. Doug explained that offspring of wealthy individuals were sometimes kidnapped, and that he had changed their name for their own safety.

Since the Breymore name wasn't listed anywhere in the articles of incorporation for Computer Innovations, he couldn't say he was totally unaware of the risks involved. The attorneys he'd dealt with had assuaged his fears, however, swearing they'd never had a problem with this particular banking institution, nor any of the outside individuals who would be handling the financial transactions on his behalf.

The reason Doug's program had not been developed in-house by Forrest Hoyt Technologies was fairly simple. Even before the merger, Forrest Hoyt Technologies, along with most of the giants in the computer industry, had been working frenetically in the development of advanced operating systems. A man like James Hoyt might have blinked a few times when on-line gambling started to surface, yet technology was exploding in so many directions that it was impossible for him to seize every opportunity. In addition, Internet gambling was extremely complex. Telinx and other major technology-based conglomerates were reluctant to do business with the kind of unsavory and paranoid individuals affiliated with the gaming industry. A virtual casino could lose millions of dollars in a matter of minutes if their system was impeached.

"Do you recall an individual by the name of Michael Milken?"

"Of course," Doug said, snapping to attention. He was a featherweight compared to a financial icon such as Milken, considered one of the greatest financial innovators in history. In one year alone, Milken had earned five hundred and fifty million in the junk-bond market. He'd served only two years in prison and managed to reestablish his position in society.

"Do you have the kind of money Milken had?" Cozzens asked. "Say an extra three or four hundred million tucked away somewhere that you earned legitimately? That's outside of whatever funds you have in this Computer Innovations account in the Cayman Islands. If you do, now would be a good time to tell me."

"No, no," Doug muttered.

Jack Cozzens was ready to have a little fun with an amateur in the field of life. "When Dante wrote *The Divine Comedy,* many people declared it unfathomable. Even if you've never had a chance to read his work, the title alone was both magnificent and astute."

"What does this have to do with Michael Milken?" Doug asked, perplexed. "What I really want to know is what does it have to do with me?"

"It's a play on words," Cozzens told him, laughing again. "I don't care much for milk. Lactose intolerant, you know."

"You're not billing me to discuss your digestive problems, I hope?"

"No," Cozzens said, his tone serious again. "As I said earlier, the last half of our conversation is off-the-record. You have just received some of my most valuable advice. Knowledge can be sold, as you well know. Genius is many times imprinted in a human's genetic code. Wisdom, however, is priceless."

Doug was ready to jump out of his skin. A shrill tone blasted forth from the speakers, then a voice came on issuing the five-minute warning for them to return to their cells. "Look," he shouted, stepping aside as several inmates marched past him. "I paid you three hundred grand to represent me. I don't need to listen to all this philosophical baloney. Start doing something to get me out of this mess, or I'm going to hire another attorney."

"You've got plenty of time to think about the things we've discussed tonight, maybe even solve my little riddle," Jack Cozzens said caustically. "Regardless of who represents you, Mr. Kuhlman, you can kiss the money you have in this offshore corporation good-bye."

A lie was still a lie, Doug thought, tasting the harsh reality of his moralistic upbringing. Even in the world of mathematics and programming, his father's words held true. If you made a lie your root, no matter how many years you worked at a problem, the result would ultimately be worthless.

EIGHT

I AN DECKER dialed his mother's number from the pay phone in the lobby of the Economy Inn. The Rubinskys had sent him out to pick up food. Just as he heard his mother's voice, Gary stepped up behind him and yanked the phone out of his hands, then pressed the button to disconnect the call. "I knew you were doing things behind our back, you stupid prick!"

"I wasn't doing anything wrong," Ian said. "I just wanted to see if my mother was okay."

"What did I tell you?" Gary said, spitting the words at him. "Your mother's poison. If I ever catch you talking to her, I'll wring your neck like a chicken. Where's the damn food?"

"I . . . I haven't gone to get it yet," Ian stammered. "I don't understand why I can't drive the car anymore. I don't like to walk when it's dark."

"Forget the food," Gary said, staring at something through the window. He made a motion for Ian to follow him, leading him up the back staircase to their room.

Tom was asleep on the bed. Gary walked over and shook him. "I'm almost positive I saw a cop car parked across the street, and I caught Ian trying to call his mother. For all we know, he's already told her where we're staying."

"You think the police found out we swiped the car?"

Gary paced around the small room like a caged animal. "No," he said. "We're cool with the car. We could probably drive the Chrysler another three months and get away with it. I found the paperwork in the glove box the other day. The car's only been on the storage lot for six weeks. Since it's been wrecked, the insurance company must have totaled it. My bet is the owner's already been paid off and ABC is just waiting to get the paperwork pushed through so they can sell it."

Tom popped open another can of Budweiser. "Then why are you all worked up?"

"They're waiting for us to do something so they can slam our butts back in jail," Gary told him, walking over and snatching the can of beer out of his brother's hands. He took a swig, then handed it back. "They're not gonna put me back in one of those cages. No one leaves this room except you until we figure out another place to stay."

"Why me?" Tom exclaimed. "What if I get stopped? Maybe Ian's mother found out the car was missing from the lot. She knows Ian doesn't have the Firebird anymore."

"The cops aren't interested in Ian," Gary said, a wild look in his eyes. "We're the ones they're after. What if they saw us leaving the skating rink?"

"You're paranoid," Tom said, flopping down in the chair. "Are you certain that's regular pot you're smoking? You haven't been using crack, have you?"

Ian had a puzzled look in his eyes. "You guys went skating?"

Tom laughed before he realized his brother had made a mistake by mentioning the skating rink. "We thought we could score some more pot from a guy we know who deals around there." He tilted his head to one side. "You need to think every now and then, Ian. Do you really think Gary and I went skating? We're in big trouble here."

Tom's brother had been seconds away from killing Ian the day they'd robbed the Quick-Mart. A car full of kids had pulled up, and Tom and Gary told them Ian was drunk and had fallen down. Then they had placed Ian in the backseat of the Firebird and dropped him off at the apartment before they had gone on to the skating rink.

"We can't stay in this room until the trial is over," Tom told him. "It could be months. And Ian's got a thousand dollar limit on that credit card. Once the motel runs our tab, we'll be out on the street."

Ian was too afraid to speak out. With his finger, he touched the abraded spot near his hairline. He only recalled fragments of the Saturday afternoon when he'd driven Tom and Gary to the Quick-Mart. The doctor at the hospital told him it wasn't uncommon to suffer memory loss from a head injury. He said the cause of Ian's blackout could have been all the booze he'd consumed the night before. According to the brothers, he'd struck his head against the door window. He swore he'd never drink alcohol again. All he remembered was waking up in his apartment with a cut on his head and a terrible headache. On the drive home from the hospital, the police had stopped the three men and placed them under arrest. Although the clerk hadn't copied down the complete license plate, he'd reported the make, model, and color, along with the letters "FDS."

"We wouldn't have had this problem if Ian still had his apartment," Tom pointed out. "How are we going to find another place to stay without a credit card?"

"I lost my apartment because you guys kept taking my money," Ian said, brushing his hair off his forehead. "It took my mom years to get me a spot in that complex."

Gary lunged at him. Ian jumped out of his chair and flattened himself against the wall, certain the other man was going to hit him. "I don't want to hear anything about your stupid apartment anymore, get it?" Gary poked Ian in the chest with his finger, then snarled at him, "Did we take your money, huh? You gave us the money. You wanted us to have the money. Did we need your lousy money?"

Ian crept along the wall, but Gary punched him in the stomach, causing him to double over in pain. Ian grabbed on to the green curtain, pulling himself back to an upright position.

"Isn't that what happened?" Gary continued, swiping at his mouth with the back of his hand. "Are you going to try and say we robbed you? Is that what you've got on that idiotic brain of yours?"

"No, Gary." Ian heard a rip, then saw a piece of the curtain had torn off in his hand. "Please, don't hurt me."

"Then say it," Gary Rubinsky yelled. "You heard me. Say it!"

Tears were streaming down Ian's face. "You didn't take my money. I wanted you to have it because we were friends."

"Fine," Gary said, panting now. "And did we rob the Quick-Mart?"

"No," Ian answered. "All you did was go in for some beer."

"When we came out of the store," Gary went on, his breath hot and rancid on Ian's face, "what did I have in my hand?"

"A sack," Ian whimpered, wiping the tears from his face with the scrap of green fabric. "A sack with beer in it. That's all you had, Gary . . . just a sack of beer and some cigarettes."

"Did I have a wad of money?"

Ian shook his head, his hands locked into fists at his side.

"Have you ever seen the gun the police say we used? Do I even have a cell phone or anything that looks like that gun?"

"No . . . Gary . . . please," Ian pleaded, his shoulders shaking as he sobbed. "You don't have a cell phone. You don't have a gun. I never saw any money. I promise I'll never say anything except what you tell me. Only what you tell me, Gary. Only what you tell me."

Gary snatched the beer off the table and finished it in one swallow, then crushed the can in his fist. "See what you started," he said to his brother. "Now the baby is crying. And you think we can trust him. Think again, Tom."

NINE

WHEN JOANNE arrived at her office, the receptionist at the front desk handed her a large envelope, advising her that Arnold Dreiser had left it for her. She assumed it contained the records she had requested on Ian Decker. As Joanne was heading to her office, she ran into Dean Kennedy, the elected district attorney. He stopped, which surprised her. Generally Kennedy whisked past her without so much as a nod. "How's your trial coming along? That new gun is frightening."

"More complicated than I expected," Joanne told him, eager to research the materials before she discussed them. "Dreiser claims Ian Decker is developmentally disabled, that he was unaware that he was participating in a crime."

"I see," Kennedy said, glancing down as he thought. At thirty-nine, he had a thick head of brown hair, rust-colored eyes, and a tall, lanky frame. No one under forty had ever held his position. His brilliance was uncontested, his grasp of the law rivaling that of any Supreme Court justice. People speculated that his post as district attorney was only the first step in what would turn out to be an exceptional career.

He spoke in short, choppy sentences, always concise, and was known to make almost instantaneous decisions. He seldom made mistakes, yet when he did, he was the first to admit it. "Is this person mentally incompetent to stand trial?"

"No," she answered. "At least, not according to the present standards for competency. I need to go over Decker's school and psychological records before the hearing. I'll keep you informed."

"Dreiser is cunning," Kennedy cautioned, holding up a finger. "Make certain that whatever records he gives you are authentic. He's had some serious personal problems."

Joanne stepped aside to let another attorney pass. "I know about his son's suicide." She paused and took a breath. "I've had problems as well. That doesn't mean I would falsify documents."

"This has nothing to do with your situation."

"Are you questioning Dreiser's integrity?"

"No," Kennedy said crisply. "When you finish going over the information, stop by my office. I want to be apprised of all the particulars before you respond to this motion."

Joanne watched as he took off down the corridor. His gait was stiff and his arms hung loosely at his sides.

Most of the clerical staff were just reporting to work. A number of attorneys had already been at their desks for hours, poring over police reports, examining evidence, dictating pleadings, reading victims' statements, or attempting to interpret California's convoluted legal system. Unlike other professions in contemporary society, much of a prosecutor's work had to be done at the office. Any item considered evidence such as criminal history files, and other highly sensitive or irreplaceable documents, were not allowed to leave the building.

Joanne's office was located down a corridor on the right side of the floor. The front was enclosed in glass, yet there were no windows, and the room was about the size of a walk-in closet. Her co-workers constantly complained about the lack of offices with windows. Even in the jail, they said, many of the prisoners could see the outside world. Removing her key, she inserted it into the lock and stepped inside. She had no interest in having a window. When a person looked out the window, they contemplated. Inside her office, Joanne's only goal was to concentrate.

A little more space would be nice, she told herself, having to step over several cardboard evidence boxes to reach her desk. Even that wasn't a necessity, however, as the size of the room made it easier for her to find whatever books or files she needed. Since she possessed no compulsion for order, a little clutter here and there didn't bother her. As long as she remained focused, her surroundings disappeared. One of the male prosecutors insisted he couldn't work unless every object on his desk remained in exactly the same position. He pitched a fit if the cleaning staff moved so much as a stapler.

Placing her backpack on the floor, Joanne ripped open the envelope Dreiser had left, dropped down in her chair, and began reading.

"We have a problem," Dreiser said, waiting for Joanne outside the doors to the courtroom.

"I reviewed the paperwork," she told him. "It doesn't make sense to continue voir dire if Spencer rules to sever the cases."

Dreiser's face twisted into a grimace. "Will you please just listen to me," he said forcefully. "Ian is gone."

"You mean he failed to appear?"

"The Rubinskys told their attorneys he skipped out last night," he told her. "I don't believe them."

"I have to inform Spencer so he can issue an arrest warrant," Joanne said, her mind clocking at lightning speeds. "I guess this guy isn't as innocent as you thought, Arnold."

She tried to push past him when he stepped in front of her. "The police have already been notified," he said. "I just left Spencer's chambers. That's why I didn't wait to speak to you after I dropped off Ian's paperwork. Spencer is signing the arrest warrant as we speak. The case has been postponed until next week. We tried to call your office but your machine picked up."

"I thought you were a defense attorney," Joanne told him, annoyed. "Now you're doing my job for me. Thanks, Arnold. Why did you make me go over Decker's records if you already knew he'd disappeared? It's not as if I don't have enough to do. Between yesterday and this morning, you've wasted hours of my time."

"I'm certain the Rubinskys are lying," the attorney said, placing his hand on her arm. "Elizabeth is waiting in my office. Come, I want you to talk to her in person."

"How far away is your office?" Joanne pulled away from him. "I can't simply walk out of the building. I have to get permission from Kennedy, verify that the warrant has been issued. We have to make certain the police are notified that Decker may be armed."

"I'd be less worried if Ian was armed."

"What does that mean?"

"You have a cell phone, right?"

"A real cell phone," Joanne said, trying to assimilate the conflicting information. "I can't push a button and kill someone with it. All I can do is make phone calls. And you have the gall to tell me you'd prefer Decker . . ."

"Forget it," Dreiser said, cutting her off. "Use your cell phone and get permission to leave the building. The longer we procrastinate, the less of a chance we have to get Ian back alive. They may be holding him somewhere until the trial is over."

"The Rubinskys?" Joanne asked. "I'm lost, Arnold. Didn't you just tell me Gary and Tom Rubinsky are the ones who advised the court that Ian had absconded? Why would these men show up in court if they'd kidnapped or murdered your client?"

"Only Tom showed up," he explained. "He claims Gary is looking for Ian. Regardless, they want to make it look as if Ian pulled off the robbery without their knowledge. I told you there were problems with this case when we had lunch yesterday."

"Then Gary failed to appear as well?" Joanne said, resting her back against the wall.

"Technically," Dreiser said. "Whatever these guys do, they do together. Tom told his attorney Gary was on his way to the courthouse. When Tom found out the judge was going to continue the case, he called Gary and told him not to come."

"I want an arrest warrant issued for both of these men," Joanne insisted. "This whole situation stinks."

"Spencer said the same thing," Dreiser told her. "About the case . . ."

"What about the case?"

"The fact that the victim picked all three men out of a lineup isn't significant. They've never denied that they were at the Quick-Mart. The only thing they're denying is that they committed the robbery."

"Why are we talking about this now?" Joanne said. "I thought you wanted me to go to your office immediately."

"I do," Dreiser said, gritting his teeth. He paused and took a deep breath. "I'm trying to explain what I think is happening here. The man who identified Decker's car just got out of drug rehab. He didn't see the robbery go down. He didn't see the gun or hear the gunshot. He was just walking by picking up cans. Do you want to listen to what I have to say now?"

When Joanne just glared at him, Dreiser continued, "Tom Rubinsky said the three of them have been holed up at the Economy Inn for the past week. Ian evidently used his credit card to book the room. I didn't know where they were staying, and neither did Elizabeth. She called all over town trying to find him."

"Couldn't she track him through the credit card company?"

"Because the card was in Ian's name," Dreiser explained, "the company refused to give her any information." Arnold glanced at his watch, knowing Elizabeth was waiting for them. "The card is maxed out now, so Ian can't use it."

Joanne cleared her throat. "Finish what you were saying earlier."

"According to Tom," Dreiser continued, "Ian said he was going out to get something to eat last night around ten. He came back shortly after eleven with a suitcase, telling Gary and Tom that his mother had given him money and told him to leave town because she couldn't stand the possibility that he might go to prison."

"Have you asked Elizabeth if she saw Ian last night?"

"Of course," he said. "Elizabeth swears she didn't give Ian money nor has she seen him. The most important aspect of the Rubinskys' story is that they're claiming that while Ian was in the bathroom, they opened his suitcase and saw a canvas bag containing both the money from the robbery and the gun. Ian wrestled it away from them and took off. Does that sound plausible to you? You went over his history this morning, right? The Rubinsky brothers are huge. Do you really believe Ian could take anything away from these men?"

"This is their official statement, what they intend to tell the police?"

"Precisely," Dreiser said. "That's why Tom showed up in court this morning. What we're dealing with here could be far more serious than a convenience store robbery. I think they killed him. They killed him because he knew too much and because he was weak. People with Ian's disabilities aren't good liars. They knew he'd break down on the witness stand."

"I'll follow you," Joanne said. "Meet me in front of the building in five minutes."

TEN

A PPROXIMATELY TWENTY minutes later, Joanne pulled up next to Arnold Dreiser's black Cadillac Escalade in the parking lot of the Bank of America building. On the drive over, she'd spoken to Judge Spencer and the Ventura PD, as well as Dean Kennedy, confirming that warrants for the arrest of Ian Decker and Gary Rubinsky were issued for armed robbery and failure to appear. Kennedy had instructed her to report back to his office as soon as she concluded her interview with Elizabeth Decker. He said he would have one of the other attorneys prepare a search warrant for the room the defendants had been using at the Economy Inn, then have Judge Spencer sign it.

Dreiser's law firm was housed on the eighth floor of the Bank of America building. Behind the double oak doors, there was a nicely furnished reception area, a conference room that doubled as a law library, and three spacious offices with floor-to-ceiling windows. "One of my partners quit," he said, escorting her down a carpeted hallway. "Want to resign your job with the county?"

"Don't tempt me," Joanne told him. "Right now, I'm scraping the bottom of the barrel financially. I couldn't handle representing men like the Rubinskys, though, no matter how much money was involved. Putting them behind bars is more gratifying."

Elizabeth Decker stood and extended her hand as Joanne entered the room. "I appreciate your coming," she said, her voice strained. "They've done something terrible to my son."

"I wouldn't jump to conclusions," Joanne told her, clasping the distraught woman's hand. "Right now, all we're dealing with is failure to appear. This type of thing is extremely common. Either the police will pick up your son, or he'll come back voluntarily."

"I woke up early this morning," the woman said. "My nightgown was dripping wet from sweat. I was certain Ian was in the room with me."

"Could he have come into the house without your knowledge?" Joanne asked, wondering if the Rubinskys' story might be true. "Were you missing any money?"

"No," Elizabeth said, sitting back down in a chair facing Dreiser's desk. The two attorneys took their seats as well. "I was wide awake. Ian wasn't in the house. He doesn't even have a key anymore. Once he started hanging out with Gary and Tom, I took the key away from him. My son and I were very close before those awful men came into his life. Even when he was a toddler, I could always sense when he needed me. If something happened at school, they didn't even have to call me. I'd drop whatever I was doing and go straight to the school. By the time I got there, Ian would be waiting on the front steps."

"My children were missing for two years," Joanne said, attempting to maintain her perspective. "Neither one of them was on trial for robbery. Your son is an adult, Mrs. Decker. Even if he weren't facing criminal charges, adults disappear by choice all the time. It doesn't mean they've been killed, or that some other dreadful thing has happened to them."

"My son is dead."

Joanne rubbed her forehead. "Are you trying to say you're psychic?"

Elizabeth's back stiffened, her voice was edged with bitterness. "I know things, okay? I'm not a psychic, and I'm certainly not insane. Look at how you're talking to me, like you think I'm some kind of nutcase. I'm a mother who loves her son. Having a special kid like Ian is one of God's greatest blessings. I feel honored that Ian is my son, that God entrusted this life to me. You lawyer people think you're so smart. You've got all these fancy degrees, but you miss what's really important in life. You'll find out, though. Everyone finds out eventually."

"I didn't mean . . ."

"You think Ian knew what those thugs were doing?" Elizabeth continued. "You think my son is a criminal, don't you?"

Joanne crossed her legs, then uncrossed them. She remembered all the nights she'd bolted upright in her bed, certain she'd heard Mike or Leah calling for her. Elizabeth had every right to be offended. "Your son's guilt or innocence will be determined by a jury," she said quietly. "That is, if the police locate him. I'm just a prosecutor. All I do is handle whatever cases I'm assigned."

"They killed him!" Elizabeth shouted, rising several inches from her chair. "Those terrible men have murdered my son. You don't care. No one has ever cared about Ian. All my life I've fought his battles, taken care of him, made certain he was safe."

"Calm down," Dreiser said. "Ms. Kuhlman is only trying to reason with you, Elizabeth. Tell her what you know about the Rubinskys."

Elizabeth stared off into space. A few moments later, she removed a tissue from her purse to wipe her eyes. "Gary's a bully and a liar. He even hit his own mother one time."

"Did she report it?"

"I don't think so," Elizabeth said. "When it's your kid, you sometimes look the other way. I think Gary was about sixteen at the time. I guess his mother tried to discipline him, and he beat her up. All I remember is she had a black eye and some nasty bruises."

"What about Tom?"

"Tom," Elizabeth said, "is basically a follower. Ian and Tom were close until Ian got pulled out of regular classes. All Ian's friends dumped him then. From that point on, Ian never had any friends that didn't use him or hurt him. After a while, he stopped trying to fit in and retreated into his own world. He liked television, movies, animals. He was studying welding, you know, until the Rubinskys got their hands on him. I'm not certain if he would have completed the course. He was scared of the equipment, afraid he'd burn himself. Around the time he started hanging out with the Rubinskys, he'd asked me to see if I could get him transferred to another program. Nothing was available. I knew these men had befriended him because they wanted to use his car. I threatened to take the car back if he didn't stop seeing them. I couldn't bring myself to do it. Ian loved that car. The car and his apartment were his first steps toward independent living."

"Do you know the Rubinskys' parents?"

"Yes," she answered. "They still live in the same house, about five doors down from us. Louise kicked Gary and Tom out years ago. She continued to give them money, though, which was a mistake in my eyes. Neither one of them has ever been able to keep a job longer than a few months. They were into drugs, alcohol, all kinds of things."

"I spent several hours this morning going over your son's school and psychological records," Joanne told her. "I thought there might be a possibility of letting him plead guilty to a lesser offense. By fleeing, though, Ian has made himself appear even more culpable."

Dreiser decided to bring the meeting to a close before Elizabeth became upset again. "Perhaps we should wait and see what happens over the next few days. You've already called all the local hospitals and nothing has turned up. The next step is to begin checking other cities."

"Your son will probably contact you," Joanne told Elizabeth, leaning forward. "He's going to contact you because he'll run out of money—whether he got it from you or someone else. He doesn't appear to be strong or resourceful enough to make it on his own for very long."

"I swear," Elizabeth said, wiping more tears from her face with a tissue. "I didn't give him any money. And I would never encourage him to leave. I put my house up as collateral for his bail. If he doesn't come back, I'll lose my home."

"When and if Ian contacts you," Joanne continued, "you must do everything in your power to encourage him to surrender to the authorities. Because of the uniqueness of the gun involved in this crime, the police may open fire on him."

Elizabeth was on the brink of hysteria. "Now you're telling me the police are going to kill him! Oh, my God! My poor baby."

"I didn't say that," Joanne said, a line of perspiration breaking out on her forehead. "Whether you realize it or not, Mrs. Decker, I'm trying to help you. You think I'm your adversary. That isn't true. I have children of my own. I care about your son. When I looked at his school papers this morning, I could see how hard he's struggled. Guilty or innocent, I don't want him to get hurt. That's why I'm telling you these things."

Joanne stood, walked over to Arnold's desk, and picked up a yellow notepad and pen. "Here," she said, handing the items to Elizabeth. "Write this down. Make several copies and tape them near every phone in your house. Instruct anyone who answers the phone to follow the instructions I'm about to give you." She paused, waiting as Elizabeth pulled a law book off the shelf behind her and placed the notepad on top of it.

"Okay," Joanne continued, pacing in front of Dreiser's desk as if she were in a courtroom, "the reason I want you to write this down is the following. When your son calls, you're going to be so relieved to hear from him that you're going to forget what to say. Also, he probably won't stay on the line for fear the police will be able to trace the call."

Elizabeth looked up. "Ian isn't that smart."

"Don't kid yourself," Joanne said, arching an eyebrow. "He's been associating with the Rubinsky brothers for some time now. Not only that, he watches television. Even a fifth grader would suspect that the phone might be tapped."

"What do you want me to write?"

"That he should not under any circumstances buy or use a cell phone," Joanne told her, holding up a finger. "Mark that as number one on your list. Second, if he does have the decoy gun in his possession, tell him to deposit it in a trash bin behind the closest police station, then call and tell you where he left it so someone else doesn't retrieve it and use it in the commission of another crime. Firearms have a long life on the street. Sometimes the same gun is used in hundreds of crimes. The last set of fingerprints on that gun will be your son's if the person who finds it uses gloves."

"I don't believe Ian ran off," Elizabeth said, scribbling down Joanne's words as she spoke. "Even if he did get scared and leave town, he'd never go anywhere near a police station for fear they'd arrest him."

"Then that's your job to convince him," Joanne said, locking eyes with her. "Do you understand?"

Elizabeth nodded, shoving a limp strand of hair behind one ear.

"The next thing you must tell him is how to conduct himself if he's stopped by the police," she said. "Instruct him to place his hands over his head or somehow make certain the officer can be assured he isn't going to shoot him. Tell him not to reach for the glove compartment, a piece of paper, or anything that even vaguely resembles a cell phone or a firearm. Police officers are trained to use the word 'freeze' for a reason. It's not just a catchy phrase."

Joanne picked up her backpack to leave. "I'm sorry, Mrs. Decker. Regardless of your son's guilt or innocence, he's in grave danger. In that respect, I completely agree with you."

"Don't leave yet." Elizabeth wanted to ask her something, but her mind had gone blank. She glanced down at the notes she'd made, hoping she had written them correctly. The prosecutor was a wise woman. In a crisis, it *was* easy to forget. "I've been through so much lately, I don't know how much more I can stand. Is what you said going to happen? Are the police going to tap my phone?"

"Not yet," Joanne said. "Right now, I'm going to treat this as nothing more than a failure to appear. I am, however, going to attempt to find out if the Rubinsky brothers are lying. We'll get a search warrant for the room at the Economy Inn. If the Rubinskys did harm your son, they're going to be two of the sorriest men ever to walk the face of the earth."

ELEVEN

THE SKY was awash in dazzling colors. Aboard the *Nightwatch*, Eli Connors was savoring the sunset, waiting until the last touch of pink turned to gray before he opened the hatch and went below.

The main section of the ship resembled a miniature version of the war room at the Pentagon. Eight monitors were lined up along the walls, connected to eight Celestron Nexstar 8 telescopes mounted in various locations on the deck. With his feet resting on a teakwood shelf that served as a credenza, Eli was finishing a bowl of home-made beef stew. He rolled his chair sideways, flipping various switches to rotate the telescopes. The white Lexus had just appeared on one of the monitors, and he had to make the proper adjustments. This had turned out to be a far more expensive operation than he'd anticipated. He'd had to purchase several more telescopes. Because of the terrain and the lack of lighting, they had to be equipped with infrared capabilities. He wasn't focusing on one house, but the en-tire community. Even though he didn't mind upgrading his equipment, he'd been experiencing problems with his generator. The *Nightwatch* was not structurally able to hold anything larger, and it would take years to outfit another vessel.

"Why did she have to move into this place?" Eli grumbled, setting his bowl down. At least Joanne didn't close the drapes in the front of the house, he thought, watching as she exited the car and entered the Spencers' house.

After another hour passed and the Lexus remained parked in the driveway, Eli switched one of the monitors over to a news channel. Another massive earthquake had struck, this time in India. The death toll was expected to be over a hundred thousand. He stared at the gory images, longing for the days when people didn't regard death, destruction, and misery as forms of entertainment. How many earthquakes did it take? How many hurricanes, floods, tornados, plane crashes, train wrecks, explosions?

An hour passed. Eli stood and stretched, deciding it was time to drop the dinghy and go ashore, maybe put his feet on some solid ground. He raised his eyes to the star-filled sky. "You're talking, Boss," he said. "The only problem is no one is listening."

"She can't go, Mom," Mike said, glaring at his sister. "She'll tell everyone that I'm only twelve. She'll ruin everything. I've waited all week to go to this party. I didn't take your car and go joyriding in the middle of the night. Leah did. She's always doing things behind your back."

"Jerk," Leah said, picking up the plates to load into the dishwasher. "I was invited too. All my friends are going."

"Mike is right," Joanne was seated at the kitchen table. "Taking my car was a serious thing, Leah. You don't deserve to go to a party. Let Mike have a little fun for a change. As long as he follows the rules, I don't see any harm letting the kids around here think he's a few years older."

"So he can lie, right?" Leah said, placing her hands on her hips. "Dad is such a bad person you won't even drive us to L.A. to visit him. But it's fine for Mike to lie about his age." She flung her arms in the air. "I guess I can start telling everyone I'm twenty-one."

"Stop it, Leah." Joanne turned to her son. "Did you purposely tell people you were older?"

"No," he said, shrugging. "No one even asked me my age. They just thought I was in high school because I'm tall. Maybe I act older. How do I know?"

"We're going to be moving soon, anyway."

"I thought you said all I had to do was cook dinner and clean the kitchen," Leah argued. "Now you're grounding me."

"Just for tonight."

Leah smashed the plate in the sink. "I hate you!" she shouted. "No wonder Dad left you. You're a bitch. The only reason he took us away is because you threatened to turn him in to the police. He would have paid back the money. You didn't give him a chance."

"That's it," Joanne said, narrowing her eyes at her daughter. "Clean up the dish you broke. You're grounded for the next two weeks."

"Clean it up yourself," Leah said, storming out of the kitchen.

Joanne marched into her daughter's room.

"What are you doing?" Leah eyed her suspiciously.

Joanne bent down and unplugged the modem from the wall, then picked up her daughter's laptop. "No computer, understand?"

"You can't do this to me," Leah cried, trying to wrestle the computer away from her mother. "I won't be able to do my homework. How can I talk to my friends?"

"You'll talk to your friends at school," Joanne told her, determined not to give in. "As far as your homework is concerned, you'll do it the same way I did." She looked at the bookcases on the walls. "You have a set of encyclopedias. And if you need to type something, there's an old Smith Corona in the garage."

Joanne carried the computer to her bedroom, then locked it inside a nine-by-twelve-foot hidden room behind her closet, placing the key in her wallet. Inside was a panic button. Judge Spencer had built the room as a safety precaution. In case an intruder came into their home, he and his wife could lock themselves inside the room and hit the panic button linked directly to the police station. Also installed was a separate phone line and enough food and water to last for several weeks. It reminded Joanne of a bomb or tornado shelter. Neither Leah nor Mike was aware the room existed. When Judge Spencer had agreed to rent her his second home, he'd shown her the room in case she ever needed it, then instructed her not to tell anyone about it.

Even in an area as secure as Seacliff Point, Spencer wanted to make certain his family was safe. Fifteen years earlier, when he'd resided in Rhode Island, a man he'd sentenced to prison had broken into his home and held him at knifepoint. His wife, Anne, had been outside working in the garden. Seeing what was happening through the window, she'd walked in and cracked the attacker's skull open with a shovel.

"Sorry, Mom," Mike said, when Joanne returned to the kitchen. "I didn't mean to cause a scene." He walked over and began picking up the broken ceramic pieces and placing them into the trash can. "The party isn't such a big deal. Why don't we go to the store and rent a movie?"

Joanne embraced him, then kissed him lightly on the forehead. "You're a good kid, Mike," she said. "Go get dressed for your party. Your sister can sulk tonight. I'm going to drop by the Cove and have a glass of wine, see if I can't put this week behind me."

"Make sure you take the car."

Joanne smiled. "You are mature," she told him. "As long you don't step out of line, I'll let you get away with passing yourself off for sixteen. Only for tonight, though. And you better watch out. You're a handsome guy. Don't let some girl take advantage of you."

"You're the greatest mom in the world," Mike gushed. "I love you."

"I love you too," Joanne said. "More than you'll ever know."

Her son fell serious. "I wish Dad hadn't done the things he did. Maybe you'll find someone else. You know, a really nice man."

"Another man is the last thing I need," Joanne told him. "My daughter hates me, one of my defendants disappeared, and I have to find another place for us to live. You're my number one guy, Mike. Think you can handle that?"

"You bet," he said smartly.

"Good," Joanne told him, "because you don't have a choice."

Realizing the Cove would be packed on a Friday night, Joanne decided to drive down to the beach instead, thinking a few moments of solitude might clear her head. She saw a bonfire on the opposite side of the beach with a few young people milling around as they prepared for the party. Slipping her shoes off, she trudged barefoot through the damp sand, heading in the direction of the north cliff where she knew she wouldn't be bothered.

Leah's angry remarks had been hurtful. Joanne had never once told her mother that she hated her. Her father would have mopped the floor with her if such words had ever left her mouth. She grew up in another era, though, where the parents ran the house instead of the children. Everything seemed upside down in today's world. The legal system was absurd. In the state of California, a person could end up serving a longer term for white-collar crimes such as Doug had committed than they would if they committed a murder. Parents were terrified of disciplining their children for fear they would cause psychological damage. Envisioning what the future might hold was frightening.

Joanne's own situation was tough all around. Things would more than likely get worse before they got better. Due to the enormous amount of money Doug had embezzled and her own position as a prosecutor, the media would have a field day once the case went to trial. Several newspapers had already published articles—another reason she felt justified in taking Leah's computer away. The girl was disturbed enough without reading about her father's exploits over the Internet.

At least she wasn't in Elizabeth Decker's position.

Judge Spencer had issued the search warrant for room 734 at the Economy Inn. Fearing that they indeed might have a homicide investigation on their hands, Joanne had pressured the police into executing the warrant that afternoon. Kennedy had given her permission to be present while the police conducted the search. After two hours, they'd walked away with nothing even vaguely suggestive of a crime—no blood, no body, no decoy gun. All they'd discovered was a piece of fabric that had been torn from one of the green curtains. Even though the manager of the motel denied it, for all they knew, the curtain had been torn before the three men had rented the room.

Of course, Joanne told herself, the Rubinskys could have easily removed all traces of a crime prior to Tom appearing in court that morning. The possibility still existed that the crime could have occurred at another location. She wasn't certain that Arnold's theory regarding the Rubinskys holding Ian somewhere until the trial was over made sense. Even if the brothers were acquitted on the robbery charges, what would they gain? Once they released Decker, he would run straight to the police. Then the Rubinskys could be tried for kidnapping, even if they had already been acquitted on the robbery charges. The only reason she could think of for them to hold Decker hostage somewhere would be to buy time.

The next question was why?

Were there more crimes involved than she or the police knew about? Did the Rubinskys need time to retrieve the money and arrange their own getaway? Maybe that's what Ian Decker was doing, getting things in order for them. Although Tom had sworn he was in contact with Gary, he could easily have been lying to protect his brother. For all they knew, Ian and Gary could have teamed up as crime partners, cutting Tom out of the picture. As Joanne had argued all along, just because Ian had a learning disability didn't mean he wasn't intentionally breaking the law.

Joanne turned her thoughts to the most urgent question: Had the Rubinskys murdered Ian Decker? The more she thought about it, the more possibilities unfolded. The Rubinskys convincing a jury that Decker had committed the robbery without their knowledge might have sounded farfetched that morning, yet she could see how it might play out to their benefit. The Rubinskys had simply taken Arnold and Elizabeth's version of how the events had occurred and reversed them. As Joanne had explained to Elizabeth that morning, the defendants' fate would be decided by twelve individuals who would eventually make up the jury panel. And, should Gary surface, and he and his brother show up in court, while Decker remained outstanding, reasonable doubt would be created in the eyes of the jury.

Joanne's thoughts turned to Arnold Dreiser. Kennedy's concerns were certainly worthy of consideration. Arnold's son's suicide could have pushed him over the edge. It wouldn't be the first time a fine legal mind had came unglued. She recalled the 1989 case involving Joel

Steinberg, a once brilliant attorney who had been convicted of manslaughter in the death of his six-year-old adopted daughter. The Steinberg case had made the world realize that child abuse was not restricted to low-income or uneducated parents, and that governmental agencies were many times understaffed and ineffective to protect the children placed in their care. What had made the case so sensational was that Steinberg and his wife had been able to adopt another child while actively abusing the first child.

Could Arnold Dreiser have provided Ian Decker with the necessary funds to leave town? Joanne considered herself a good judge of character, though, and this line of thinking didn't seem plausible. Not only could the attorney be disbarred, he could be charged with aiding and abetting a criminal, as well as with obstruction of justice.

Decker's psychological evaluations and school records had only confirmed what Arnold had already told her. Holding Decker's exam papers in her hands had brought tears to her eyes. Every other page had the dreaded "F" letter scrawled across the top, whereas the papers themselves had shown the mark of tremendous effort.

Elizabeth Decker was a unique woman, Joanne told herself. The majority of people considered a person with a disability to be a burden. Yet Elizabeth had told Joanne that to be entrusted with a child like Ian was an honor.

Reaching the cliff, Joanne climbed up onto a ledge with a flat surface, listening to the waves. Every so often, it was possible to watch grunion runs from here. Grunions were small fluorescent fish that came to shore during the late evening or early morning hours to spawn. The local radio station would broadcast an approximate date and time the grunion were scheduled to appear. The homeowners' association put on a party every year, awarding prizes to the person who caught the most fish. People would roll up their pants and wade out into the surf, scooping up the fish with their hands, then depositing them in plastic pails. When the grunion spawned, the shoreline was illuminated with thousands of dancing lights.

Joanne wrapped her arms around her chest, chastising herself for not bringing a heavier jacket. After growing up in St. Louis, the climate in California had always annoyed her. She favored seasons—the changing colors of fall leaves, waking up and seeing the ground covered with snow in the winter, the wetness of spring, the blistering heat of summer. In California, she never knew what kind of clothes to wear. A person could pass through several seasons in a single day. It was February, and the air was cold and damp, yet earlier the temperatures had been in the upper sixties. She recalled one Christmas when it had been so hot, she'd had to turn on the air conditioner.

Immersed in her thoughts, Joanne became aware of a strange noise. It reminded her of the squishy sound a person's shoes made when they were filled with water. She held her breath and listened. A few moments later, she saw a large shadowy figure rapidly moving toward her.

T W E L V E

MIKE WAS warming his hands by the fire, standing next to a redheaded girl with freckles and pale skin. She wasn't bad looking, but she wasn't Tess Fourney. "My cheerleading coach designed our new uniforms," Stacy said, smacking on a wad of gum. "They're going to be fabulous, much better than last year. I tried mine on the other day. The stupid seamstress jabbed me with a needle. Look," she said, lifting up her sweater and exposing a tiny mark near her navel. "I might never be able to wear a bikini again."

"Terrible," Mike said, deciding he'd rather go home and stare at the wall than listen to such nonsense.

Leaving the girl standing there, he pushed his way through the throng of young people. Not everyone present was a resident of Seacliff Point. Kids had invited their friends from outside. Some were huddled around the fire, talking and laughing, while others were stretched out on blankets. Tess Fourney was the girl Mike wanted to see. Her father was a scientist. Not only was she pretty, she was smart.

And she was only fourteen. Two years wasn't such a big span in age. Even if he told her the truth, maybe she wouldn't care. Every guy at Seacliff Point was in love with Tess Fourney, though, so his chances were about one in a zillion. And not because she was wild. It wasn't even her looks, although she was extremely pretty. Tess just had a way about her. She drew people to her like a magnet.

Mike stopped and spoke to another girl, their neighbors' daughter. Julia Merritt was a senior in high school. Her brother, Patrick, had just graduated from Notre Dame. Both of the Merritt children were spoiled because their parents were rich. As an early graduation present, Julia's parents had given her a 2001 Porsche Boxster convertible. The color was called Ocean Jade, a metallic turquoise. Porsche must have manufactured only a handful of cars in that color, because no one had ever seen a car exactly like it. Mike thought Julia's father was a sneaky guy and wanted to keep tabs on his daughter. Either that, or he wanted to make certain she didn't forget where she parked her car at the mall.

Even though Emily Merritt and Mike's mother were friends, the Merritt kids had never had anything to do with Mike or his sister. He guessed it was because his family was only renting, which placed them lower on the social ladder. Even though Seacliff Point was a great place, many of the residents were snobs.

"What are you doing here?" Julia Merritt asked. "Isn't it past your bedtime?"

Mike's little charade was about to come tumbling down. He'd forgotten about his mother's friendship with Emily Merritt, and the fact that she probably knew everything about him, even the embarrassing stuff about his dad. "They asked me to carry the firewood. Did Pat get a job yet?"

"All the decent jobs are in Los Angeles," Julia told him. "Pat doesn't want to live in the city."

Mike suddenly saw Tess smiling and waving him over. He pushed past Julia and through the crowd like a linebacker. "I haven't seen you for awhile," he said, trying to act nonchalant. "How's it going?"

Tess was a small girl with long blond hair, hazel eyes, and gorgeous skin. Her best feature was her smile, though. She had perfect teeth and two deep dimples in her cheeks. "Want to go for a walk?"

"Where do you want to go?" Mike glanced back at the bonfire. "Looks like the party is just getting started."

"I've lived here all my life," Tess told him, pointing her toe and drawing a circle in the sand. "These things get old, you know. Why don't we walk down by the cliffs? I'd rather look at the stars than stand around and talk."

Mike was certain the bells had just rung in heaven.

THIRTEEN

FEARFUL SHE was about to be assaulted, Joanne scrambled up the steep cliff from the ledge where she'd been sitting. A circle of light surrounded her, and she glanced over her shoulder toward the shadowy image below her. The light moved several feet away, and she saw the person's hands moving rapidly. Eli Connors spun the flashlight in his hand like a baton, illuminating his face. "Remember me?"

"Eli?"

"Yeah," he said, grinning mischievously. "What the hell are you doing? Don't you know better than to climb rocks at night? Let me help you before you hurt yourself."

"Hurt myself," Joanne grumbled in anger. "Where did you come from? You scared me to death."

Eli laughed with delight. "I came to shore in the dinghy. Come to think of it, that word fits you perfectly."

"What word?" Joanne said, allowing him to place his large hands around her waist and lift her off the ledge.

"Dinghy," he said. "You know, like looney. Wasn't that the name of your family doctor?"

Joanne looked perplexed. "When did I tell you the name of our family doctor?"

"Forget it," Eli said, falling serious. "All these gated communities are the same. I told you when the Spencers offered to lease you their house that this place wasn't secure. You want to be safe, you have to live in a building, know what I mean? A building with one entrance and one exit, both of them manned with guards and cameras."

"Seacliff Point is secure by land," Joanne argued, dusting herself off. "The average criminal doesn't have a dinghy, nor could they afford to convert a fishing boat into a high-tech office. I thought you'd already left for Bali?"

"Don't you ever look out your window, woman? I've been anchored in your backyard ever since I dropped your lousy ex-husband off at the jail."

Joanne squinted, seeing the faint outline of a vessel off in the moonlight. "That's the *Nightwatch*? How would I know that? What happened to your lights? Are you pretending you're on some kind of covert mission?"

"Generator problems."

"Too many toys," Joanne remarked, employing the same tone she used for her children. "You don't work for the government anymore, Eli. You could end up in prison if the Coast Guard catches you. And I probably haven't seen half of what you've got on that boat."

"Let's go for a drink," Eli said. "You can bring me up to date."

Joanne had missed the detective. His size alone made her feel safe. His services didn't come cheap, but he got the job done. He'd managed to find Doug and bring her children home. Of all the men who'd passed through her life, Eli Connors would always stand out as one of her heroes. "Before we do anything, tell me why you're here."

"Did you think I was going to forget you just because you ran out of money? Even behind bars, I don't trust your ex-husband."

Joanne jerked her head back, startled. "Are you saying Doug might hire someone to hurt me?"

"Anything's possible."

"Doug isn't violent," Joanne told him as they walked toward her car.

Eli seized her by the shoulders and spun her around. "Listen to me," he said. "Your husband has enough money tucked away to hire a private army. I might bend the rules now and then, but I don't kill people. The weapons and surveillance equipment I have on board the *Nightwatch* are to keep innocent people like you from getting themselves killed."

"You're paranoid," Joanne said. "If something happened to me, Doug would be the prime suspect."

"What about the kids?"

"He loves the kids."

"Your husband is furious right now," Eli continued. "He'd just hit the big time when I found him. And we're not talking small change here. He sold a software program he designed for on-line gambling casinos to Forrest Hoyt Technologies for fifty million dollars."

Joanne stopped walking, not certain she'd heard him correctly. "Did you say fifty million dollars? The DA in L.A. told me Doug had sold some kind of program, but they didn't mention a sum anywhere near that amount."

"Fifty mil, sweetie," Eli said, turning the collar up on his nylon jacket. "Put yourself in his shoes. The man's worked years developing this program. Even when I tracked him down and handed him off to the authorities, he wasn't worried. With that kind of bread, he figured he could pay back whatever money he had embezzled, serve a couple of months in jail, then walk out a rich man. That isn't going to happen now."

"Why not?"

"Because he got caught with his pants down," Eli told her. They were standing next to Joanne's Lexus in the parking area adjacent to the beach. He watched as she fumbled in her purse for her keys. "Why don't you get a clip or something to hold your keys? Do you know how many women have been assaulted while they were trying to find their car keys?"

"Just finish what you were saying," Joanne said, not in the mood to listen to another of Eli's lectures. Pulling her keys out, she waved them in front of him, then unlocked the car door. "Get in," she told him. "We'll stop by my house first, then we'll go to the Crow's Nest in Ventura."

Once Eli had squeezed his enormous frame into the passenger seat, and Joanne steered the car in the direction of Circular Road where her house was located, Eli continued to explain the situation to her. "Because of your husband's gambling debts, he had to use a fictitious name to set up a corporation. The corporation then established an off-shore bank account. The name Douglas Kuhlman is nowhere on this account, nor is he listed in any of the articles of incorporation. The off-shore holding company accepts the funds, then when Doug's corporation files the appropriate requests, the money is wired to another individual in the islands who is employed by your husband. This individual then transfers the money to Doug's dummy corporation."

"There's a fine line on some of this stuff," Joanne said. "Not every shelter or holding company is illegal. The more money people make, the less taxes they pay. That's how the world works. A smart attorney or business manager knows where the cracks in the system are and merely presents them to his client as an alternative." She paused and then continued, "And please stop referring to Doug as my husband. The divorce is final. Call him anything you want, but don't call him my husband."

"A shelter is one thing," Eli explained. "This was a scam from day one. Doug's first mistake was to steal from a company as big as Telinx."

"He didn't steal fifty million, though," Joanne said. "I'm not certain all the numbers are in yet, but the last time I spoke with the L.A. prosecutor, it was nowhere near that amount."

"Let me explain how this works," Eli said, clutching the door handle as Joanne swerved around a corner. "Pull over and let me drive."

"This is my car, Eli," Joanne told him, sick of men who drove like maniacs, then started whining like babies as soon as a woman took the driver's seat. "You talk, I drive. If you want, I can stop the car and let you off."

"Tough broad," Eli remarked, gritting his teeth as she fishtailed around another sharp curve.

"I don't have a choice," Joanne told him. "I'm a single parent, and I have a mountain of problems—both professionally and personally. The only way I can survive is to take control of my life. When I was married, I was a weak and foolish woman. I let my husband make all the decisions. The rest of the story you know."

Eli remained silent until they pulled into her driveway. "Once they find a person with this much dirty money," he told her, "the IRS, the state, and every governmental agency involved work around the clock to freeze the assets so they can later lay claim to them. The only problem is the minute they alert the holding company that a crime is involved, the outside agent usually skips out with the money."

"Good grief," Joanne said, gripping the steering wheel with both hands. "You're telling me that a complete stranger walked away with fifty million? Half of that money should belong to my children. How could this happen?"

"Because your ex-husband and lots of other idiots believe these people are trustworthy, that's why," Eli told her. "I'm not certain the money is gone. I've managed to obtain a good deal of information, but in this case, too many agencies and countries are involved. The account holding the fifty mil is listed under the name of Jorge Baudelaire. Mr. Baudelaire can legally wire the money to any account he wants. No one can touch him. Your husband listed this individual as the president and CEO of his corporation. He was in such a rush to get his hands on the money once the Forrest Hoyt Technologies deal was finalized that he didn't even appoint any other officers in the corporation. The more people involved, the less chance you have of someone taking you for a ride."

"I still don't understand," Joanne said, overwhelmed. "Why would he want more people involved? Wouldn't that increase the chances of someone discovering what he was doing?"

"That's the way I would have handled it," Eli said. "All the parties involved have to agree to take the money. Then they have to trust each other."

Joanne placed her hand over her chest. "How could someone smart enough to invent such a valuable computer program be this careless?"

"Hey," Eli said, shrugging. "You were married to the man."

Joanne felt sick to her stomach. "Is there more?"

"I'm afraid so," the detective said. "Doug paid Baudelaire to use his name in all the negotiations with Forrest Hoyt. As far as Forrest Hoyt Technologies is concerned, they purchased the program from Jorge Baudelaire. Even if Doug was completely legit, which he isn't, he'd have trouble collecting his money. In most instances, though, the people who funnel the money back and forth have an established track record with whatever banking institution refers them. What I'm trying to say is that not everyone gets ripped off. Millions of dollars run through this pipeline every day and nothing goes wrong. But when you dangle fifty million in front of someone, then tell them the rightful owner is a crook, even Honest Abe might be tempted to jump on it."

"Discounting the financial side of this thing," she said, "I still don't understand why you think I might be in danger."

"Not just you," Eli said, turning sideways in the seat. "How about your kids, huh? Your husband owes a fortune to an Apache Indian tribe, the owner of one of his favorite on-line gambling sites. They may think you're sitting on the money, that you've got it buried under Judge Spencer's house and have been in cahoots with your husband all along."

"That's absurd."

"You're wrong," Eli said. "What if they snatched one of the kids, thinking it would force you to tell them where the money is hidden? I mean, I spent two years tracking down your husband. That's why I decided to hang around. You're a fine lady, Joanne. You don't deserve any more misery."

"I think we should pass on the drink," Joanne told him, not wanting to leave Leah in the house alone. "I let my son go to a party at the beach tonight. Should I go and get him?"

"No," Eli said, exiting the car. "I'll keep an eye on all of you for a few more days."

"Don't you want me to drive you back to the beach?"

"Not necessary," the detective said, pointing to a black pickup truck parked across the street.

"That's the Robertsons' place," Joanne said, shocked. "They're at their other house in Florida. How did you get past the gate?"

"All I did was print myself up one of those fancy stickers that say Seacliff Point," Eli said, already walking toward his vehicle. He yelled out over his shoulder, "Then I pasted the sucker on my windshield. But you don't need me to protect you. I'm just a guy with too many toys."

Joanne shouted, "How can I reach you in case of an emergency?"

"Call 911," the big man said. "I'm not a cop, remember."

"Don't do this to me," she said, jogging across the street. "Forget what I said about the Coast Guard and your equipment. At least someone cares enough about my safety to look out for me. For God's sake, you've been working all this time for free. With the kind of fees you charge, you could have bought another boat."

"I don't mind if you call the *Nightwatch* a vessel," Eli told her, leaning back against his truck. "But please, don't call her a boat again. Everything I own is on that ship."

"I know you lost your job with the CIA because they framed you," Joanne said, reaching out and touching his arm. "They lost a good man."

"Don't worry, " Eli said, clicking the alarm button for his truck to disarm it. "You still have my pager number."

FOURTEEN

ELIZABETH DECKER was resting on the sofa. She had gone to mass that morning, then spent the remainder of the day praying, asking God to send her son back. The phone rang just as she got up to make another pot of coffee. "Ian?"

"Tom and Gary killed Ian," a strange male voice said in hushed tones. "They buried him in a field off of Interstate 5 near Magic Mountain. The field is maybe five or six miles from what I think they said was a truck stop. They also mentioned going through the drive-through at McDonald's."

"No, God!" she cried. "My son is dead? You're lying! Tell me it isn't true!"

"Check the storage lot at your business."

"Don't hang up," Elizabeth said. "The phone isn't tapped."

When she heard the dial tone, she sank to her knees on the floor. A searing pain entered her back. An unknown force pushed her forward, and she fell face forward onto the floor. Her body contracted into the fetal position. She was in a cocoon of darkness. She was certain her son was in the room with her, trapped in the dimension that followed death.

Elizabeth finally surfaced from the dark tunnel and regained her eyesight, although the images in front of her were murky and distorted. She struggled back to her feet. Now of all times, she had to be strong. She had to be strong for Ian. She had to lead him, comfort him. "It's okay, baby," she said softly, wiping the tears away with the back of her hand. "I'm here. Mom's here for you. Don't be afraid."

She clenched her eyes shut, tilting her chin toward the ceiling. She couldn't indulge in self-pity. She would have the rest of her life to cry, stare at his pictures, relive memories. Now she had to make certain his killers were brought to justice. This was the time to work. Just as she had once carried him inside her body before his birth, she would now carry his soul. She would be Ian's arms, legs, hands, eyes, ears, mouth, feet—his human and willing host.

Without conscious effort, she walked down the narrow hallway to her son's room and sat on the edge of his bed. She wasn't certain how much time had expired. In this dimension, hours could pass without notice. Elizabeth was in a space where the clocks had all stopped.

Elizabeth's feet took her to Ian's old stereo. Her finger depressed the play button. Her ears were assaulted with the thumping bass of a rock band. She reached for the volume control, then yanked her hand back. Ian liked the music loud. Her eyes roamed to the posters on the walls—the Rolling Stones, the Doors, Sting. When he'd moved to his own place, Elizabeth had left the room intact, fearful he wouldn't be able to make it on his own.

Tonight her worst fears had been realized.

She drifted into the kitchen, pouring a glass of milk and opening the pantry door. The word "chips" popped into her mind. She didn't have any potato chips. A river of tears streamed down her face. Such a small thing, yet so monumental. How could she have forgotten to buy potato chips? Ian liked salty foods. She poured salt on her finger and licked it, then made a crunching sound with her teeth.

A logical person could never accept Elizabeth's behavior, even knowing she had just been told her son was dead. She would be labeled insane, moronic, certifiable. In the past, they would have classified her as a madwoman and locked her away. Whatever humiliation came along she willingly accepted.

Elizabeth possessed an ability to lead and shelter souls. Her grandmother had taught her mother. Her mother had taught her and her sisters. How far back the lessons went, no one would ever know, possibly to the onset of creation.

Elizabeth Decker had no formal education, no fine clothes or expensive homes. She had no stocks, bonds, awards, or certificates. What she possessed, however, were the necessary tools for the long and tedious task ahead of her.

No other gift could be more valuable.

FIFTEEN

WHEN JOANNE returned from a conference regarding a pending rape case, she discovered a message from Dean Kennedy on her voice mail. "I'm returning his call," she told his secretary.

A few moments later, Kennedy came on the line. "Arnold Dreiser and Elizabeth Decker are waiting in the lobby."

Joanne made it her habit to enter the office via the side entrance, not wanting to run into an irate attorney or defendant in the lobby. "What's going on?"

"Mrs. Decker received an anonymous phone call last night," Kennedy told her. "The caller said her son had been murdered and buried in a field near Magic Mountain."

"Why wasn't I notified?" Joanne asked. "Dreiser has my home number. Do you think he's trying to go over my head for some reason by contacting you?"

"He claims he tried to call you at home several times last night," Kennedy stated. "Your line was busy. You better check your phone and see if it's out of order. In the meantime, I'll notify the front desk to send them to my office."

Joanne called her home number. After seven rings, she hung up. Because the Spencers didn't want to change their phone number, and Joanne had rented their house for only a short time, she didn't have voice mail outside of her cell phone. She kept her cell phone on all the time, but Dreiser didn't have the number. Thinking she might know why no one had answered the phone when Dreiser had attempted to contact her, she opened the zippered section inside her wallet where she kept the key to the safe room. The key was gone. Leah must have rifled through her purse while she was in the kitchen. Then, after Joanne left the house, her daughter must have unlocked the room to retrieve her computer. The main phone line had probably been busy because Leah had been on-line either chatting with her friends or surfing the Internet. Like father, like daughter, Joanne thought, marching down the corridor to Kennedy's office. She hadn't thought either of her kids knew about the secret room. She must have left it unlocked once, and one of them had accidentally discovered it. Joanne used that room to store various paperwork related to her divorce, as well as items related to her former husband's criminal activities—items she didn't want the children to see. Knowing Leah, she'd probably been intrigued by the room and told her friends about it. Now Joanne knew she'd have to tell the Spencers that their safe room was no longer a secret. Great, she thought, striding past Kennedy's secretary and into his office.

Dreiser stood politely, looking almost as bedraggled as Elizabeth Decker. The woman was dressed in a pink sweater and black sweatpants, her hair uncombed and her eyes red and swollen.

Kennedy's office was located on one of the four corners of the floor. Not only did his office have floor-to-ceiling windows, it was twice the size of Joanne's. In one corner was a conference table and eight chairs. Kennedy's secretary, Edith Mathews, a gracious woman with short red hair and a lovely oval face, entered the room carrying a tray with coffee and a bucket of ice filled with bottles of Evian water. Now that Joanne was present, Kennedy gestured for them all to take a seat at the conference table.

"Have the police been notified?" Joanne asked, scooting her chair closer to the table.

"Yes," Kennedy said, turning his attention to Elizabeth. "Mrs. Decker, please tell Ms. Kuhlman about the phone call you received last night."

Elizabeth spoke slowly as if she had to force each word out of her mouth. "I'm not certain of the time," she said. "I had supper around six, then watched television. I don't think I fell asleep, but I was resting on the sofa, so I might have dozed off for a few moments. My guess is the man called after seven o'clock. I know it was between seven and nine, because I called the police and my brother, Carl, a few minutes past nine."

Elizabeth related the details of the phone conversation. "I tried to get the man to stay on the line," she told them, her eyes roaming to each individual who was present at the table. "I told him the phone wasn't tapped, but he hung up." She stopped speaking, sitting there with a blank look on her face.

"Are you okay?" Joanne asked, pouring her a glass of water.

"Yes." Elizabeth was now speaking in a monotone. "The police said my call wasn't an emergency. An hour later, a sergeant called me and told me that there was a warrant issued for my son's arrest. He said nothing else was necessary." She stopped, then continued, "The sergeant did write down what the man on the phone told me. I think he said they would file what he referred to as an incident report. I tried to get them to send someone out to the field where the caller said my son was buried, but he refused to help me."

"What about the storage lot at your business?"

Dreiser spoke up, "Elizabeth's brother started taking an inventory of the cars on the lot last night. He finished about five o'clock this morning. Two vehicles are missing. One is a Chrysler Cirrus, and the other is a Ford Taurus. Both cars were involved in accidents and never claimed by the owners. They were preparing paperwork to auction them off in order to collect the towing and storage fees. Both vehicles have now been reported stolen."

Joanne asked, "Why would they steal two cars?"

Elizabeth answered meekly, "I don't know."

"I'm sure the word is out on the street that your son is missing, Mrs. Decker," Kennedy told her. "The call you received last night might have only been a prank."

"My son is dead," Elizabeth said, her chin thrust forward with dignity. "If he isn't dead, he's in terrible trouble."

Joanne was seated next to Elizabeth and reached over and lightly touched her hand. "Try to remain positive," Joanne said. "The fact that two cars are missing could be a *good* sign. I know you don't want to believe your son was a willing participant in the robberies, but what this anonymous caller told you is far worse. Ian might have taken one car, and Gary Rubinsky took the other."

Joanne realized that, with everything going on, she'd failed to ask if anyone knew the whereabouts of the Rubinskys. Since the court hearing had been postponed, Tom was not obligated to appear in court until Wednesday morning. She glanced over at Arnold. "Does anyone know where the Rubinskys are? Have they been in contact with their attorneys?"

"I spoke to both Joe Watkins and Marilyn Cobb about thirty minutes ago," Dreiser told her. "Neither one of them has spoken to either Gary or Tom. The police interviewed the clerk at the Economy Inn this morning. He said Tom showed up last night, and he told him the police had searched the room. It would have been nice if the clerk had notified the police when Tom returned, since he knew there was a problem. We may never hear from the Rubinskys again."

"Watkins and Cobb don't have any way to get in touch with their clients?" Joanne asked. "Is that correct?"

"No," Dreiser said. "Don't forget, Ian's car was impounded at the time the three men were first arrested. They could have stolen the cars off the ABC lot the next day. I didn't give much thought to how they were getting around. I assumed they were using a friend's car or someone was dropping them off at the courthouse each day. They may have transported Ian's body in the first car, then decided to dispose of it. This would give them a reason to go back to the lot for a second car."

Regardless of whether her son had been murdered or not, Elizabeth Decker had been repeatedly victimized. Joanne could tell by the stern look on Kennedy's face that he was ready to take action.

"Prepare a petition to revoke the Rubinskys' bail," Kennedy told Joanne, brushing his finger across his upper lip. "Notify the Ventura PD that all three men are now wanted on suspicion of auto theft. Verify that both vehicles are entered into the national system. Call Chief Adams and fill him in on what we have to date." He paused, thought a few moments, then continued, "Adams will have to contact the Valencia Sheriff's Department. There's a lot of open ground around Magic Mountain and more than one truck stop with a McDonald's. A thorough search will require an enormous amount of manpower and equipment. The sheriff in Valencia covers the entire Santa Clarita Valley all the way up to Frazier Park. This is the worst possible place to attempt to find an unmarked grave."

Joanne saw the myriad of problems unfolding. The Rubinsky brothers could have killed Decker on the same spot where they buried him. Then the case would fall under another jurisdiction. "Are you saying we should hold off on the search?"

"Picking up the Rubinsky brothers is the first priority," Kennedy said. "Killers aren't known to check in with their attorneys unless they're in custody. As to the search, the sheriff in Valencia may not be willing to deploy the necessary manpower without additional evidence. We might be jumping the gun here."

Elizabeth stood, so weak she had to hold on to the back of the chair to keep from collapsing. "I didn't come down here to listen to speculation or complaints about manpower. Right now, I don't care what happens to the Rubinsky brothers. All I want is to find my son so I can give him a proper burial. Is that too much to ask of you people?"

Before anyone could respond, Elizabeth walked out of the room. She had dealt with the police years before, when a drunk driver had killed her husband. As soon as she got home, she would call her relatives and friends, organize her own search party. She didn't need their dogs, their officers, their high-tech equipment. She would find Ian herself.

SIXTEEN

UNTIL THEY knew whether or not the trial would resume the following week, Kennedy didn't want to assign Joanne any additional cases. When she came to work Tuesday morning, she checked in with the sheriff in Valencia. The sheriff's department had dispatched a search and rescue team at approximately one o'clock Monday afternoon. As Kennedy had pointed out, however, the reference points given to Elizabeth Decker encompassed too large a territory. Dozens of truck stops and rest areas lined Interstate 5 in the vicinity of the Magic Mountain amusement park. Five of them had a McDonald's restaurant in close proximity, and there were miles of open fields and pastures. Without specific coordinates, the Valencia authorities doubted if they would ever be successful in locating a body. They had already flown over the area with a helicopter, sent men out in four-wheel-drive vehicles, and even collected some of Decker's clothing so the dogs could be trained to recognize his scent. The next step would be to divide the area into grids and have men go out on foot. Without definitive proof that a homicide had been committed, the sheriff would only agree to deploy manpower for another twenty-four hours.

Joanne was reviewing an assault case in preparation for the preliminary hearing to be held the following month. She found it difficult to concentrate as her mind kept returning to the Rubinskys/Decker matter. She tended to favor Arnold's line of thinking, that the Rubinsky brothers would not be heard from until the police apprehended them.

Joanne was reaching into her backpack for her lunch when the phone rang.

"This is Lieutenant Warren with the Ventura Police," he said. "One of our officers just arrested a subject by the name of Tom Rubinsky. He was driving a 1994 Ford Taurus that was reported stolen this morning."

"Where is he?"

"The officer has him in the back of his patrol car," Warren told her. "We were told your office wanted to question him before we booked him. He's asking for his attorney. I doubt if he's going to talk to you."

Joanne's immediate concern was the arresting officer's safety. "Did he have what looked like a cell phone on him?"

"No," Warren said. "We issued a bulletin on this new decoy gun. Our officers are jumpy, you know. Last night one of our rookies almost killed a fourteen-year-old kid. Everyone has a cell phone these days. This damn gun is a nightmare. There's no telling how many innocent people are going to die because of it. The worst part about it is we're the ones who are going to take the fall."

"Rubinsky might be able to lead us to the person selling the guns," Joanne told him. "Call Marilyn Cobb, Tom Rubinsky's attorney. Then instruct the arresting officer to bring Rubinsky to my office. Notify Chief Adams as well. He should be present during the interview because of the ramifications of this new weapon. Don't allow anyone near the car. Use the same standards you would at a major crime scene. Dispatch several of your officers to guard the car until the crime lab sends out a flatbed truck. Rubinsky may have transported a body in that car."

Joanne hung up and immediately called Kennedy.

At approximately 4:45 P.M., Joanne, Kennedy, Dreiser, Chief Colin Adams, and homicide Detective David Bernard of the Ventura PD were waiting outside the door to the main conference room on the third floor of the district attorney's office. The front desk had just advised them that two police officers had arrived with a prisoner.

Handcuffed and shackled, Tom Rubinsky was mumbling profanities as the two officers held him under the arms and almost carried him down the hallway. His clothes were filthy, and he reeked of alcohol and body odor. "Get these bastards to take the cuffs off," he barked. "My hands are numb. They can't do this to me. This is police brutality."

Dreiser exchanged glances with the individuals present. "Miss Cobb is on her way," he said, a look of disgust on his face.

"Didn't you hear me, damn it?" Tom yelled. "The cuffs are too tight! I can't feel my hands."

Chief Adams told one of the officers. "You need to loosen the handcuffs."

"What about the chains on my legs," Tom said. "I can't even walk."

Kennedy shook his head. Tom was a powerful man, and they couldn't afford to take any chances. Once the officer had escorted Tom into the conference room, the other individuals followed. A yellow notepad and several pens had been placed on the table in front of each chair. In the center of the table was a triangular-shaped microphone linked to the county's recording and dictation system. A transcript of the interview would be typed and distributed to the appropriate individuals by noon the following day. Two television monitors were mounted on the front and rear walls.

Kennedy took a seat at the head of the table, gesturing for the officers to deposit their prisoner in a chair at the table. "He might need to use his hands to write," he said. "The shackles remain, but you can remove the handcuffs."

Marilyn Cobb rushed through the door, taking a seat next to Tom Rubinsky. Her curly red hair was secured in a clip at the nape of her neck. She cupped her hand over her mouth and turned to confer with her client. Tom rubbed his wrists and glared at the two officers as they walked over and stood guard by the door.

Joanne pulled out a chair directly across from the defendant on the opposite side of the table, with Chief Adams and Detective Bernard on her left and right.

Tom Rubinsky scratched the top of his head, then stared around the room. "Who are these people?"

"The individual on my left is Chief Adams with the Ventura Police Department," Joanne told him. "This is Detective Bernard, also with the Ventura PD. The gentleman at the head of the table is Dean Kennedy, the district attorney."

"I thought you were the district attorney," Tom said. "Why is he here?"

"Mr. Kennedy is my boss," Joanne explained. "He's the head of this agency. My title is ADA, or assistant district attorney." She asked Marilyn Cobb, "Are you ready to continue?"

"Yes," Cobb said, digging Tom's file out of her briefcase.

Tom said belligerently, "You'll have those two goons break my neck if I don't talk to you."

"No one is going to physically harm you," Joanne told him. "You requested that your attorney be present. That request was granted. We have the right to question you, but you do not have to answer. The Fifth Amendment affords you the right against self-incrimination. Would you like to exercise that right and terminate this interview?"

Again, Tom turned and whispered something to Marilyn Cobb. "My client agrees to the interview," she told them.

"Good," Joanne said, assuming the public defender had told Tom that he would be better off cooperating. Although he had already been read his Miranda rights by the arresting officer, to cover all the bases, she recited them again. Finally, they were ready to proceed with the interview. "Please state your name and place of birth."

"Tom Rubinsky," he said. "I was born in Fresno."

"Can you give us your full name?"

"Thomas Arthur Rubinsky."

"How did you come to be in possession of the 1994 Ford Taurus you were driving at the time of your arrest today?"

"My brother gave it to me."

"Are you referring to Gary Rubinsky?"

"Yeah," Tom said, sneering, "who do you think I mean?"

Joanne rolled her neck around to release the tension. The man sitting in front of her sickened her. How could he have participated in the killing of a developmentally disabled individual? She forced herself to appear relaxed and nonjudgmental. She wanted the interview to be productive. "Where is your brother, Tom?"

"Don't know," he said, shrugging. "The judge said we didn't have to be back until this week. Gary must have gone somewhere to chill out."

"Are you aware of the terms and conditions of your bail?" Joanne asked, tapping her pen on the table. "The court restricted both you and your brother from leaving the city until the case was resolved. Your brother also failed to appear in court on Friday."

"I didn't say Gary left town," Tom answered, his words slurred.

"Maybe he just wanted to go somewhere and be alone. Sometimes a man needs to clear his head, know what I mean?"

"And your brother gave you the Ford Taurus?"

The bourbon Tom had consumed the night before was still flooding his system. His head was pounding, and his throat was parched. "Gary didn't give me the car," he told her, contradicting himself. "Ian's family owns a towing company. Elizabeth loaned him a car until you guys release his Firebird. We intended on returning it after Ian split. We just didn't get around to it."

"Where would your brother go without a car?"

"Look, lady," Tom said, "you can ask me all the questions you want. I swear I don't know where my brother is right now. We got into a fight, and he walked off and left me in a bar."

"When did this occur?"

"Last night," Tom said. "Around eleven, I think. Gary's probably staying with one of his girlfriends. I mean, there isn't a law that says I have to keep tabs on my older brother."

"Mrs. Decker didn't loan you that car," Joanne said. "ABC Towing and Storage reported two vehicles stolen this morning. One was the Ford Taurus you were driving at the time of your arrest, and the other was a 1996 Chrysler Cirrus. Is Gary driving the Chrysler?"

Tom craned his neck around. "I'm thirsty."

Marilyn Cobb went to the credenza and poured a cup of water. Tom gulped it down, then crinkled the cup in his fist. "I don't know where Gary is or how he's getting around," he said, leaning forward over the table. "How many times do I have to tell you? Gary does what he wants." He stopped and smirked. "Trust me, there's hell to pay if anyone tries to stop him."

"What do you mean by that statement?" Joanne asked. "Is your brother violent?"

Tom slipped down lower in his chair. "He's my older brother. All I'm saying is he's tough. You know, he doesn't let anyone push him around."

Joanne flipped through her papers to her notes from her first conversation with Elizabeth Decker, the morning after Ian had failed to show up in court. "Isn't it true that Gary once struck your mother?"

Marilyn Cobb spoke up, "I don't see how discussing his brother's past behavior is relevant to the current case."

Joanne watched as Tom repeatedly swiped at the side of his nose, as if he had just developed an itch. Body language was sometimes better than a lie detector. This was the first time he had made that gesture. She reminded herself to pay careful attention if and when he made that particular gesture again. "When was the last time you saw Ian Decker?"

"I already told you people," Tom said, the chains rattling as he moved his feet under the table.

"Just so we're clear," Joanne said calmly. "Could you confirm what you told Ms. Cobb?"

"Friday night."

Joanne wrote "FRIDAY" in large letters on her notepad, thinking this was the first valuable information they had obtained since the onset of the interview. When people lied, elements of the truth had a way of slipping out. Tom had told the court that Ian Decker had left Thursday evening, not Friday. Since Decker had consistently denied seeing the decoy gun used in the crime, if he had found the gun, it could have given the brothers a motive to kill him. It was possible that they held Decker hostage Thursday night until they made their final decision, and then they had taken him out to the field Friday night and shot and buried him.

"May I speak to you outside?" Joanne asked Kennedy, wanting his approval before she confronted Tom with the information Elizabeth had received from the anonymous caller.

As soon as the door to the conference room was closed, Joanne said in a hushed tone, "How far do you want me to go? Should I confront him, tell him he and his brother are suspects in a homicide?"

"I don't see why not," Kennedy said. "He's not going anywhere. Start hammering away at him. Get him to crack and give us what we need. What if Decker isn't dead? He could be bleeding to death in a ditch somewhere while you're playing twenty questions with his killer."

"You're welcome to take over," Joanne said, stung by his sharp remarks. Her face flushed in embarrassment. Kennedy refused to acknowledge her. He was chastising her by his silence, letting her know that the situation was far too serious for her to take his comments personally. "We can't restrict him from making a phone call," she continued, linking gazes with him. "The less we tell him, the greater chance we have of apprehending his brother. Gary might not know that he's now a murder suspect. That's why I've been . . ."

"You've got one suspect in that room," Kennedy said, his eyes blazing with intensity. "We didn't bring these people down here to talk about stolen cars. I'm not interested if Gary Rubinsky hit his mother when he was a teenager. Valencia is borrowing men from other departments. Crush this man, Joanne. You've got enough bottled up frustrations to castrate five guys. Imagine this idiot's your ex-husband and rip him to shreds."

"Fine," she snapped, flinging open the door to the conference room.

Taking her seat, Joanne spread her hands out on the table. "You killed Ian Decker," she said, her voice booming out over the room. "You killed him and buried him in a field near Magic Mountain."

Tom's face turned ashen. Beads of perspiration popped out on his forehead. His eyes darted frantically to Marilyn Cobb, then back to Joanne. "I didn't kill anyone," he said, his voice shaking. "I don't know what the hell you're talking about."

"Stop lying," Joanne demanded fiercely. "Ian found the gun. He confronted you, and you killed him. Gary doesn't care what happens to you. How do you think we know where he's buried?"

The underarms of Tom's shirt turned dark with perspiration. A muscle in his face was twitching.

"We know everything, Tom," Joanne continued. "The grave is near a truck stop off of Interstate 5. The truck stop is next to a McDonald's restaurant. How do we know these things? Who do you think told us? Can't you figure it out, Tom?"

With both hands, Joanne shoved the yellow pad of paper across the table. Tom jerked back, almost knocking over his chair.

Marilyn Cobb opened her mouth to protest, then closed it. Not only was she inexperienced, it was obvious that she didn't like Tom Rubinksy and assumed he was guilty.

"Draw us a map to the grave," Joanne said, unrelenting. "We've got an army of men in that field. They're going to find him. Your brother sold you out, understand? Save us some time and the court will look more favorably on you. Otherwise, your days are numbered. Either draw us a map, or you'll be using that pad of paper to start marking off days. We're talking premeditated murder, Tom. Killing Ian Decker is the same as killing a kid or a senior citizen. You know he wasn't the same as you and your brother. The law takes that into consideration." She stopped and took a drink of water.

"Not only that," Joanne continued, "you killed Ian to keep him from testifying against you. Listen carefully." She paused, one side of her top lip curling in contempt. "We're not talking life in prison, Tom. You're going to be executed."

A cloak of silence fell over the room, the only sound Tom's heavy breathing. He gripped the arms of his chair. The area around his mouth became chalky white. A few moments later, he leaned over and vomited. One of the police officers brought over a trash can. Marilyn Cobb grabbed a stack of napkins and handed them to him, then she filled up another paper cup with water. Ignoring the napkins and water, Rubinsky wiped his face with the edge of his shirt. His chin dropped to his chest, and the fear was replaced with rage.

"Here," he snarled, picking up the yellow pad and hurling it across the room, "draw your own fucking map."

One of the two police officers twisted Tom's arms behind his back, snapping on the metal handcuffs. Rubinsky lunged forward against the restraints, his eyes bulging. "You're the one who's a liar. You're trying to trick me."

The larger of the two officers grabbed Tom from behind, prepared to take him to the ground. Joanne leapt to her feet, gesturing for them to wait. "Who else would tell us these things?" she shouted. "You let Gary talk you into it, didn't you? He said you could get away with it. All you had to do was get rid of Ian and everything would be fine. Isn't that what Gary told you? Did Gary shoot Ian? What did he do? Make you watch while he killed your childhood friend?"

Marilyn Cobb had no choice but to intervene. "My client refuses to answer on the grounds that it may incriminate him."

"He doesn't have to answer," Joanne said, taking a deep breath. "While your brother is free, you're going to hear it. In the middle of the night you're going to hear it. When you're awake you're going to hear it. While you're sitting on death row, you're going to hear it."

"What?" Tom said. "What am I gonna hear?"

"You're going to hear the pitiful screams your friend made when you killed him."

Joanne finally broke him. Tom began sobbing hysterically. Kennedy was nodding in satisfaction.

"You don't mind taking the rap for Gary," Joanne continued, thrusting her finger toward the ground. "You don't care that Ian Decker is buried in a cold grave, a grave you and your brother dug for him. What's the big deal, right? Isn't that what Gary said? Ian didn't have a future anyway. If you and Gary didn't kill him, someone else would. He was a sitting duck, right? An accident waiting to happen?"

"Book him," Kennedy said, pushing himself out of the chair. "Chief Adams, I'd like you to assign every officer available to this case, as well as assist Valencia in recruiting extra manpower and equipment so we can expand the search for the victim's body. Joanne, as soon as you get the pleading prepared and typed, bring it to my office for my signature."

"How do you want me to write it?"

"First-degree murder with special circumstances," Kennedy stated, pausing and pointing at Tom from the doorway. "You're a guilty man, Mr. Rubinsky. You made a mistake by not telling us the truth. That mistake will cost you your life."

SEVENTEEN

Tuesday, February 13, 2001, 3:30 P.M.

WHEN SCHOOL let out that afternoon, Leah walked over to a handsome sixteen-year-old with shoulder-length blond hair and a golden tan. "I need to see my dad," she said. "Didn't your parents go to Aspen on a ski trip?"

"Yeah," Nathan Salinger said, "but my aunt is staying with us. I could never sneak the car out without Irene finding out."

"What about one of your friends?" Leah asked. "Can't you think of someone who could drive me?"

"Why doesn't your mother take you to see your father?"

"Because she hates him," Leah said bitterly. "I'm afraid to even go home today. She took my computer away because I talked back to her. She hid it in this secret room in the back of her closet. I stole the key to the room from her backpack and took my computer out. When she finds out, she'll probably send me to reform school."

"Don't be silly," Nathan told her, laughing. "Your mother can't send you to reform school. You didn't break any laws. Wasn't this room in your own house?"

"Don't you know what my mom does for a living?" Leah asked. "She sends people to prison. We don't own the house in Seacliff Point anyway. We're renting it from Judge Spencer and his wife. Maybe some of that stuff in the room belongs to them."

Nathan was leaning against a large oak tree, a toothpick dangling from one corner of his mouth. His mother said he had an oral fixation. Because gum wasn't allowed in school, he chewed on toothpicks. "Tell me about this room," he said, grinning mischievously. "Is this where the Spencers keep their dirty stuff, like porno magazines and X-rated movies? Hey, maybe it's their dungeon. You know, whips and chains, that type of thing."

"You're disgusting," Leah said, shoving her long hair to one side of her face. "All you ever talk about is sex."

"I'm a guy," he told her. "Guys talk about sex. If you want to talk about clothes or something, hang out with one of your girlfriends."

Leah kicked a rock across the grass, slowly raising her gaze to him. "Do you think you're my first boyfriend? I've had boyfriends since I was twelve. When we lived with my dad, he was never around. I had a different guy over every afternoon. I used to give my brother five bucks to leave the house."

Nathan snapped to attention, looking around to see if anyone was in earshot. "Why are telling me this? Are you trying to make me jealous?"

"You're the one who started talking about sex."

"I was just joking around," he said. "I'm your friend, Leah. I care about you. I've been trying to help you. I just can't solve all your problems."

"Every guy starts out saying they want to be my friend, then the next thing I know, they're trying to get in my pants. You're the same as all the others. Why don't we talk about what you did to me at Trent's party?"

A group of students were walking toward them, either to their parents' cars parked in front of the school or to board one of the two school buses. Nathan took Leah's elbow and steered her in the direction of the restrooms.

"Where are you taking me?" she protested. "I'll miss my bus."

"Don't worry," Nathan told her. "I'll make sure you get home."

The boys' restroom was unlocked. The custodian stayed until five o'clock, then locked all the rooms after he'd finished cleaning. Kicking open the door, Nathan pulled Leah inside, blocking the door with his body. "Listen to me," he shouted, holding her by the shoulders. "I didn't force you to do anything against your will. You wanted to be with me. You insisted I go in the bedroom with you. You stripped naked, then climbed on top of me."

Leah had an icy look in her eyes. "I was drunk on that vodka punch Trent made. That didn't mean I gave you permission to have sex with me." She moved closer, her breath hot on his face. "I was freaking passed out! A person can't give their consent when they're unconscious. I hope you enjoyed yourself. All I remember was waking up in Trent's bedroom. Did you guys trade off, huh?"

"I can't believe this," Nathan said, shocked at what he was hearing. "You're trying to blackmail me. Do you want money? Are you trying to force me to take you to see your father? I'll hire a car service if that's what this is all about."

"Forget about my stupid father," Leah shrieked uncontrollably, her frustrations spewing out. "My father's a criminal. Just because I've had a few boyfriends doesn't mean I had sex with them. I was lying when I said those things. I wanted to get back at you. I'm only fifteen years old."

"Calm down," Nathan said, placing his hands on her shoulder.

"I wish I were dead," Leah said, wrenching away from him. "I got drunk so I could forget about my miserable life for a few hours. I thought you were a nice guy, that we were just going to play around. I guess I was wrong."

"I'm sorry," he said, reaching out to her. "Please . . . I thought . . ."

Leah backed into a corner. "Don't touch me."

Nathan turned around in a small circle. "You're not going to say I raped you, are you? God, Leah, you'll ruin my life. My parents will disown me, and I'll go to jail. Then I won't be able to get into a decent college. No one in my family has ever been charged with a crime. Most of them are doctors, lawyers, bankers. I'm begging you, please don't do this to me."

Nathan shook his head, blaming himself for ever getting involved with her. She'd pursued him from the first day she'd enrolled at the Waldorf School. She knew his family had money, that his father was one of the wealthiest men in Santa Barbara. He'd never suspected she might be an opportunist. Her mother was a district attorney. She lived in an exclusive community. When she'd told him about the problems with her father, he'd felt sorry for her, wanted to comfort her. "I made a mistake," he said. "We should have never gone to Trent's party. Things always get out of hand with that crowd. I swear on my mother's life, Leah, I thought you wanted it. I didn't realize you'd passed out. I don't even remember how it happened. I thought I was dreaming or something. Trent must have poured enough vodka in that punch to make an elephant pass out. I don't even like booze."

"Yeah, right," Leah said, picking a piece of lint off her black skirt. "Don't worry. I'm not going to call the police and tell them you raped me."

Nathan released a long sigh of relief. "It stinks in here," he said, reaching for the door handle. "We can talk at my house. I'll get my aunt to drive you home later."

Leah placed her hands behind her back. "What am I going to do? I'm pregnant."

Nathan's mouth fell open. For a few moments, he was speechless. When he finally spoke, his voice was elevated several notches—the voice of a young boy who suddenly found himself in serious trouble. "I thought you were just trying to get my attention. Are you really pregnant?"

A tear rolled down one side of her face. "The home pregnancy test came back positive," she told him, dabbing at her eyes with her finger. "I'm sure my father will wire me money for an abortion if I ask him. I tried to tell him over the phone the other night, but my brother kept walking in. Besides, knowing my mother, she's probably recording our phone calls in case my dad says something they can use against him in court."

"How far along are you?"

"It's been over two months since Trent's party," Leah said. "I haven't gained any weight, but I was sick to my stomach yesterday morning."

Nathan pulled her into his arms, gently pushing her head down onto his shoulder. "Everything's going to be okay, Leah," he said, inhaling the fragrant scent of her hair. "Maybe the test was wrong. My grandfather left me some money, so you don't have to worry. Before you even think about getting an abortion, though, I want you to see a doctor. Sometimes those tests are wrong. You might not have read it right."

"They'll call my mother," Leah said. "I couldn't stand it if she knew. She already thinks I'm a juvenile delinquent. The only person I've ever been able to talk to is my dad. They're going to send him to prison. Then I won't have anyone."

They took a shortcut to Nathan's house, using one of the hiking trails laced throughout Santa Barbara. Both of them were silent. Tall trees shaded them, the leaves crunched under their feet. He clasped her hand protectively, pushing aside several protruding branches so they didn't strike her in the face. In three months, he would turn seventeen. Just a few weeks after that, he would graduate. He came from a family of staunch Catholics. His mother went to mass every Sunday, and his grandmother went every morning.

Nathan glanced over at Leah's profile, her elegantly slanted nose, her pronounced cheekbones, her delicate, flawless skin. People told him he was handsome, that his family had good genes. Other images appeared in his mind. He tried to push them away, but they were too vivid. Their child would be beautiful. How could he allow her to kill it?

Nathan and Leah reached an area where the trail branched off into separate directions. He suddenly stopped walking, dropping Leah's hand and staring off into space. All the stories he'd read about arriving at the fork in the road, then having to decide which path to take. Like the night he'd had sex with Leah, the moment had felt surreal, as if he were locked inside another dimension. What decision would he make? He turned and gazed at Leah. This wasn't only his decision. They might not agree. Was a life worth the sacrifices they would both have to make?

Yes, Nathan told himself, taking Leah's hand again in confidence.

EIGHTEEN

A STORM FRONT moved in early that morning. Joanne almost didn't make it to the office. Several times she nearly lost control of the Lexus in the torrential downpour. A mud slide had brought traffic to a standstill on the 101 Freeway. The storm was so severe that Seacliff Point and most of the surrounding areas had suffered a blackout. She decided to keep Mike and Leah home from school, calling Emily Merritt and asking her to check in on them.

Carrying her galoshes in her hand, Joanne removed a pair of black pumps from her backpack, dropped them on the floor just inside the main entrance to the courthouse, and was about to step into them when she spotted Kennedy standing by the elevator. Rushing to catch up to him, they rode to the third floor together. "Quite a storm," he remarked, fastening the snap on his umbrella. "You had a longer drive than I did. I'm surprised you made it in today."

"At least we have power here at the courthouse," Joanne said. "My kids are at home without electricity."

"You're renting the Spencer house, right?"

"Yes," she answered. "They plan to move back in March. At first they told me May, but I guess their big house sold ahead of schedule. They intend to make the house at Seacliff Point their primary residence. I assume you've heard that Judge Spencer is retiring next year."

Kennedy looked down at the floor. "I hate to be the bearer of bad news."

Joanne gasped. "They found the body."

"No," Kennedy said, "I'd classify that as good news."

The elevator stopped and they stepped out. Joanne attempted to keep up with him as he headed down the back corridor to the entrance to his office. He had long legs and walked fast, so much so that even some of the male ADAs couldn't keep up with him. He stopped in front of the back door, waiting for her to remove her key and unlock the door, rather than bothering to use his own.

"The authorities in Valencia have called off the search," Kennedy told her. "They were going to extend it through today, but the weather made it impossible. Now they're dealing with traffic accidents, mud slides, flooding, road closures. According to the weather bureau, the storm is due to last through the end of the week. The area where they've been searching must be a swamp by now."

"Will they resume the search when the weather breaks?"

"Not without additional evidence."

"Mrs. Decker will be shattered," Joanne said, her brows furrowing.

"There's nothing more we can do," Kennedy said, disappearing down the hallway.

Inside her office, Joanne removed her raincoat, then checked her voice mail. She wanted to get a cup of coffee, yet she forced herself to make the call to Elizabeth Decker. The woman should know immediately that the authorities had discontinued the search for her son's body. When a recording came on, she left a message, relieved that she could postpone the conversation until later in the day.

Joanne opened her wallet and pulled out Eli Connors's business card. For a few moments, she sat with her palm pressed against her forehead, her mind completely blank. "Humph," she said, turning the card over in her hand. For the amount of money she'd paid him, his card struck her as odd. All it had on it was his name and pager number. The paper was thin, and the edges appeared to have been cut with a pair of scissors. With the technology available today, most people had discarded their pagers for cell phones, Palm Pilots, and other means of communications. Of course, Eli was generally at sea.

Joanne had seen the *Nightwatch* last evening from her bedroom window, and had wished the detective could have come ashore. Joanne didn't know what to do about her daughter. When she'd arrived home from work, she'd discovered that Leah had not come home from school. At first, Mike had thought Leah had missed the bus, but after calling several of her friends, he'd started to worry that something had happened to her. Just when Joanne was about to call the police, Leah walked in the door, ran to her room, and barricaded herself inside for the remainder of the evening. Joanne was left to wonder what she had done to deserve such disrespect from her daughter. Her children were physically under her wing again, yet her husband still controlled Leah.

Setting her own problems aside, Joanne realized why she'd pulled out Eli's card. If anyone could find Ian Decker's body, it would be Eli Connors. Since there was nothing to validate the detective's concerns about her or her children's safety, she suspected he would take off as soon as the weather cleared. He hadn't worked in several months, and maintaining a vessel like the *Nightwatch* was costly. Elizabeth couldn't afford to pay him, though, and Joanne certainly didn't have any extra money lying around.

Before she knew it, however, Joanne found herself dialing his pager number. She had no idea how many times she'd called him during the two years Mike and Leah had been missing. She tossed his card aside, wondering why she'd taken the time to retrieve it. She'd long ago committed his number to memory.

Eli had been her rock, her counselor, her guardian angel.

Joanne walked down the hall to the small kitchen, poured herself a cup of coffee, and took a sip as she headed back to her office. She heard her phone ringing as soon as she walked through the door. Reaching over her desk to answer it, she knew that it was Eli.

"You need something?"

"Where are you?"

"In the parking lot."

Joanne asked, "What parking lot?"

"Look out your window."

"I don't have a window," Joanne told him. The detective never failed to amaze her. "Are you trying to tell me you're in the courthouse parking lot?"

"Yeah," he said. "Nasty day, huh?"

"Come up to my office," she said. "I have something I'd like to run by you."

"I don't go inside government buildings," Eli answered. "With my luck, the damn thing will blow up, and they'll blame it on me."

"That's absurd."

"No," Eli said, "it's realistic."

"Where do you want me to meet you?"

"Go through the underground tunnel to the jail," Eli told her. "I'll pick you up near the motor pool."

"Why in God's name are you in the parking lot of the government center?"

"You paged me," Eli said, disconnecting.

* * *

Thirty minutes later, Eli and Joanne were sitting in a booth at Lulu's Café, a hole-in-the-wall coffee shop near the wharf in Ventura. Some of the locals gathered at Lulu's for breakfast, but because of the storm, the restaurant was deserted. Eli had just finished a stack of pancakes, a side order of bacon, two eggs, and sucked up about four cups of coffee. Joanne had already eaten breakfast at home, and was nursing her second cup of coffee. The detective removed his baseball cap, then ran his hand over his bald head, tucking the hat inside the pocket of his windbreaker. "Are you certain this Decker guy didn't just skip town?"

Joanne slouched in the booth. "I should have brought a tape of the interview with Tom Rubinsky," she said. "Then you'd know what we're dealing with." Kennedy had failed to compliment her on the interrogation, which had been disheartening. Although Rubinsky hadn't confessed or drawn them a map to Decker's grave, she thought she'd done a good job under the circumstances. Kennedy had been willing to file first-degree murder charges, which told her he was convinced that Decker hadn't simply absconded. Without a body, though, they might never be able to convict Tom Rubinsky of anything more serious than robbery and auto theft. The most appalling fact was that Gary, if the police failed to apprehend him, might suffer no penalty whatsoever. No matter how offensive Tom's behavior had been during the interview, she still considered Gary the more dangerous of the two brothers.

Dean Kennedy was an aloof man. Joanne shouldn't have expected any pats on the back. He seldom wasted time telling a subordinate something that he felt they should already know. She wondered about his wife, if he ever told her he loved her. Some men thought if they told you once, it should last a lifetime. An intensely private person, Kennedy didn't mix his private and professional life. He didn't always treat his staff with the same respect. She'd been shocked when he'd brought up the situation with Doug.

"My boss would never file first-degree murder charges if he had any doubts," Joanne told the detective. "Without more evidence, we can't justify continuing the search. Another problem is that the location where the caller said the body is buried falls outside our jurisdiction. That means we're at the mercy of the Valencia authorities."

"Ultimately," Eli reminded her, "jurisdiction will be determined on where the crime occurred not where they dumped the body. How big is the area?"

"Valencia has been searching within a twenty-mile radius of Magic Mountain," Joanne told him. "Decker could be stashed in a meat locker, or buried in someone's backyard. I believe his mother would have heard from him by now if he was alive. The anonymous phone call is what bothers me. What if one of the brothers disguised his voice and called Elizabeth, purposely feeding her erroneous information? We could have underestimated these men." She paused, thinking over the scenario she'd just described. "Don't you see how brilliant something like that could be?"

"Not precisely," Eli said. "But I'm sure you're going to tell me."

Joanne shoved her coffee cup aside and folded her arms on top of the table. "Once we deploy a large amount of equipment and manpower without success," she said, "the case will eventually become inactive. By sending us on a wild-goose chase, the Rubinskys may have saved themselves from a facing a murder rap. Our robbery case has some serious problems too. Should we fail to gain a conviction, all these men will be looking at is auto theft."

"Did you put a tap on the mother's phone?"

"Since the call, yes," she said, asking the waitress to refill her water glass. "We can't rule out the possibility that the Rubinskys may have another crime partner. I was certain they'd transported the body in the Ford Taurus, the car Tom was driving at the time of his arrest. I was wrong. The crime lab says the car is clean."

"They probably took it to a car wash."

"We're checking the car washes now," Joanne advised. "There's a ton of car washes, Eli. People in California wash their cars more often than they do their children."

"Good line," Eli said, chuckling.

"There's nothing funny about this," Joanne snapped. "I'm supposed to be at the courthouse, not in some dive watching you slop down pancakes." She pointed at his stomach. "You're going to have a heart attack if you don't lose some weight."

"That's the least of my worries," Eli said, patting his stomach. "I'm more worried about a bullet than a heart attack." He pulled out a package of chewing gum. When Joanne waved it away, he popped a stick in his mouth.

"You've never told me exactly why you had to leave the CIA."

Eli frowned. "You know I can't tell you what happened. Why do you think I live the way I do? If what I know got out, I'd have all kinds of people gunning for me."

Joanne was intrigued. She'd approached this subject before and always got the same reaction. "Have I heard about it?" she asked, resting her chin on her fist. "Did the situation have any racial connotations?"

Eli had a pained expression on his face.

"Well," she said, "you are black."

"Gee," he said sarcastically, "I hadn't noticed. Has anyone ever told you that you're white?"

"Stop it, Eli," Joanne said, knowing he was going to make her work for every morsel of information. "Would I have heard about it on television? Was it written up in the newspaper?"

"Yeah," Eli said, nervously scratching his neck.

"You weren't with the Secret Service, were you?"

"Something went wrong, okay?" he said, looking around to make certain no one was in earshot. "I saw something I wasn't suppose to see."

"What did you see?" Joanne probed. "Come on, Eli. You're going to drive me crazy if you don't tell me."

"I witnessed a murder in the White House," he said, speaking in hushed tones. "It was either a murder for hire or a massive cover-up. What I know for a fact is that they moved the body and set it up to look like a suicide."

"Lord, Eli, was it Roland Milhouser?" Milhouser had been attorney general for six months when he'd been found dead of a self-inflicted gunshot wound in the study at his home in Georgetown. Joanne had never heard any rumors that the attorney general's death might have been a homicide. Speculations were that he'd been having an affair, that he was mentally ill, that he'd been an alcoholic. Eli had been involved in something far more serious than she had imagined.

"You understand why I can't tell you," Eli said. "I'd be putting you at risk. Washington is a dangerous town. People think it's money that causes all the problems. It's not, it's power."

"I don't want to hear any more," Joanne said quickly. "I'm sorry I asked."

Eli gestured for the check. "Are you willing to provide me with everything I need on this Decker matter?"

Joanne stared out the window, trying to decide how far she was willing to go, particularly now that she'd heard Eli's story. She certainly didn't want to find herself in his position, always having to look over her shoulder. She doubted if Eli Connors was even his real name. Had he left a wife behind, children, a home?

She listened to the wind howling. The rain was coming down in transparent sheets. Lightning zigzagged across the sky, followed almost immediately by a loud clap of thunder. She suddenly felt a gust of cold air and pulled her jacket tighter around her body. Ian Decker's image came to mind, glancing over his shoulder at her the last day he'd been present in the courtroom. She knew now what it was she'd seen in his eyes—resignation. Had he had a premonition that the Rubinsky brothers were going to kill him? Had he felt powerless to stop it? This was what hurt Joanne the most, that a person as vulnerable as Decker had found no protection from evil. Instead of the massive resources of the government working on his behalf, they'd been attempting to imprison him. Joanne was ashamed. When Dreiser first brought Decker's problems to her attention, she'd felt burdened and disinterested. Should he turn up dead, the entire criminal justice system would have blood on its hands.

"I'll get you copies of the police reports along with my personal notes," Joanne blurted out. "That's as far as I'm willing to go."

Joanne's thoughts turned to Elizabeth Decker. The police said she'd been searching every day, occasionally with her daughter but most of the time alone. She was probably out there right now, oblivious to the rain and lightning, driven by a force far stronger than nature.

"I'll need to see everything you've got if you want me to find this man."

"You know I can't take evidence out of the building," Joanne snapped back at him. "I want to help his mother, but I don't want to place my career on the line. I have kids of my own to consider. You, of all people, should know what my family has been through."

"It's your decision," Eli said.

"The tape from the convenience store is distorted. And you can't take a chance by approaching the witnesses," Joanne told him. "Finding out who has been distributing this decoy gun could lead us to Gary

Rubinsky, but I don't want you involved in that end of the investigation. You'll end up butting heads with the same people you're trying to avoid. Every law enforcement agency in the country is trying to find the source of those guns."

"I might be able to enhance that film," Eli said. "Let me take a look at it?"

"The crime lab already looked at the tape," Joanne argued. "Don't tell me you have more sophisticated equipment than we do."

"Sometimes it's not the equipment, it's the talent," Eli told her, his tone more fact than boasting. "And don't forget, the county crime lab handles thousands of cases. Most of their work is done under duress, trying to meet mandatory deadlines. I don't have a crew on the *Nightwatch*. It looks like I'm going to have some time on my hands riding out this storm."

"Let's forget about the evidence for right now," she told him. "Are you going to work for free?"

Eli cracked his neck, his enormous frame cramped inside the small booth. "There's a lot of sad cases," he told her. "We can't right every wrong, Joanne. And no matter how much I'd like to offer my services without charge, I've got to cover my own expenses. With you, well, I guess you could say this became more than a business arrangement. I would have never hung around this long if I didn't think of you and your kids like family. And I certainly wouldn't have ever discussed the reason I left the agency unless I was certain I could trust you."

"Elizabeth Decker can't afford to pay you, Eli," Joanne said, seeing the clock on the wall and realizing people were probably looking for her. "She mortgaged her home to get her son out of jail."

"Who posted the Rubinskys' bail?"

"I don't really know," Joanne said. "They went through a bail bondsman. I have to get back to the office, Eli. I haven't even notified Arnold Dreiser that Valencia has discontinued the search."

"Dreiser, huh," the detective said, pulling out his baseball cap. "I think I've heard of this guy. Isn't he a well-known attorney?"

"His specialty is medical malpractice," Joanne said, sliding out of the booth. "He's related to Elizabeth Decker, otherwise he wouldn't be involved."

Eli pulled a ten out and left it on top of the bill. "Dreiser won a major class-action suit several years back. If my memory serves me correctly, it involved a defect in a car. The wheelbase was too short, causing it to roll. I don't recall the exact amount of the settlement, but I think the numbers were high."

Joanne was surprised she hadn't come up with the idea of getting Dreiser to pay Eli's fees. "Do you know about his son?"

"No," Eli said, holding the door open for her as they exited the restaurant.

"The boy committed suicide," Joanne said, opening her umbrella before they stepped out into the rain.

"Don't tell me he thinks it was a murder," Eli said, grimacing.

"No," Joanne said. "My opinion is Dreiser thought if he got Decker cleared he would make amends for whatever guilt he's carrying over the death of his son. Now that we suspect that the Rubinskys may have killed him, Dreiser's become even more emotionally involved."

"Are you willing to do your part, get me what I need to put this together?"

"Handing over my files is the limit, Eli," Joanne said, stopping in the parking lot. "I might sneak you into my office one night and let you pick through the evidence. But I refuse to let you take anything out of the building. This is a first and last for me, understand? When it comes to my work, I play by the rules."

"Good," he said, grabbing the umbrella out of her hand and holding it over both their heads as they huddled together in the rain. "Then we're in the same ballpark."

"What does that mean?"

"Well, I have my limits too. I don't steal, and I don't kill people."

"What about everything else?"

Eli hit the button to disarm the alarm on his truck, then held the door open for her. "Everything else is up for grabs."

NINETEEN

ELIZABETH DECKER exited her red-and-bronze Chevy Blazer on a farm road approximately ten miles from Magic Mountain. Already soaked, she didn't bother with an umbrella. The plastic visor would keep the rain out of her eyes, and she'd borrowed some of her daughter's ski clothes. Dressed in a black jumpsuit with red stripes on the sleeves and four zippered compartments, her feet were encased in red insulated snow boots.

In the rear of the vehicle were two sturdy shovels, a hoe, two rakes, and a grocery bag containing Elizabeth's gardening tools. The day before she'd lopped off the metal portion at the end of one of the rakes. At the moment, all she needed was the wooden pole. If she found something that appeared to be evidence, she would return for the other rake. On the drive over, she had checked her phone messages from her cell phone. Dreiser had called her, Joanne Kuhlman had left a message, and a detective at the Valencia Sheriff's Department had tried to get in touch with her. She didn't need to speak to them. She knew why they were calling.

Since three o'clock that morning, Elizabeth had been working at her dining-room table, mapping the area where she believed her son's grave was located on large sheets of white paper, then dividing the area into grids. To distinguish one grid from another, she'd purchased fifty yellow plastic stakes at Home Depot the previous evening. She placed a small hammer into one of the zippered compartments of the ski suit, a hand shovel into the other. Her plan was to insert the plastic stakes into the muddy soil to establish the outer perimeter of the grid. She picked up the stakes and placed them in one of the heavy blue plastic garbage bags the sanitation department distributed, knowing she would have to return to the car and retrieve more once these were positioned. Even though the stakes were plastic, they were cumbersome and she couldn't carry them all at one time.

Elizabeth had hoped to receive another phone call from the anonymous informant. But now that the police had set up the wiretaps at her home, she felt certain that the man who had told her about her son's murder would never be heard from again.

She rubbed her hands together, wishing she had remembered to bring along a pair of gloves. Already her fingers were stiff and cold. It couldn't be more than forty degrees. When she exhaled, she could see her breath.

Elizabeth didn't mind the flashes of lightning, though, the drumrolls of thunder, the transparent sheets of rain, the slippery streets, the traffic-clogged roadways. In a way, she found it gratifying. Her son's cries for help had been heard. The storm was her affirmation. An unspeakable act had been committed against a holy and treasured soul.

Heaven was outraged.

Elizabeth compared life to an unending series of examinations. When asked to find an adjective to describe Ian Decker, the majority of people would check the boxes marked "pathetic," "retarded," "burdensome," "useless," "annoying," "stupid," "blundering," along with hundreds of other words with negative connotations. The box they should have checked was "none of the above." What one saw with the human eye or heard with the human ear did not always constitute reality. Ian Decker was a special soul, a vessel, a bridge from the past to the future. Even in death, he would be eternally cherished and protected. His mother no longer attempted to explain the inexplicable. Some knowledge was not meant to be shared.

Trudging out into the open field, Elizabeth poked the ground with the wooden pole, making certain it reached a depth of at least twelve inches. The Rubinsky brothers were lazy. Her son's grave would be shallow. In addition, the rain had made her task easier. The day before the ground had been dry and hard. Physical stamina, however, would not be a problem. To others she might appear to be on the verge of collapse, her face haggard with dark circles etched under her eyes, yet she would be given the strength to work tirelessly until her mission was accomplished.

Every fifty feet, Elizabeth would bend over and hammer a yellow stake into the mushy soil. She then turned to the right and counted off another fifty feet, continuing in the same pattern until she had established a grid. Back and forth she marched, plunging the plastic stakes into the ground. When she struck something solid, she dropped to the ground and scooped out the object with the small hand shovel. She dug up rocks, soda cans, and hubcaps, and wasted half an hour unearthing the remains of a rusted-out hibachi grill.

Her hands raw and bleeding, her clothes and face smeared with mud, Elizabeth climbed inside the passenger seat of the Blazer at precisely five o'clock. She circled the area she had covered on her hand-drawn map with a black Magic Marker, then folded the paper carefully and stored it inside the glove compartment. Once she got home, she would bathe, eat, sleep, then get up in the morning and return. She would continue expanding the radius until she found Ian. Were it not for the rain, she would have used flashlights and continued to search until dawn.

After dinner that evening, Joanne asked Mike to go to his room, then sat down at the kitchen table to have a serious talk with her daughter. "Where did you go yesterday?"

"I didn't go anywhere," Leah told her. "I forgot one of my books. I needed it to do my homework so I went back to my locker to get it. I thought I had enough time, but by the time I got back, the bus had already left."

"How did you get home?"

"My friend's aunt drove me."

"What friend?"

"His name is Nathan."

"Is he a boyfriend or a friend?"

"A friend," Leah said, deciding it was time to smooth things over with her mother. "There's a group of kids. We all hang out together. I'm not going out with him or anything." Nathan had already made an appointment for her to see a doctor tomorrow afternoon in Santa Barbara. The doctor was a woman, and Nathan said she was a friend of the family. Leah had been shocked that he would take her to a doctor who knew his parents. It was okay, he told her. This was a person they could trust. At first, Leah had thought he was arranging for her to have an abortion, but she'd been mistaken. Nathan only wanted the doctor to verify that Leah was pregnant. After that, they would decide how to proceed. Although she was anxious, she was also relieved. Her secret was out. She no longer had to carry the burden alone.

Once they'd reached his house, Nathan had made them a snack and spread a blanket out on the lawn. He'd been exquisitely gentle, stroking her face and telling her that no matter what happened, he wouldn't abandon her. Maybe it was only an act, but Leah needed to believe his statements were genuine. Had she not passed out that night at Trent's party, she would have consented to have sex with him. Even before the evening had begun, she'd set out to seduce him. Most of her girlfriends had already had sex. She envied the attention they received from their boyfriends. Her father had always made a fuss over her, but now he was no longer around.

"Nathan's a nice guy, Mom," Leah told her, twirling a strand of her hair around her finger. "A bunch of kids are going to a movie tomorrow after school. Nathan asked me to go with them. Mike and I were stuck in the house all day today. Can I go?"

Joanne rolled her neck around. A person knew they were getting old when their bones ached every time the weather changed. "Does he drive?"

"No," Leah said. "Nathan's aunt is going to drive us. His parents are away on a ski trip. Don't worry. We're not going to be alone in his house or anything. Like I said, we're going with a group."

"You're supposed to be grounded," Joanne told her, wondering what had caused Leah's disposition to change so drastically. She hadn't been this bubbly in months. "You had no right to go in my purse and unlock the room behind the closet. And taking the car was wrong. You also hurt my feelings when you told me you hated me. I'm certain you didn't mean it, but 'hate' is a terrible word."

"I'm so sorry, Mom," Leah said, walking over and kneeling on the floor by her mother's chair. "Please," she pleaded, holding her hands in a praying position, "I'm begging you to forgive me. I know I've acted terrible lately. It's been tough because of Dad. I promise. I won't ever disrespect you again."

Joanne placed her head in her hands. She hoped her daughter's newfound attitude was sincere and not merely an act to get what she wanted. "Okay," she said, peering at Leah. At few moments later, Joanne reached over and clasped her daughter's face in her hands. "You can't possibly know how much I love you, how terrible it was for me during the time you were gone. How could you believe the things your father said were true?"

"It wasn't easy for Mike and me, either," Leah told her. "Dad told us you never wanted to see us again. We didn't believe him at first. We called the house. We called the courthouse. We didn't know that Dad had fixed it so the phone numbers we were calling rang in his office, and that he'd told some lady what to say. Since you never got in touch with us, we decided Dad must have been telling us the truth."

"But it still seems like you resent me," Joanne told her. "Don't you know that what your father did was terribly wrong? He didn't just hurt me, Leah, he hurt all of us."

Leah got up and returned to her chair at the table. "He's still my father," she said, a spark of defiance surfacing. "Dad didn't want to go to jail. He didn't stab or rob anyone. I know what it feels like to be afraid. People make mistakes when they're scared."

"I want you to be happy," Joanne said, "but I can't let you walk all over me. The next time you disrespect me, the penalties are going to be severe. I'll take your computer away forever, understand?"

"I need it to do my schoolwork."

"No chat boards," her mother said, standing. "They tried to call me from the courthouse several times and the line was busy. I don't want you to use the modem. Things will be different once we move. Right now, I need to keep the line open for emergencies."

"You mean I can't use the modem ever again?" Leah asked. "Why don't we just go live in a cave? You can't be serious."

"You can use it now and then," Joanne told her. "But only with my permission." She started to leave the room, then stopped in the doorway, turning back around. "If you defy me this time, I'll disconnect the phone."

"You can't do that!" the girl said, her eyes widening. "What would we do if there was an emergency? They could charge you with child abuse."

Joanne laughed, the first pleasant moment of the day. On the drive home, she'd tried to figure out a way to curtail Leah's rebellious behavior. An idea had popped into her mind that just might work. She would be able to tell by her daughter's reaction if it was worth pursuing. The child abuse comment was classic.

"Listen carefully," Joanne told her. "I adore you, but I also want you to understand my position. A parent is obligated to feed you, clothe you, educate you, and put a roof over your head. They don't have to provide you with a computer, a modem, a phone, an allowance, even your own room for that matter." She leveled her finger at her. "Disobey me again, and I'll do exactly what I just said. I'll have the calls forwarded to the Spencers' other number, and buy Mike a cell phone. Then if there's an emergency, your brother will handle it."

"Buy Mike a cell phone!" Leah shouted, throwing her hands in the air. "That's the lamest thing I've ever heard. He's only twelve. I'm the one who should have a cell phone, not my stupid brother."

"You're the one who's been acting immature," Joanne told her, slapping open the door leading out of the kitchen. From the other room, she shouted, "Don't forget to clean up the kitchen."

TWENTY

ARNOLD DREISER navigated the steep hill leading to his home on Crest Drive in the foothills above Ventura. He noticed that the city had already placed sandbags in strategic locations. The previous year, several homes had been damaged by mud slides. Arnold had purchased the house from his ex-wife after their son's suicide. Susan had found Jake. He was only thankful he'd been spared that agony.

Having already made plans to take Jake to brunch at the country club that morning, Susan Dreiser had knocked on her son's door around ten o'clock. When he didn't respond, she had no reason to be concerned. Like most teenagers, Jake often slept in on the weekends. Once he'd reached puberty, though, he'd demanded a lock on his bedroom door. She'd misplaced the spare key, and Jake's lock was the type that couldn't be picked with a paper clip or some other sharp object. Deciding to have another cup of coffee and finish reading the Sunday paper, she waited forty-five minutes and then tried calling his private number. When the voice mail picked up, she became alarmed.

Returning to her son's room, Susan shouted his name repeatedly and beat her fist against the door. Certain now that something was wrong, she went to the garage for a hammer and flew back up the stairs in a panic. She pounded on the lock until she broke the door handle.

The bed had been soaked with blood. Jake's body was cold and rigid, his eyes were open and fixed on the ceiling. Their son had slit both of his wrists with a razor blade, bleeding to death while his mother slept only a short distance away. The coroner had fixed the time of death between eleven and twelve the night before. The two boys Jake had gone out with that evening claimed he'd been quieter than usual, yet they didn't notice anything about his behavior that gave them any indication that he was considering taking his own life.

Everyone had told Dreiser he was a fool to move back into the house. For sixteen years, however, Jake Dreiser had lived inside the three-story yellow adobe house at the top of the hill. His father couldn't abandon the structure that had once been filled with his son's laughter. Perhaps in the beginning, Dreiser had been looking for answers, thinking that if he remained in the house long enough, he'd find something, anything that would explain why Jake had committed suicide. Two years ago, Dreiser had reached a level of acceptance. To bring additional closure, he'd hired a contractor to knock out the ceiling in his library and raise it to the second floor where his son's room had been located. Dreiser thought it was somehow appropriate that the site of such horror and sadness was now an open, airy space surrounded by lovely cherry-wood shelves and leather-bound books.

As a labor of love, Dreiser had done most of the carpentry work himself. His father had been a finish carpenter, and Dreiser had worked in his shop after school until he'd graduated from college and entered law school. For the past nine months, he'd spent every weekend in his garage, carefully cutting, sanding, and finishing the shelves for the new library. The top shelves could only be reached by means of a ladder, so this is where Dreiser placed his collection of first-edition books, each encased in plastic dustcovers. Most of them were family heirlooms that he had intended to pass on to Jake. In another symbolic gesture, Dreiser had refused to purchase or build a library ladder. The books could be reached with a metal work ladder he kept in the garage but once the volumes had gone up, he'd never taken them back down. They were Jake's books now, he'd decided, and they would remain in the open space that would forever belong to his son.

The first floor of the house was divided into two sections separated by a stairway. On one side was a two-car garage, on the other was a home gym. He opened the door to the gym, then quickly closed it, ascending the stairway to the main floor. Last year, he'd sold off the antiques and redecorated, choosing light Danish woods and contemporary designs. Since most of the fabrics were in neutral tones, he'd painted the walls in an assortment of colors, mixing the paint himself. The living room was a robin's-egg blue, the kitchen a cheerful yellow, and the dining room was what he called a serious shade of green. He seldom had people over for dinner, but whenever the crystal chandelier was lit, the dark green walls and his collection of battleship etchings provided a warm, masculine atmosphere.

Dreiser headed to the kitchen, opening the refrigerator and staring inside. Twice a week, a woman came in to clean and prepare food for him. Removing a plate of chicken, vegetables, and a baked potato covered in plastic, he popped it into the microwave, then opened the door to the liquor cabinet. His fingers closed around a bottle of Bombay gin. Yanking his hand back, he quickly closed the cabinet. Today was the anniversary of his son's death. For the past five years, he'd spent these evenings alone, drowning his sorrows in alcohol as he sorted through old photographs. Outside of an occasional glass of wine or a few beers,

Dreiser usually wasn't much of a drinker. With the Decker situation, he couldn't afford to nurse a two-day hangover. He glanced at the stack of photo albums by the fireplace, then forced himself to go upstairs. What good did it do to put himself through such misery?

Jumping in the shower, Arnold decided he would forget about eating in, and would call a friend and go out instead. The phone rang just as he stepped under the hot water and began lathering his body with soap. He started to let the answering service pick up, then became concerned it might be Elizabeth.

"Arnold?"

"Joanne?"

"I was expecting to get your voice mail," she said. "What are you doing? Am I disturbing you?"

"Well," he said, "right now I'm dripping water all over the bathroom floor. I was in the shower."

"Are you naked?"

Dreiser laughed, the sound bouncing off the tiled walls. "Are you interested?"

"Maybe," she said, walking over to the window and seeing the lights burning inside the cabin of the *Nightwatch*. "But not now."

With only a few words, Joanne Kuhlman had pulled off a small miracle. She had not only called him at precisely the right moment, she'd managed to get him to laugh on a day he'd never thought it possible. "Are you implying that you'd like to get together at a later date? You're not one of those people who goes back on their word, I hope."

"No, no," Joanne said, embarrassed. "I think you're a nice man."

"Just nice?" Dreiser asked, a playful smile on his face. "Can't you come up with a better adjective? You know like 'great,' 'sexy,' 'brilliant,' 'irresistible.' I'd certainly rank you a few notches above 'nice.'"

"Really?" Joanne said, her face flushing. "How would you rank me?"

"Ah, let's see," he said, pausing a moment. "I'd probably place you in the 'remarkable' category."

"'Remarkable,' huh?" she said. "I'd prefer to be 'beautiful,' 'desirable,' 'determined,' and 'heroic.'"

Again Dreiser laughed, a feeling of warmth spreading throughout his body. "You only gave me one adjective."

"I think we should get back to why I called," she continued. "Have you talked to Elizabeth today?"

Dreiser hit the button for the speakerphone so he could dry off and get dressed. "I talked to Elizabeth's daughter," he said. "Pauline is a nurse at Holy Cross Hospital. She went out alone today."

"In a storm like this?"

"According to Pauline," Arnold said, "before the rainstorm, Elizabeth had been staying out there until three or four in the morning. She would have gone with her mother today, but they needed her at the hospital."

"I want you to meet a friend of mine," Joanne told him. "He tracked down my ex-husband. I think he might be able to find Decker's body."

"Not a private detective," Dreiser said. "I don't put a lot of stock in those people, Joanne. Why would we bring an amateur into the picture when the search and rescue team has been working for days. As soon as the weather clears . . ."

"The search has been called off," she told him. "The Valencia authorities can't justify deploying this much manpower without more evidence."

"Tell me about your friend."

"Eli is far from an amateur," Joanne said. "We're talking former CIA."

"Why did he leave the agency?'

"Trust me," she said, sighing. "This is one story you don't want to know."

"Is this man dangerous?"

"Take me off the speakerphone!"

"I'm at home, Joanne," Dreiser said, pulling on a pair of slacks before he retrieved the handset. "There's no one in the house but me. This guy must be bad news if you're afraid to even talk about him over the phone."

"Let me use Eli's explanation," Joanne told him. "He doesn't steal and he doesn't kill people. As far as being dangerous, the answer is yes, but only to people like the Rubinskys."

"Sounds like my kind of guy," Dreiser joked. "Anyone willing to offer their services for free is welcome."

"Eli doesn't work for free."

"Who's going to pay him?"

Joanne swallowed first, then said, "You are."

The smile disappeared from Dreiser's face. "Wait a minute here," he protested. "I've already lost a ton of money on this case. My practice is out of control, and now you want me to pay some former CIA agent who sounds like trouble. Sure, I care about Ian. But before the trial, I'd only seen the guy twice in his lifetime. I don't even know Elizabeth that well, for Christ's sake."

Joanne decided to hit the defense attorney hard. The day she'd gone to lunch with him, he'd badgered her into believing Decker was an innocent victim. Now that she was in over her head emotionally, as determined to find Decker as his own mother, Arnold was ready to head off in the opposite direction. If they didn't find the body by the weekend, she'd given thought to having Mike and Leah round up some of their friends and join the search party. "You're going to think I'm cruel for what I'm about to say," she said, sucking in a deep breath. "I only say what I feel is right. That's how my parents raised me."

"It's a free world," Dreiser told her. "Say whatever you want."

"There's nothing you can do about what happened to your son," Joanne told him, walking around as she talked. "My heart goes out to you. Nonetheless, you have an opportunity to help Elizabeth."

Dreiser bristled. "As if I haven't been trying to help Elizabeth."

"Representing Ian on a robbery charge isn't the same," she said. "I admit I thought he'd just skipped out at first, but too much time has passed. A person with his limitations would have called home by now."

Dreiser felt as if she'd punched him in the gut. She'd lifted his spirits only to crush them, using his son's death to coerce him into paying for a private detective he'd never met. "Are you certain the authorities are calling off the search?"

"The word came from Kennedy himself," Joanne told him. "That's why I want you to bring Eli on board. He has the skills, the time, and the equipment. I'm not saying he'll find Decker tomorrow. If we put him on the payroll, I feel fairly certain he'll get the job done. You have to hire him immediately, though, or he's going to leave town."

A tense silence ensued.

Arnold finally asked, "What makes you think I'm rolling in money?"

"My savings account is empty," Joanne said, her voice escalating. "I don't even have a home I can borrow against. I'm only renting the Spencers' house. In a few months, I'm going to have to find another place to live. I'd pay Eli myself, but I can't afford it. I know you have a successful law practice, and you've won some large settlements. This woman needs help. Who else am I supposed to call? You're the one who got me involved. My only responsibility was to prosecute Decker for robbery."

"How much does this Eli person charge?"

"It's up to you to negotiate his fees," Joanne explained. "For obvious reasons, I can't be involved. Do you know where the Cliff House restaurant is located?"

Arnold was dressed now and seated in a chair in his bedroom. "Yeah," he said. "The place off 101 Freeway on the outskirts of Santa Barbara."

"Right," Joanne said. "Eli and I will meet you in the bar at nine o'clock. If for some reason, he can't come, give me your cell phone number." After jotting down his number, she gazed out the window again. The rain had let up for the moment. She felt certain Eli could get to shore safely if he left right away. She wondered if he'd wired her house without her knowledge and was listening to their conversation. "Oh," she added, "don't worry about bringing your checkbook. Eli gets paid in cash."

"I only have a few hundred dollars on me."

"He'll wait for the money until the bank opens in the morning."

Joanne strode into the bar at the Cliff House restaurant shortly after nine o'clock. Dreiser almost choked on his beer when he saw the hulking figure behind her. At first, he wasn't even sure it was a man. All he saw was a large, dark shadow that seemed to reach all the way to the ceiling.

Joanne made the introductions. "Eli, this is Arnold Dreiser."

Dreiser shook the man's hand, marveling at the size of it. He wasn't small in stature himself, but he felt as if he'd placed his hand inside an oversized catcher's mitt. "Pleased to meet you," he said, clearing his throat. "Should we get a table?"

"No," Eli said, his voice surprisingly soft. "Follow me."

Dreiser threw some money down on the bar, then rushed to catch Joanne and Eli as they exited the restaurant. "We'll talk in my truck," Eli told him, pointing to a black Toyota pickup in the parking lot.

"Won't it be a little cramped?"

"I can't stay," Joanne said, kissing Dreiser on the cheek before she jumped in her car and took off.

Dreiser was completely befuddled. He touched the spot on his cheek where the prosecutor had kissed him. Eli crossed to the other side of the parking lot; Dreiser remained in front of the restaurant. What was he doing? On the anniversary of his son's death, he was about to get into a car with a man who looked as if he could snap his neck like a twig. His palms began perspiring.

He saw Eli gesturing to him, standing alongside his truck.

"I left something in my car," Dreiser called out. "Just give me a minute to go get it."

"Get back here," Eli shouted, grimacing in annoyance. "I'm not going to hurt you."

"Oh," Arnold said, trying to come up with an explanation. "It's my medicine, you know. I need to take my medicine."

"Like hell you do," Eli said, slamming the car door.

In a panic, Dreiser ran toward his car. Eli tackled him, slamming him down onto the pavement. With the big man on top of him, Dreiser felt as if he couldn't breathe. "Get off me."

"Listen carefully," Eli whispered in his ear. "I'm here because Joanne said you wanted me to find some kid's body. If the way I look scares you, I'm sorry. This is how God made me."

Dreiser pleaded, "Just let me up, okay?"

"On one condition?"

"Anything," Dreiser gasped.

"Promise you'll never judge a person by the color of their skin or any other physical characteristic. Do you know how many black men are in prison because of people like you?"

"It wasn't the color of your skin," Dreiser told him. "My son killed himself. It was five years ago today. I shouldn't have come tonight. I usually stay home and get plastered."

Eli rolled off him, then stood, reaching down and offering Arnold a hand. Arnold ignored Eli, pushed himself up, then sat there, his eyes moist with tears. He hadn't been this humiliated since he'd been beaten up in the third grade. He dropped his head, hoping Eli wouldn't notice that he was crying. He found himself staring at the man's tennis shoes. The only time he'd seen feet that big was on a professional basketball player.

"How's your sea legs?" Eli asked, reaching down and clasping Dreiser's forearm, then gently pulling him to a standing position. "You know, do you get seasick?"

"No," Dreiser said, swiping at his nose with the back of his hand. "I used to have a sailboat. I sold it several years back. Why do you ask?"

"I'm going to take you to my place," Eli said. "We'll have a few drinks and talk. The ride over might be a little rough, but once we get there, I think you'll feel better. And don't worry about getting home. Wherever you want to be in the morning, I'll make certain you get there."

As they were walking back toward Eli's truck, Dreiser suddenly stopped. "That's why she kissed me."

"What are you babbling about now?"

"Today's Valentine's Day, right?"

"I haven't given it much thought," Eli answered, unlocking the passenger door for the attorney. "Is that why you ran off like that? Did you think I wanted you to be my Valentine or something? Even if I was into guys, you're not my type."

Eli doubled over with laughter. Dreiser joined in. Instead of being frightened, he now felt relaxed and comfortable, as if he'd known this man for years. Perhaps he'd needed to shed a few tears. Or it could be the man himself. Once Dreiser got over the initial shock, being around Eli made him feel safe, as if nothing could harm him. No wonder Joanne had insisted he meet him. If he could find Ian, Dreiser would consider offering Eli a job as an investigator with his law firm.

"I was referring to Joanne," Dreiser said, realizing he'd scraped his chin when Eli had knocked him down. "She kissed me. It was just a peck on the cheek. I wasn't expecting it. I'd forgotten it was Valentine's Day."

"Think she was trying to tell you something?" Eli said, a broad grin on his face. "She's one fine lady. I'm not so sure about you. Her ex-husband did a number on her. I'll have to check you out if you're thinking along those lines."

The two men were inside the cab of the truck now. "What can you tell me about this thing with her ex-husband?" Dreiser asked, fastening his seat belt. "Joanne mentioned that he is on trial in Los Angeles. What exactly did he do?"

"You'll have to ask Joanne," Eli said, gunning the engine and steering the Toyota in the direction of the 101 Freeway. "I don't discuss my clients' business."

"From what you said, you must live on a boat."

"A ship," Eli told him. "She's a beauty."

"What about the weather?"

Eli peered out the windshield. The dark clouds had passed and a number of stars were now visible. "The storm's over, my friend."

TWENTY-ONE

ELI AND Arnold were facing each other in two swivel chairs in the main cabin of the *Nightwatch*, the row of computer terminals flickering beside them. Eli picked up their cocktail glasses and carried them to the galley, returning a short time later with two ceramic mugs filled with coffee. Watching the man duck his head as he came through the portal, Dreiser was curious. "Aren't you afraid you're going to knock yourself unconscious? Does anyone ever check up on you?"

"Nah," Eli said, handing over one of the coffee mugs as he squeezed his large frame into the vacant chair. "I don't want anyone keeping tabs on me. My clients call me whenever they need me. Joanne would probably notify the Coast Guard if I didn't return her page, particularly now that she knows I'm here. That's why I didn't tell her I was still keeping an eye on her until a few days ago. With some of the stuff I've got on board this tub, the last thing I need is for the Coast Guard to come snooping around."

Dreiser had consumed several glasses of bourbon. He didn't feel in-

toxicated, however, and he was highly sensitive to caffeine. He took a
sip of the coffee to make certain Eli wasn't offended, then set the coffee mug down on the console. Eli had agreed to take him back to shore
whenever he wanted, and Dreiser needed to catch a few hours of
sleep. He had a court appearance in Los Angeles at ten o'clock, and because of the traffic, he'd have to leave Ventura no later than seven-
thirty in the morning. "What if you got sick?"

"I don't get sick," Eli said, his eyes roaming from monitor to monitor.
He spun his chair around, placed the coffee mug on top of a stack of
papers and typed in a few coordinates to reposition the telescopes.

Dreiser leaned forward, peering over his shoulder. "What are you doing, if you don't mind me asking?"

"Making certain Joanne is safe," Eli told him, clasping his coffee
mug with both hands. "Focusing on just her house wouldn't accomplish anything. I scan the entire community. The trees are a major
problem. That and the fact that there's no streetlights. Why would
someone build a fancy area like Seacliff Point, and then be too cheap
to put in a few streetlights? Doesn't make sense, you know."

"If there aren't any lights," Dreiser asked, "what good are the telescopes?"

"The telescopes have infrared capabilities," he explained. "They also
scan and record automatically. Because I don't have enough equipment to cover the entire area at one time, I have to review the footage,
then reset some of the cameras. What you're seeing on this screen," he
said, pointing to one of the monitors, "was recorded while we were on
shore. All the rest of the monitors are live. By the time an assailant
reached Joanne's house, it'd be too late. My only choice would be to
shoot him."

"I thought you didn't kill people."

Eli let out a long sigh. He'd spent the afternoon poring over the files on the Decker case. Most of the night, he'd listened to Dreiser talk about his son. The day had exhausted him. "I don't make it a habit of killing people," he told him. "You can shoot a person without killing them."

"From this distance?"

"With the right weapon." Eli said, arching an eyebrow. "And don't ask, because I have no intention of telling you what kind of weaponry I have on board. I only brought you here because Joanne vouched for you. Whatever you've seen or heard tonight is not to be repeated." He pinned Dreiser with a steely gaze. "Are we clear?"

"Absolutely," Dreiser said, having caught a glimpse of the dark side of Eli's personality. He waited until the muscles in the man's face relaxed, then presented his next question. "Do you really think Joanne's ex-husband would hire someone to hurt her?"

"I haven't ruled out the possibility," Eli said, spinning his chair back to its previous position.

Dreiser ran his hands through his hair. "What good is the film footage? I realize if something did happen, you'd have documentation, but it'd be after the fact. The point is to keep someone from hurting her. Aren't you wasting your time filming?"

"A contract killer works differently than your average criminal," Eli told him, opening a drawer and removing a bag of peanuts. He offered some to Dreiser, but the attorney waved them away. "They don't just run up to someone and blow their head off," he continued, cracking a shell and tossing a peanut into his mouth. "Doug Kuhlman has the money to hire a professional. He wouldn't take a chance of hiring some lightweight off the street for fear they'd hurt his kids. Joanne said you used to be a judge. Haven't you ever handled a murder-for-hire?"

The thought that Joanne could be in danger was chilling. "Not personally," Arnold said. "I only served six months on the bench, and I was assigned to the misdemeanor arraignment calendar. Of course, I've studied and heard about cases involving hired assassins. As far as my current law practice is concerned, criminal law isn't my speciality. Elizabeth asked me to help her, or I wouldn't be involved in this mess."

"She's your cousin, right?"

"Yes," Dreiser explained, rubbing his eyes. "Let's get back to the murder-for-hire cases. Another reason I'm not that familiar with this type of crime is most of the homicides in the Los Angeles area don't involve professional killers. Where are you from?"

"Everywhere," Eli told him, tossing a handful of empty shells into the trash can.

"Don't be ridiculous," Dreiser said. "I mean where did you grow up?"

"None of your business."

"Forget it," Dreiser said, holding up a palm. "I don't care anyway."

"Okay," Eli said, dusting his hands off, "a professional killer would spend weeks, even months watching and analyzing his victim's activities before he got down to plotting the actual crime. We're speculating this person would be a male, even though there are a number of competent female assassins."

"Where?"

"In the phone book." Eli said, chuckling. "Are you really an attorney or did you have too much to drink?"

"Look," Dreiser said defensively, "I know the law. Like I was trying to tell you earlier, most of what I know about professional killers comes from movies, newspapers, or old case law I studied in school. I'm trying to get a grasp on what you're telling me. Cut me some slack."

"You got it," Eli said, falling serious. "From my experience, a killer is considered a professional if they've killed more than once and haven't been caught. They're smart, see, devious. They're also cautious, partly because they don't want to end up in prison, and also because this is their trade. Even a killer takes pride in his work."

Eli shoved his empty coffee mug aside and picked up a bottle of water, squirting it into his mouth. "What I've been trying to do for a number of months now is to determine if this person exists. The first thing I had to do was to familiarize myself with the residents of Seacliff Point. I don't want to end up shooting an innocent man. Get the picture?"

Dreiser nodded, listening intently.

"So," Eli continued, "now that I'm familiar with all the residents, I'm looking for someone who doesn't belong. A third of the houses in this community are unoccupied. The owners use them as second homes. This makes my job even more difficult."

"Are you implying that this alleged killer might be hiding out in one of the empty houses?"

"That's what I'd do," Eli said, closing up the bag of peanuts. "Because the people who live at Seacliff Point are lulled into a false sense of security due to the gate and the cliffs. Most of the houses don't even have burglar alarms. A professional wouldn't have a problem disabling an alarm system anyway. An alarm is nothing more than an inconvenience."

"And you've been working for Joanne without pay for some time now?"

"Like I said," Eli told him, yawning, "she's a special lady. She paid me all she could afford to pay. I wasn't going to split and then find out someone had killed her. One of the reasons I'm willing to help find this Decker fellow is that I'd rather hang around until I'm certain she's not in any danger."

Dreiser said, "But you'll have to go onshore to search for the body."

"Nothing will happen during the day," the detective told him. "Outside of weekends, Joanne is at the courthouse. She's safe there, and her ex-husband would never have someone harm her when the children are awake. The crime would occur at night, and the location would more than likely be her driveway or somewhere close to her house. They'll hit her when she's getting out of her car." He opened a drawer in the console and shoved the bag of peanuts inside. "There's another element that has to be considered."

"What's that?" Dreiser asked, knowing he should leave soon. Eli had been right about the weather. The rain had stopped and the boat was barely moving.

"Kuhlman may have hired someone to snatch the kids again."

"But the guy's in jail," Dreiser said, wondering if Eli was getting carried away. For all he knew, the man might be infatuated with Joanne. Dreiser glanced over his shoulder at all the surveillance equipment. Eli certainly fit the profile of a stalker, watching her every move. What did they really know about this man? "Why would he take the kids? Who would look after them?"

Eli shrugged. "I have no idea," he told him. "According to Joanne, the authorities in Los Angeles have frozen Kuhlman's domestic bank accounts. But the majority of his money was deposited in foreign accounts under another man's name. Whoever had access to those funds has probably claimed them as their own by now. That's what happens with those offshore operations when you get yourself thrown in jail. Kuhlman could have money stashed everywhere, for all we know. That means he could hire someone to look after his children until he got out of prison, maybe ship them off to Europe where no one could find them."

"You're describing a vicious person," Dreiser said, holding on to the back of the chair. "I thought Kuhlman was just a computer genius."

"Genius or not," Eli said, "the man's royally pissed off. He negotiated a fifty-million-dollar deal, and unless there's a problem with the criminal case that I'm not aware of, he's headed to prison. And don't forget, this man took the kids and kept them for almost two years. A person has to be coldhearted to deprive a mother of seeing her children, don't you think? This bastard didn't even drop her a postcard to let her know they were okay."

"I agree he might try to get his children back," Dreiser said, a concerned look on his face. "I'm just not certain why he would go out of his way to harm Joanne."

"He blames her for his present predicament," Eli continued. "He also has a hard-on for me because I'm the one who tracked him down. I doubt if he'd go as far as to pay someone to come after me. I wish he would, to tell you the truth. Then I could bust the sucker and move on."

"Speaking of moving on," Dreiser said, glancing at his watch and noting that it was past two o'clock. "I have a court date in the morning."

Dreiser followed Eli up the stairs to the main deck. Watching as Eli began lowering the dinghy, he recalled their conversation in the car. "I thought you said you wouldn't discuss Joanne's situation without her consent."

"I got her consent," Eli told him. "I called her while you were in the head. She must think highly of you, my man. Said I could tell you anything you wanted to know."

Dreiser inhaled the brisk sea air, his mind soaring with the possibilities of what might unfold. Trust was certainly a good starting point for a relationship. Over the past five years, he'd dated dozens of women. No one had managed to hold his attention for longer than a few weeks. It didn't matter how young they were, how good-looking they were, or even what they did for a living. In most instances, he'd had to force himself to call them, just so he wouldn't have to spend every evening alone. Joanne, however, had captured his attention from the first day he'd seen her in the courtroom. How many dinners had he paid for just to listen to some daffy woman rattle on about her weight, her job, her kids, her finances? With a simple kiss on the cheek, Joanne had excited him more than all the women he'd slept with since his divorce. He felt the stirring of something he hadn't felt in years—anticipation.

Dreiser saw the lights from other vessels flickering in the distance. With the moon out, he could see the swell of the waves. The need for instant gratification had almost removed the word expectation from the vocabulary. Women expected a man to make a move on them right away. People played the stock market, dreaming of becoming rich overnight. Everyone was in a hurry. No one wanted to wait. He remembered when he was a kid counting off the days until Christmas, too excited to sleep, sitting in front of the tree every day trying to imagine what was inside the brightly wrapped packages. As soon as Christmas came, regardless of how many presents he received, there was always the inevitable letdown.

Dreiser's thoughts returned to Joanne. It wasn't unrealistic to think that Eli might have romantic inclinations toward Joanne, especially considering the effect she had on him. He stared at the sinewy muscles in the detective's arms, back, and legs. In addition to Eli's physical strength, he had access to high-powered weapons and the skill to use them. He definitely wasn't a man Arnold wanted to compete with, regardless of the circumstances.

"The wind's picking up," Eli told him, handing Dreiser a life vest. "We'd better be on our way or you're going to end up bunking with me tonight."

Dreiser suddenly realized they'd never reached an agreement. "We haven't discussed your fees."

The dinghy splashed into the water. Eli dropped the ladder, then turned around and faced Dreiser. "Ten thousand as a retainer," he told him, "and another ten when I find the body."

"What if you don't find the body?" Dreiser asked. "We're not even certain he's dead."

"If he's dead," Eli said, his voice laced with conviction, "I'll find him. The only thing I can't tell you is how long it will take me. The phone call to his mother could have been a ruse. Let's keep our fingers crossed that it was valid. You can't find a body if you don't know where to look."

"When do you need the money?"

"Tomorrow night will be all right," the detective told him. "We'll meet at nine in the parking lot of the Cliff House. Joanne told you it has to be cash, right?"

Dreiser tensed. "How am I going to explain a ten-thousand-dollar cash withdrawal to my accountant? I could use a man with your kind of expertise in my law firm. Why don't we make this legit?"

"No can do," Eli told him, shaking his head. "I thought I'd start searching for Decker first thing in the morning. It's your call."

Dreiser fastened the straps on his life vest, then began descending the ladder to the dinghy. They were far from land, it was almost three o'clock in the morning, no witnesses around, and Eli was peering down at him waiting for an answer. At a time like this, Dreiser decided, a man would agree to just about anything. "I guess I'll see you at the Cliff House tomorrow night."

Eli tilted his head back and laughed, a deep boisterous sound. "I thought you'd go along with the program," he said. "Otherwise I was going to set you adrift and let you find your own way back to shore."

Dreiser's jaw dropped. The wind had picked back up and the small boat was thrashing around, pulling against the tethers. He had to grip the bench beneath him to keep from falling overboard. He looked up and saw Eli holding two paddles in his hand. He looked for a motor but didn't see one. "Good God, you were serious, weren't you?"

"Not really," Eli said, dropping the paddles into the dinghy. Once he was in the boat and rowing them toward the shoreline, he told Dreiser,

"I spend a lot of time alone. A little amusement now and then keeps me from getting into trouble."

"Glad I could be of service," Dreiser said, annoyed. "For ten grand, I'd wouldn't exactly classify myself as entertainment. I'm your employer, even if our little arrangement isn't entirely legal."

"Not until you pay me," Eli said, intentionally splashing water into Arnold's face with the paddle. "And it's twenty thousand, remember. The ten is only a retainer."

TWENTY-TWO

WILLIE CRENSHAW was sprawled out on the rumpled sheets in his one-room apartment at 349 Lewis Street on the west side of Ventura. Fast-food containers and empty beer cans were strewn across the kitchen counter and the end tables.

"Damn," Willie said, the bright morning sunlight burning his eyes. He rolled over onto his stomach, burrowing his head into the pillow. He didn't use cocaine or amphetamines, so it wasn't drugs that were causing his bout of insomnia. Ian Decker was the problem. On the occasions when he did manage to fall asleep, Willie was plagued by nightmares. One night he dreamt he'd been buried alive. The man who lived above him threatened to call the police when he woke up screaming like a maniac.

It had been almost a week since Willie had run into Gary Rubinksy at the Sunny Day car wash on Ventura Avenue the morning after Gary and his brother had killed Ian. Why did the stupid moron have to tell him what they'd done? He wasn't in the confession business. He was already sweating out a warrant for dealing. The last thing he'd needed was to become involved in a murder. Besides, Willie abhorred anything even remotely violent. He should have never let his friends talk him into stealing the shipping container off the loading dock in Long Beach. Once Willie had seen the decoy guns inside, he'd freaked. Even your run-of-the-mill gun spelled trouble, and the guns they'd removed from the container were anything but ordinary. He'd wanted to wash his hands of it, but he was short on cash. Having the police on your tail made it difficult for a dealer to earn a living. To avoid arrest for as long as possible, Willie had restricted his sales to long-term customers like the Rubinskys.

He picked up a half-empty can of Coke off of the nearest end table. Although the soda was flat, his throat was parched and he didn't feel like going out for breakfast. He never hit the street before ten or eleven. A man could peddle heroin or crack around the clock. The only people looking to score marijuana this early in the morning were schoolkids, and Willie didn't sell to minors.

Reaching underneath the mattress, Willie pulled out a wrench, then walked over to the defunct radiator where he kept his product. Squatting on the floor, he used the wrench to remove the radiator cap. Setting the cap aside, he probed inside the radiator, his fingers clasping on to the knotted end of a rope. He gently pulled on the rope until an industrial-strength plastic bag popped out.

Depositing the bag on the bed and dropping the wrench on the floor by the end table, Willie rummaged around in his bureau drawers. He removed a pair of Levi's, a plain black T-shirt, and some clean underwear. He never wore clothes with emblems or any kind of distinctive design on them. Those were the kind of things people remembered. He got his hair cut every two weeks at a different barbershop, did his best to wear clean clothes, tried to switch vehicles whenever possible, and he didn't have a single tattoo on his body. Staring at his image in the mirror, he decided he looked pretty good. He wasn't buffed like a jock, nor would anyone mistake him for a pencil pusher. His goal was to blend in, to pass as an average working-class guy.

Before he got dressed, Willie went to the bathroom and relieved himself, then he brushed his teeth and dabbed at his underarms with a sliver of stick deodorant. He tossed the empty container of deodorant into the trash. He'd have to go to the market. He knew he should take better care of his room, throw out all the trash, and change the sheets on his bed. Right now, though, his surroundings didn't matter.

After he'd dressed, Willie stuffed all the dirty clothes piled on the chair into an army-style duffel bag. Then he picked up the sack of drugs off the bed, wanting to take a quick inventory. Dropping down in the brown leather chair, he counted twelve bags, each bag containing an ounce of marijuana. In addition to the twelve bags of pot, he also had four ounces of hash that he'd picked up from a dealer in Oxnard a few days before he'd seen Gary at the car wash. Although Gary had admitted he and his brother had been drinking and drugging for days, Gary had flashed a roll of bills and asked for something stronger than normal. Willie had suggested he try the hash.

Gary had looked ragged and tense that morning, but Willie hadn't noticed anything to make him think the man had committed a murder. The only thing that struck him as strange was that Gary was washing the blue Chrysler Cirrus the men had been driving since Ian's Firebird had been impounded. The Rubinskys were pigs. When they'd had the Jeep Pioneer, the only time the car was anywhere close to clean was the day after a rainstorm, and that was only the exterior.

Not only was Gary washing the Chrysler, he was doing a bang-up job of it, even scrubbing out the trunk and the backseat. Sunny Day was a self-service operation. Gary must have gone through ten bucks. For that kind of money, he could have gone to the Wind Tunnel down the street. Gary even bought a stack of those paper towels they sold out of a dispenser, making certain he went over every square inch of the car. At first, Gary lied and told him the car had to be clean because Tom was making a deal with a guy to buy it.

Willie left the Jeep parked on the street near his apartment. Now that he thought about it, when Gary traded their car for that newfangled gun, Willie should have realized that the Rubinskys were out of control. Once again, Willie'd acted on impulse. He'd needed a new set of wheels and although the interior of the Jeep was trashed, the engine was in fairly good condition.

Gary had wanted to go to the beach and sample the hash before he handed over the money. Willie didn't mind, because whatever Gary sampled was added to the buy. Even when a customer didn't ask to sample his goods, Willie always ended up getting a free smoke because he carried a rolling machine and papers. He was amazed at how many potheads didn't even know how to roll a decent joint, and none of them ever had papers. Everyone was always impressed with the way the rolling machine turned out neat little joints that looked just like cigarettes. Willie got a kick out of the amount of attention he got from such an inexpensive device. Practically every head shop in town sold rolling machines, so it wasn't as if he'd reinvented the wheel.

Willie stared out over his one-room apartment, traveling back in time to his childhood. He remembered Ian giggling as he jumped through the sprinklers on a hot summer day, his skinny arms and legs burned to a crisp by the sun. A few moments later, his mind's eye saw the two of them huddled together in Scottie Defoe's treehouse, playing Monopoly on a Saturday afternoon. Ian had been a cute kid. He was always doing funny things—tripping over his shoelaces, using the wrong words, repeating what people said like a parrot. Now that Willie thought about it, Ian giggled more than he talked. If he wasn't giggling, he was clapping. Years later, Willie figured out that Ian didn't understand half of what people were talking about and that the giggling and clapping were his primary means of covering it up. Before they started school no one ridiculed him, though. They were the neighborhood gang. Ian's clapping had given some of the parents headaches, but the fact that he laughed a lot didn't bother anyone. His giggling was contagious, uplifting. The others boys would find themselves laughing over nothing, laughing so hard they'd fall on the ground.

Firing up another joint, Willie sucked the acrid smoke deep into his lungs, then moistened his throat with another gulp of lukewarm soda. It wasn't right that Ian was dead, that the Rubinskys had used him and then killed him. He got up and started pacing back and forth, his T-shirt already damp with perspiration.

While they had been smoking dope at the beach that afternoon, Willie started teasing Gary about washing the Chrysler. Gary blurted out that they'd shot Ian and placed his body in the trunk of the car. By that time, Gary was so high that it was hard to make sense out of what he was saying. Willie wasn't sober either, which didn't help. Gary mentioned a stretch of land near Magic Mountain several times, and later talked about stopping for coffee at a McDonald's restaurant off Interstate 5. When Willie asked him where they had came up with the money to buy the Chrysler, Gary had admitted that he and Tom had coerced Ian into stealing the car from his mother's business.

Before he'd called Elizabeth, Willie had tried to piece together the various fragments of his conversation with Gary. If the information he'd given Elizabeth had been accurate, the police should have found Ian's body by now.

Walking over and staring out the window, Willie decided that if he had to judge who'd accomplished more, Ian would win the prize. Willie wasn't smart enough to have become a doctor or lawyer, but he knew that there was only one thing wrong with his brain. His brain craved marijuana. And it craved marijuana because he'd taught it to crave marijuana just like he'd trained his cocker spaniel to catch a Frisbee.

Willie needed marijuana like a man in the desert needed water. Since the age of thirteen, his life had passed in a drugged-out fog. He now consumed a lid of grass every day. He took his first puff within an hour after he woke up, his last before bed. Recently he'd developed a hacking cough. Would he quit? Not unless someone handed him a million bucks, and even then, he'd probably start smoking again. Without marijuana, the world was full of sharp edges, grating sounds, tasteless food, and obnoxious people. When he was high, everything was mellow and cool. If someone insulted him, he'd just smile and walk away.

Willie knew he could have worked at a bank like his father, or maybe one day he could have owned a small restaurant like his grandfather. His parents were decent people. He had nothing to complain about in that respect. A few years back, he'd told himself that one day he'd stop, turn around, and take off in the right direction. He'd already served one term in prison. With a prior for possession-with-intent-to-distribute, by the time he walked out of the joint the next time, he'd be too old to make anything out of his life.

As ironic as it might seem, Willie had always respected Ian. With all of his limitations, Ian had still managed to graduate from high school. Willie had called it quits after the ninth grade, and for no reason other than to party and hang out with his friends. When he'd heard that Ian was enrolled in the welding program at Franklin Junior College, he'd felt a spark of hope. If Ian could do it, why couldn't he? By then, however, Ian was in over his head with the Rubinsky brothers.

Had Tom and Gary really killed Ian? They both had a tendency to shoot their mouths off. Gary was a pathological liar. The guy would lie when there was no reason to lie. Of course, telling someone you'd committed a murder was one humongous lie. He reminded himself that Gary had only told him about what they'd done after smoking the hash. People said all kinds of ridiculous things when they were under the influence of drugs. For all he knew, Ian was alive.

Just then, Willie heard someone pounding on his door. His adrenalin started pumping, certain it was the police. He leapt out of the chair, and was headed to the bathroom to flush the drugs down the toilet when he recognized Gary Rubinsky's voice.

"Open the damn door!"

"Wait, for God's sake," Willie said, his fingers trembling as he frantically unlocked all four dead bolts. Flinging the door open, he stepped back as Gary stormed into the room.

"Lock it up," Gary said, hyped to the gills. "Every cop in town is looking for me."

"Sure . . . right away." Willie hastily shoved all the bolts back into place. He cowered in the corner between the door and the bathroom, reaching in the pocket of his jeans for his lighter.

Gary was dressed in a black leather jacket, a white shirt, and black slacks. On his feet were a pair of scuffed brown leather cowboy boots. He removed the dark sunglasses he was wearing, swinging them back and forth in his hand as he paced. He hadn't shaved, and his face was partially obscured by a stubby beard. He stopped abruptly, pointing his finger at Willie. "You called Elizabeth, didn't you?"

"No way, man," Willie said, shaking his head. He stared longingly at the joint he'd been smoking in the ashtray across the room. Dealing with Gary without marijuana wasn't going to be easy. He had to convince Gary he was telling the truth, though, or he'd end up in an unmarked grave next to poor Ian.

"Don't lie to me," Gary said, kicking over the green duffel bag. "You must have called her. No one knew anything except you."

Willie raised a hand in the air. "I swear, Gary. I don't even know anyone named Elizabeth."

"Ian's mother," Gary spat at him. "You know Ian's mother. You used to hang out with the guy even more than Tom did. You went to his house every day after school to raid their refrigerator. Don't try to tell me you don't know Elizabeth."

"Hey," Willie said, scratching his head, "that hash we smoked the last time I saw you wiped me out. My brain is fried anyway. I don't remember half of what we talked about that day. I'm lucky to remember things that happened an hour ago."

"Like hell you don't," Gary shouted. "The police have been searching for Ian's grave. I heard on the radio that they're looking for me. They know I'm driving a blue Chrysler. They even know the license plate. I need the Jeep back." He held out his hand. "Give me the keys."

"A deal's a deal," Willie told him, angry now. "What am I supposed to drive? The Chrysler? You carried Ian's body in that car. The cops will bust me for sure. I might have a warrant out, but I didn't kill anyone. You're out of your frigging mind if you think you're gonna pawn that car off on me."

The light in the room faded. Willie blinked several times, uncertain if another storm was moving in or if the stress of the situation was affecting his vision. He then saw Gary's hand extended in front of him, a small rectangular object inside it. He had to squint before he realized that it was the decoy gun. "Jesus Christ, Gary," he pleaded, dropping down on his knees. "You don't want to shoot me. What have I ever done to hurt you? Why would I tell the cops you killed Ian? I don't want to have anything to do with the cops."

Gary was standing with his feet spread apart, his right arm extended and braced with his left. He appeared only seconds from depressing the trigger, yet his eyes were flashing with fear. "I don't have a choice, Willie," he told him. "You could use what you know about Ian's death to cut a deal."

"Here's the keys to the Jeep," Willie said, removing them from the clip attached to his jeans and tossing them across the floor. "I'll drive the Chrysler out in the desert somewhere. I promise, Gary. No one will ever see that car again. If you want me to, I'll dismantle it and bury the parts."

Gary's face was beet red. Sweat was pouring off his forehead. He let his arms fall limp at his side, then wiped his runny nose on the sleeve of his jacket. "We shouldn't have shot him, Willie. It was a mistake. He was a loose cannon though, you know. He wasn't right in the head. Once they put him on the stand, we wouldn't have stood a chance."

Willie spoke in a low, consoling tone. "I know, Gary. I would have probably done the same thing. Take the Jeep and . . ."

"You don't understand," Gary said, his face twisted in anguish. "Ian found the gun. We had to take the stuff out of the locker at the skating rink because the manager was getting suspicious. Until then, Ian believed we were innocent. We had him convinced that two other guys robbed the Quick-Mart . . . that the police only busted us because the clerk remembered our car when we stopped off to pick up some beer."

"Is that why you killed him?" Willie asked. "Because he saw the gun?"

"Yeah," Gary said. "Tom dropped the gun on the floor like a fool. Ian thought it was a phone and almost shot us. When he realized it was the gun they'd been talking about in the courtroom, he went crazy on us. He knew we'd been lying to him all along."

Gary staggered over to the chair and collapsed. He placed the gun on the end table, then buried his head in his hands. Willie started to go for the gun, then stopped. Even overwrought and exhausted, Gary possessed razor-sharp reflexes. Before Willie made it across the room, he'd be a dead man. He wasn't sure why Gary hadn't shot him earlier. Was he stalling, struggling with the thought of killing another childhood friend?

Maybe the gun wasn't loaded, Willie thought. Something else came to mind. Gary had always been the loudmouth, the bully, the one who made all the decisions. Tom was almost like his shadow, as if he had no identity outside of the fact that he was Gary Rubinsky's brother. Working the street all these years had taught Willie a lot about human nature. Things were not always as they appeared. Contrary to what people had always thought, Gary may have never been the strong one. Without Tom in the picture, his older brother seemed lost and confused.

Willie was standing at the crossroads. He could either keep his mouth shut and pray that Gary would take the Jeep and leave, or he could put his neck on the line and see just how deep the weak spot ran.

"Where did you bury Ian?"

"What?" Gary barked, yanking his head up.

"You heard me," Willie said, pushing himself to his feet. "And where's Tom? Did you kill him too? Did the cops bust him?"

Gary unsnapped his leather jacket. "My chest hurts," he said, breathing heavy. "I've been living in the car, trying to lay low and figure out what to do, where to go. I think something is wrong with me. I feel like I'm dying."

"Tell me about the night you shot Ian," Willie said, taking a few steps toward him. "I want to help you. I can't help you unless I know exactly what happened that night. If I don't know the truth, I could make things worse for you guys."

Gary acted as if he hadn't heard him, bending over at the waist in pain. "Could I be having a heart attack? Ain't I too young?"

"I've seen eighteen-year-old kids croak with heart attacks," Willie told him, rubbing his hands together. "Most of them were snorting coke, but you never know." Willie wanted the upper hand, and if Gary was convinced he needed immediate medical attention, the greater the chance Willie had of staying alive. "I know a lady down the street who used to be a nurse. I hate to say it, Gary, but you look pretty bad. Maybe something is really wrong with your heart."

Gary clutched his chest again. "I've had this sharp pain for days."

Willie took two more steps. Just a few more feet and he'd be in arm's reach of the gun.

Gary saw him and grabbed the gun off the end table. "Get back," he said. "Come closer and I'll shoot you."

"Don't you know what's wrong with you?" Willie said. "You've got to talk it out, Gary. Go to any shrink, and they'll tell you the same thing. You can't keep something like this to yourself."

When Gary spoke this time, Willie had to strain to hear him. Gary stared off into space, his voice a dull monotone. "I shot Ian in the back," he said, sweeping his tongue over his lower lip. "He was about five feet away. After I shot him, Tom and I picked him up and put him in the trunk of the car. We were going to stop somewhere and just dump him out on the road, but Tom said we had to bury him."

Willie stood perfectly still, afraid to move. He had to keep him talking. Gary hadn't showed up at his apartment simply to get the Jeep back. He had come to kill him. "Did you bury him near Magic Mountain?"

"I still can't believe all of this has happened." Gary pulled his collar away from his neck as if it were strangling him. "These are Tom's clothes I'm wearing. We knew we couldn't go back to the Economy Inn. We cleared our stuff out of the room before we left."

"Did you and Tom get into a fight?" Willie asked. "Why isn't he with you?"

"Don't you have anything to drink in this place?" Gary asked, his tone of voice shifting. "My throat is burning. I must have smoked two packs of cigarettes already and it's still morning." He turned toward the left side of the room. "Where's the refrigerator? Didn't you used to have a refrigerator in this place?"

"I sold it," Willie said, embarrassed that he'd fallen so far down the ladder. He then wondered if he wasn't the one who needed to see a shrink. How could he feel ashamed? He didn't cheat people. Only on rare occasions did he steal. He didn't rob, maim, or kill. Even when he was in prison, he had managed to stay out of trouble. "I can get you a glass of water."

"Anything," the other man said, clasping the gun firmly in his hand.

Willie went to the bathroom and filled up a plastic glass with tap water. He frantically searched the room, looking for something he could use as a weapon. He might be able to knock Gary unconscious with the wrench he'd used to remove the cap on the radiator. He'd have to get close to him to hand him the water. The wrench was on the floor next to the end table.

When Willie walked out of the bathroom, his friend was waiting for him.

"I'm sorry," Gary said, aiming the gun and firing.

The gunshot resounded in Gary's ears. The bullet struck the center of Willie's forehead, leaving a hole about the size of a quarter. Willie fell backward with a thud, one arm underneath his body and the other at his side. Gary stood and watched as a pool of blood began to form on the floor around Willie's head, then he leaned down and listened for a heartbeat.

Once he was sure that Willie was dead, Gary hurriedly stuffed the plastic sack of marijuana inside his jacket, scooped up the keys to the Jeep and struggled with the bolts to the door. Slamming the door behind him, he stepped over an older gray-haired man curled up on the floor in the corner.

"Was that a gunshot?" the man asked, peering up at him.

"No," Gary said, covering his face with his jacket. "Nothing but a car backfiring. Go back to sleep."

TWENTY-THREE

JOANNE WAS returning to her office after a pretrial hearing on a domestic violence case when Dean Kennedy stopped her. "Do you have any news regarding the homicide?"

"What homicide?" Joanne said, crushing a manila file folder against her chest. "Did you try to reach me?"

"A Ventura detective was looking for you," Kennedy said, glancing at his watch as if he were late for an appointment. "Maybe they called the wrong courtroom."

As Kennedy continued down the hallway, Joanne unlocked her office and went inside. She skipped several of the messages on her voice mail and jotted down Detective Lieutenant David Vogel's number on a yellow pad. A few moments later she reached him at the crime scene.

"You might want to drive over here," Vogel advised. "We recovered the Chrysler Cirrus that was stolen from the ABC Towing lot. It was parked across the street from the apartment complex where the shooting occurred. The crime lab is sending a truck to transport it back to the lab. The address is 349 Lewis Street."

"Tell me about the victim." Joanne sighed, looking at all the boxes and files crammed inside her office.

"Name is Willie Crenshaw," Vogel told her. "White male, twenty-one, average height and weight. County's holding a warrant on him for sale and distribution of marijuana. Rap sheet shows he served a stint at Chino a few years back. Cause of death appears to be a gunshot wound to the head."

"Is the murder weapon the decoy gun used in the Quick-Mart robbery?"

"We won't know anything until ballistics has a chance to examine the bullet."

"I'm on my way," Joanne said, jotting down the address. "Are you in charge of this investigation?"

"Looks that way," Vogel said, disconnecting.

On the drive over, she called Dreiser's office, but his secretary said he was in court in Los Angeles. The attorney wouldn't be allowed at the crime scene anyway. She only wanted to alert him of this new development. Even without knowing all the details, she was fearful that they were now dealing with two interconnected homicides. Since Tom was incarcerated, Gary Rubinsky had to be the killer.

Joanne parked several blocks away because of the number of emergency vehicles. Four black-and-white police cars were parked on Lewis Street, along with the crime-scene van and several units from the coroner's office. One of the county's tow trucks was attempting to navigate down the narrow street to load up the Chrysler. Before she got out of the car, Joanne dialed her home number.

"Hi, sweetheart," she said when her son answered. "Put Leah on the phone."

"She isn't here," Mike told her. "Didn't you tell her she could go to a movie or something after school? She wasn't on the bus."

"I forgot," his mother said. "Listen, something came up. If your sister doesn't show up by seven, call me on my cell phone. I'm not sure what time I'll be home tonight."

"Can I walk up to the Cove and have dinner?" Mike said. "What if Leah doesn't come home? I'll starve to death."

"You're being a little melodramatic, kid," Joanne told him. "If you can pass yourself off for sixteen, I think you can manage to fix yourself something to eat."

"Do you have a date or something?" Mike asked, having noticed that his mother was acting strange lately. She was spending more time on her hair and makeup, wearing slightly shorter skirts, dousing herself with cologne.

"I can't talk now," Joanne said, fishing her ID out of her backpack. "Make yourself a sandwich. There's plenty of food in the house. And to answer your question: No, I do not have a date."

Joanne left her backpack in the car, slipped her phone into the pocket of her jacket, and depressed the alarm activation button on her key ring to lock the Lexus. When she'd come to work that morning, it had been overcast and drizzling. The sky was clear now and the sun was slowly setting on the horizon. Enjoying the beauty of the sunset didn't seem appropriate, however, considering that she was on her way to look at a corpse.

The building was a dilapidated five-story structure erected in the seventies. The police had cordoned off the area with yellow evidence tape, and officers were stationed at opposite ends of the street to keep people from entering the crime scene. Flashing her ID at one of the police officers, Joanne asked where she could find Detective Vogel. "Third floor," the officer told her, reaching for the microphone clipped near his left shoulder. "The command post is in apartment 3B. I'll let the lieutenant know you're on the way up."

Joanne headed up the narrow stairway, having to inch her way past the various descending officers. David Vogel was waiting for her. An attractive, slender man in his late thirties, he had unruly blond hair, fair skin, and dark circles under his hazel eyes. Dressed in a tweed jacket, white shirt, and brown slacks, he tilted his head toward an empty apartment. "Let's talk in here before we go in," he told her. "We've got too many people in the victim's apartment right now. The lab is still collecting evidence."

Joanne started to take a seat on a stained beige sofa when Vogel scowled. "I don't know if I would sit there," he said, pulling up two rickety wooden chairs. "The landlord told me the former tenant was a prostitute and crack addict. He evicted her last week."

"Great," Joanne said facetiously, dropping down on one of the chairs.

"We have something close to a witness," Vogel said, taking a seat across from her. "I can get one of my men to bring him in if you want to interview him. He's a little like the sofa, though. I'm not certain he's worth anything outside of establishing a time line—and even there, we've got problems. The guy's sixty-eight, and he's probably been drinking for fifty years. We're talking major alcohol dementia."

"Not again," Joanne said, crossing her arms over her chest. "The Rubinsky brothers are the scum of the earth. One of the witnesses in the Quick-Mart robbery had just been released from rehab, and the victim doesn't speak English. Now you're telling me the only witness to this crime is a burned-out drunk. Heaven help me."

"I think they took the day off," the detective told her, fiddling with his watch.

Joanne asked, "Who took the day off?"

"Heaven," Vogel said, giving her a lopsided grin. "This place is about as close as you can get to hell, know what I mean?" He paused and then continued, "We've got a dead dope dealer, a stolen car, and a lousy witness."

Joanne wondered why the detective had asked her to come out. She rubbed her temples. During her last year of law school, she'd suffered from excruciating migraines. For the past week or so, she'd had a headache almost every day. If they got any worse, she'd have to see a doctor and start taking medication again. "Don't forget about Ian Decker," she told him. "What if this person kills again? Make certain your men perform a thorough investigation, Vogel. You may think you're dealing with a skid-row killing . . . that no one is going to care what happened to this person. I won't allow you to take that position."

"Until someone either finds Decker's body or arrests him, we're classifying him as a suspect in this crime in addition to the Quick-Mart robbery. Nothing new has turned up regarding his disappearance. All you have is a tip from an anonymous caller."

"You're missing the point." Joanne glanced behind her, then lowered her voice so the people outside the room wouldn't overhear. "Don't botch this investigation, Vogel, or Kennedy will have both our heads on a platter. Our stats are down at the agency. Kennedy hasn't been in the best mood lately. No margin for error. Are we clear?"

"We lucked out on the coroner," Vogel told her, ignoring her comments. "Charley Anthony is handling it."

"Good," Joanne said, thinking he'd finally told her something worthwhile. Charles Anthony was one of the best forensic pathologists on the West Coast. She'd heard rumors that he was exhibiting some bizarre behavior recently, yet there was nothing to indicate that it was interfering with his work.

"Okay," Vogel said, lacing his hands together. "Here's the rundown. Leon Carter heard what sounded like a gunshot. He didn't check the time. His statement was the following: 'I bet it was around ten 'cause that's when I usually wake up to pee every morning.'"

"Horrors," Joanne exclaimed, slouching in the chair. "What kind of description did he give you of the assailant?"

Vogel had slept only four hours in the past two days. He had a wife and four kids. The baby had been sick with the flu, and his oldest daughter had broken her arm earlier in the week. He worked two jobs, and still had trouble paying his bills. He yawned, stretching his arms over his head. "He said it was a man."

Joanne waited for the detective to continue speaking. Instead, he just stared at her, wanting her to get a taste of the frustrations he'd been dealing with for the past four hours. He was also offended that the prosecutor would insinuate he might botch a murder investigation. Although he was a meticulous and intuitive investigator, David Vogel had a hair-trigger temper. He'd once beaten a suspect within an inch of his life.

"Did he know the person?" Joanne probed, gesturing a circle with her hand to get things rolling. "Did the physical description match up with Gary Rubinsky? I don't care if the witness is brain dead, Vogel. He must have seen something."

The detective stood, picked up the chair, then dropped it back on the floor. "Want me to have him brought in? I'm trying to keep from wasting both your time and mine. It took a pot of coffee and two hours just to get Carter to identify the suspect as male. He doesn't care. He isn't sure. He doesn't know." He placed his hands on his hips. "You want to listen to that crap, go right ahead."

"Settle down," Joanne said, not wanting things to get out of hand. Whether their personalities clashed or not, they would be working together until the case was resolved. "I apologize," she said. "We're both tense. We got off to a bad start."

"All Carter knows is that he heard a loud noise that sounded like a gunshot," Vogel told her, his face muscles softening. "He thinks he was in his apartment and came out to see what was happening. A male voice said there was nothing to be concerned about, that what he'd heard was a car backfiring."

"He can't describe the man's features or clothing?"

"What I've been trying to tell you," the detective said, "is Leon Carter's got about three brain cells left, and even those aren't firing right."

"No one else in the complex saw anything?"

"If they did," Vogel answered, "they're not talking. Even Carter may not have seen the killer. For all we know, the person who spoke to him was one of the other tenants." He paused and pointed at his chest. "You think I'm happy about this situation? I brought you out here so you could see firsthand what kind of case we've got on our hands. Finding the car was a lucky break. And if Rubinsky and Decker are the killers, they're both dumb enough to have left evidence all over that apartment. Bottom line . . . We're not going to solve this case with witnesses. The name of the game is evidence."

A young dark-haired police officer had been standing in the doorway, waiting for them to finish speaking. "They're asking for you, Lieutenant," he said. "The coroner says he's ready to transport the body."

Detective Vogel stood. Joanne followed him to apartment 3F. Willie Crenshaw's body was outlined in chalk only a few feet from the front door. Charley Anthony was dictating some last-minute notes on a small recorder, so Joanne and Vogel waited. A body bag was unzipped and open on the floor, and two lab techs were waiting on the outside landing with the gurney. "Who called this in?"

"Mr. Gonzales, the landlord," Vogel told her. "Gonzales brought someone up to look at the vacant apartment at eleven-fifteen this morning when he saw the victim in the doorway."

"Did the killer leave the door open?"

"Not necessarily," the detective advised. He pointed at the row of dead bolts. "Gonzales said the original latch bolt doesn't work. The apartment was burglarized several years ago. The owner's too cheap to fix it. Crenshaw installed the dead bolts after he moved in. My guess is the killer didn't realize the latch was busted. He must have slammed the door hard enough that it sprang back open."

Charley Anthony peeled off his rubber gloves and shook Joanne's hand. A heavyset man in his fifties, Anthony had curly gray hair and a ruddy complexion. "How's it going, sweetheart?" he asked, as if he'd just run into an old girlfriend in a coffee shop. "I haven't seen your pretty face in a month of Sundays."

"I haven't tried a homicide lately," Joanne responded, glancing down at Crenshaw's face. Although he hadn't discussed it with her, she suspected Kennedy had purposely lightened her caseload due to the problems with Doug and the children. Inhaling the stench of death made her question whether she was emotionally able to handle a homicide even now. She was spreading herself too thin, making too many impulsive decisions. She shouldn't have allowed Eli access to Decker's files. Glancing at her watch, she reminded herself to call Dreiser later and find out what he'd decided regarding the detective. Doug was scheduled to go on trial in two weeks. Kennedy would have to bring in another prosecutor. How could she handle a chain of homicides when she would have to testify in her husband's trial in Los Angeles? The throbbing in her head intensified.

"You're looking good," Charley Anthony said, leering at the outline of Joanne's breasts through her jacket. "We should get together now that you're single." He reached into his pocket and handed her his card. "Call me tomorrow. I'll take you out for a nice dinner."

Joanne couldn't believe her ears. Her feet were two inches from a pool of blood and Anthony was trying to put the make on her. "I'm seeing someone," she lied. "Nice man, you know."

Anthony's eyelids fluttered. He knew she was lying. He rubbed his hands together, more determined than ever. "I know where to find you," he said. "Nice guys don't last that long. I'll give you a call in a couple of months."

Joanne jerked on Vogel's jacket sleeve, pulling him to the other side of the room. "Did you catch that?"

"Yeah," Vogel said, chuckling. "He's something else, isn't he? I hear he pops Viagra pills like candy. I'm scared to call him out if the victim is a woman. Nastiest old goat I've ever seen. Look at his pocket. That's the edge of a porno magazine. I think he jerks off six times a day."

Joanne's tension erupted into laughter. She ducked her head behind Vogel, then peeked over his shoulder at the coroner. Charley Anthony had struck up a conversation with a young blonde technician. They burst out laughing again when they heard the coroner repeat the same lines and give the woman his card. "You've got to hand it to him," Joanne whispered in Vogel's ear. "He's persistent."

"Too persistent," Vogel said, scowling. "This is a crime scene, not a singles bar. Forget Anthony. Come, take a quick look at the victim's wounds. I'm ready to lock this place up and go home."

As soon as Joanne walked over and bent down beside the body, her nostrils were assaulted by the putrid orders of body gases, excrement, and blood coagulating in the warm room. She opened her mouth, certain she was about to vomit. Vogel quickly unwrapped a piece of chewing gum and stuck it in her mouth. The gum was strong, causing Joanne's eyes to water. The stench of death was instantly replaced with peppermint.

"This usually does it for me."

"Thanks," Joanne said, deciding she and Vogel would get along just fine.

TWENTY-FOUR

Friday, February 16, 2001, 5:35 P.M.

LEAH WAS ten weeks pregnant.

Nathan Salinger pulled out his wallet to pay for their sodas at the Burger King on State Street, a block from the doctor's office. They'd taken the bus to town after school. Dr. Sarah Malloy had tested and examined Leah without charge, but she'd encouraged both Nathan and Leah to tell their parents about the pregnancy. Dr. Malloy also recommended that they speak to a counselor before making any decision related to an abortion.

Leah scooted to the far side of the booth near the window, stabbing her straw through the plastic cap attached to her soda. "I'm not going to tell my mother," she said, her jaw set in defiance. "She'd go ballistic. You'll have to arrange for one of your doctor friends to give me an abortion. Make sure the appointment is after four. That way, I won't have to skip any of my classes. I'm already behind."

Nathan sucked in a deep breath, then slowly exhaled. He'd learned a valuable lesson, he told himself. Now he was going to have to figure out how to deal with it. Leah was less mature than he'd realized. While Dr. Malloy was speaking to them, she had rudely flipped through the pages of a magazine.

Nathan felt as if an enormous weight had been placed on his shoulders. His eyes drifted to the window, watching as two teenage girls in tight jeans and cropped tops walked by, laughing and talking on their cell phones. Their suggestive clothing and demeanor now seemed repugnant to him. He asked himself how many girls at his school had already undergone abortions. A cloak of sadness fell over him. A human life was growing inside the girl sitting across from him. Leah's attitude was appalling. She didn't want to miss a class. A class! The possibility of receiving a bad grade held more importance than the life of an unborn child.

Until Leah, Nathan had never had sex. Because of his looks and popularity, he'd played along when his friends told crude jokes and boasted about their sexual conquests. Pretense could go a long way. Even his closest friends didn't truly know him. Girls were always telling him he should be an actor, a suggestion he found absurd. Under the surface, Nathan was a shy, sensitive, and deeply serious young man. The last thing he wanted was to draw attention to himself.

A woman with a baby sat down in the adjacent booth. Nathan was transfixed as the mother gently placed the child in her lap, pressing her lips to the silky, fine hair on the top of the baby's head. Nathan found himself drawn into that intimate moment. The woman glanced over at him and smiled, her face glowing with contentment and joy. He'd seen women with children before, but this was different. Love, he told himself. He had been allowed to witness the wonder of maternal love. As long as the woman had the child in her arms, she would be happy. She didn't need material possessions. The entire world was in her arms.

Turning his attention back to Leah, she seemed to be bathed in dark shadows. Nathan couldn't lay all the blame on her, however. They were both at fault. He was angry at himself, angry at Leah. His first mistake was having gotten drunk.

What was done was done, Nathan told himself. The problem wasn't something that could be pushed aside and dealt with later. The clock was ticking. The longer they waited, the worse it would be. "Look," he said, "I agree that neither one of us is ready to get married and raise a kid. There are alternatives. . . ."

"What?" Leah said, shoving her hair to one side of her head. "You're not going to tell me to have the baby and then give it up for adoption, I hope."

"Something could be arranged," Nathan told her, one of his eyelids twitching. "Are you saying you wouldn't consider having the baby under any circumstances? You've already made up your mind. Am I right?"

"More or less," Leah told him. "How can I have the baby? I have to finish school. And why should I go through all that misery just to give the baby to a stranger? I'm not that far along. If you don't know a doctor who will give me an abortion for free, you'll have to find a way to get the money. I've been to your house. Your family is loaded. You must have a trust fund or something."

Nathan felt himself shaking. He suppressed an urge to reach out and slap her. When he spoke, however, his voice was low and controlled. "This isn't about money."

Leah shook her head. "You're crazy if you think I'm going to have this baby," she snapped at him. "It's not even a baby. It's nothing right now, understand?" She held up her fingers. "I'm only just over two months, Nathan. I could see you pitching a fit if I was four or five months. All that's inside me is a bloated sperm. And you put it there, I didn't. I was unconscious, remember?"

Nathan felt his body stiffen. An imaginary wall dropped into place, and Leah disappeared. Without speaking, he got up and walked out of the restaurant. When Leah shouted after him, he didn't hear her. He tucked his chin toward his chest and darted across the street in the middle of traffic, oblivious to the skidding tires and honking horns.

Joanne had accidentally turned off her cell phone as she slipped it into her pocket when she arrived at the scene of the Crenshaw homicide. Seeing that she had a message as she returned to her car, she hit auto dial without checking the caller ID. "What's going on?" she asked her son. "Is Leah home?"

"Nope," Mike answered, sprawled out on the sofa in front of the TV.

"Did she call?"

"Nope."

"Turn off the television," Joanne said, unable to tolerate the background noise. Hearing a repetitive pinging sound, she assumed Mike was playing a video game. Her headache was getting worse. She reached up and turned off the dome light. Even lights were beginning to disturb her. This was how she felt in the early stages of a migraine. She had to relax, put things into perspective. A migraine could last for days.

"Can't I go over to Alex's house?" Mike asked. "There's nothing on TV tonight. I'm bored out of my skull."

With her free hand, Joanne turned the key in the ignition of the Lexus. Except for two black-and-whites, the emergency vehicles had all cleared. She saw Lieutenant Vogel giving instructions to the officer who would stand guard over the crime scene.

"Don't leave the house," Joanne told Mike. "I'm worried about your sister. She should have been home by now. Have you eaten?"

"I ate a bunch of junk," Mike grumbled, an empty sack of potato chips on the sofa beside him. He'd waited until seven to see if his sister would show up. By then, he'd been ravenous. He'd wolfed down two ham and cheese sandwiches, an entire package of chips, seven cookies and guzzled three Cokes. "My stomach hurts now."

"Take some Rolaids," his mother said. "I'm on my way home. If Leah comes in, make certain she calls me. I'm worried about her."

"You should be."

"What does that mean?"

"Like, she took the car without asking," Mike said. "Like, she lies to you about talking to Dad. She screamed at you and said mean things. She even found the key to Judge Spencer's secret closet. Then she went on the Internet and told all her friends about it. You think she acts bad around you, you should see how she treats me. She's driving me nuts, Mom."

Joanne reached into her backpack, hoping she might have some Tylenol. Finding nothing, she said, "You think something's seriously wrong?"

"Duh," Mike said. "I know we were gone for a couple of years, and you're busy with your work and everything. Yeah, I think she's got a problem. I can't tell you what it is because she doesn't talk to me. Leah yells at me, she slams the door in my face. The other day, she even tried to kick me. But she doesn't talk to me. She used to talk to me when we were living with Dad. We were pretty close back then. Leah's not the same, Mom."

"I agree," Joanne said, trying to remember what she herself had been like at fifteen. Perhaps Leah was suffering from PMS. On top of the psychological problems related to her father, this might explain her mood swings and unusual behavior. Joanne would take her daughter in for a checkup as soon as possible. "Did you call me earlier?"

"No," Mike told her. "You said to call if Leah didn't come home. She didn't come home."

"Let me go," his mother said. "There's a message on my cell phone. I just assumed it was Leah and called home."

Mike tried to tell her something else, but Joanne cut him off and disconnected. Playing back the message, she discovered that it was Arnold Dreiser who had called her. She stepped on the gas and headed toward the freeway. Eli had warned her that Doug might try to take the children again. Since Mike had been giving his father the cold shoulder, Doug could have paid someone to pick up Leah. Deep in her thoughts, she realized she'd made a wrong turn. She opened the window. She could smell the ocean, but she couldn't identify any landmarks. How far had she driven? The fact that there weren't any streetlights didn't help. After driving around for another thirty minutes, she finally pulled over and parked, getting out of the car to stretch her legs. Knowing she needed to calm down before she got behind the wheel again, she returned Arnold's call. "Where are you?"

"I just handed your friend ten grand," Dreiser told her. "Have you had dinner? Why don't we meet somewhere? Eli said there was a homicide in Ventura, that the police had recovered the stolen Chrysler. I called your house and spoke to your son. He gave me this number. Is this your cell phone?"

"Yes." Joanne was puzzled. "How did Eli find out so quick? I didn't see any reporters around."

"Have you forgotten?" Dreiser said. "News travels at the speed of light these days. Everyone knows everything. With this OnStar system I have in my car, I can even have my e-mail read while I'm on the road. You need to catch up. You're still living in the past."

"Don't pick on me," Joanne told him. "I'm lost on the outskirts of Ventura, and my daughter didn't come home from school today."

"Sounds terrific," Dreiser joked. "Isn't this where we started?"

"I have no idea what you're talking about."

"Forget it," Dreiser said, hearing the tension in her voice. "Tell me what street you're on. I'll get directions for you."

"I'm lost," Joanne told him. "If I knew where I was, I wouldn't be lost."

"Listen," Dreiser said, "everything will be fine. I'll stay on the line with you. Get in your car and drive to the closest intersection. Are you east or west of Ventura?"

"I don't know," Joanne said, embarrassed. "I'll call you back."

She finally made her way to a well-lit road, jotted down the names of the streets so she wouldn't forget, and was about to call Dreiser when her phone rang.

"It's me," Leah said. "Mike said you wanted to talk to me."

"Where have you been?" Joanne exploded. "I told you to be home by seven at the latest. I was going to call the police if I didn't hear from you in the next five minutes."

After Nathan had abandoned her, Leah had missed the bus. She'd had no choice but to take a taxi. Once she got to the house, she'd co-erced her brother into giving her twenty dollars to pay the driver. "Nathan's aunt got sick," she lied. "We had to wait around for his mother to come and get us. I'm sorry. I should have called you. What's the big deal? It's only eight-thirty."

"This has got to stop," Joanne said sternly. "I want to know what's going on, why you've been acting the way you have lately. Are you feel-ing okay?"

"Nothing's going on," Leah shouted. "It's not my fault the stupid woman didn't show up. Are you going to blow this out of proportion like everything else?"

Joanne felt like hurling the cell phone out the window. She couldn't deal with her daughter's disrespectful attitude—not even over the phone. "We're going to have a long talk when I get home."

"Not tonight," Leah said haughtily. "I have a history exam tomorrow.

I have to ace this test, or I'm going to get a *D* in the class. You don't want me to get thrown out of school, do you?"

Her daughter was manipulating her. And like her father, Leah was shrewd. She knew Joanne had to pinch pennies to send her to Waldorf, that the money would have been squandered if her grades were poor. "Put your brother on the phone."

A few moments later, Mike picked up the extension from his bedroom. "I'm watching a movie," he told her. "Can't you stop bothering me? Go hang out with the lawyer who called here a few minutes ago. The guy with the funny last name. He must be the dude you've been fixing yourself up for."

"Don't be silly," Joanne said. "Mr. Dreiser and I are working on a serious case right now."

"High heels, perfume, short skirts," Mike said. "Since when do you wear high heels to work? You told me they give you a backache. I think you've got a crush on this guy. What's the big deal? You're not married to Dad anymore."

Joanne had skipped lunch. No wonder she had a headache. She hadn't been eating right lately. Dreiser's suggestion that they have dinner together was beginning to sound appealing. "He asked me to go to dinner," she said. "You really think I should go?"

"You need a man around here," Mike told her. "He didn't sound half bad. I mean, I would have preferred a movie producer, a doctor, or maybe a rocket scientist. But hey, if he can kick Leah's ass, we'll take him. Oh, one more thing."

"What's that?"

"Make sure he can cook."

"Cute," Joanne said, smiling. "I love you, kid."

"I know," Mike said. "Now can I finish watching the movie?"

TWENTY-FIVE

DREISER AND Joanne were nestled in a secluded booth at the Bayside Bar and Grill in Ventura. "Would you like another gin and tonic?" Dreiser asked.

"How many have I had?" Joanne asked, her speech slurred from the alcohol.

"What difference does it make?" he said, having watched her consume three cocktails in less than thirty minutes. "Don't worry, I can always drive you home. You've had a tough week."

Joanne raised her glass in the air, peering at the contents. "I usually drink wine. This isn't bad. My headache is gone, and I've almost forgotten my daughter's obnoxious behavior."

"Want to tell me about it?"

"There's nothing to tell," Joanne told him, tapping her fingernails on the table. "That's the problem. As hard as I've tried, I haven't been able to get through to my own child."

The waitress, a young brunette, whisked past their table. Dreiser asked her to bring them another round. "When children rebel," he said, brushing shoulders with Joanne, "it isn't always just a stage they're going through. Is she seeing someone? You know, a psychologist?"

"Of course," Joanne told him. "She hardly says two words to the woman. The point of taking her to a psychologist was for her to talk out her problems. She goes for an individual session and we go in together too. Her behavior is getting worse though. Even her brother is concerned about her. I'm going to take her in for a physical checkup. It could be something as simple as PMS. I've also considered switching over to a psychiatrist. Maybe she needs to be on some type of medication."

"Try everything," Dreiser told her, his eyes misting over. "Look at the positive side. At least your daughter is sending you signals that something is wrong. Jake kept everything bottled up inside. If I'd known he had any thoughts whatsoever of killing himself, I would have moved the universe for him. I didn't get that chance. Everyone that knew him . . . teachers, friends, relatives . . . they all saw him as a happy, well-adjusted young man." He paused, shifting in his seat. "If only I knew why. I've accepted his death. All I want to know is why."

"Things sometimes happen for no reason," Joanne said, wishing she'd kept her problems to herself. Leah was alive. Nothing else was important. "From what you've told me, I doubt if there was anything you could have done." She hesitated, trying to think of a way to change the subject. Since they were already there, she decided to ask a question that had been nagging at her since he'd told her about his son's death. "Did they do an autopsy?"

"I wanted them to conduct an autopsy," Dreiser said. "I'm surprised you mentioned it. This was a major point of contention between my wife and me. An autopsy would have prolonged things. I was afraid Susan might have a breakdown. She's the one who found him. We were already divorced then. Jake was living with her."

Once the waitress brought their drinks, a thought-filled silence ensued. Joanne sipped her gin and tonic. "Let's get out of here," Dreiser said, tossing some bills down on the table. "Right now, I want to hold you. Keep drinking, and I'll end up carrying you."

Joanne's stomach fluttered in excitement. She grabbed her backpack and scooted out of the booth. Her knees felt like rubber. After staggering a few feet, Dreiser's strong arm encircled her waist, steadying her. She could feel the warmth of his breath on her face. He was only inches away. She was certain he was about to kiss her.

"I'm sorry," he whispered, motioning toward the front of the restaurant, "I'm not one for public displays of affection."

"Oh," Joanne said, shaking her head, "neither am I."

They stepped into a dimly lit entryway. A separate door led to the parking lot. Dreiser blocked the door to the restaurant with his body, then scooped her up in his arms. Joanne felt his hands pass from the center of her back to her hips. His hands swept over the curves in her body like a person admiring a sculpture. Every nerve ending in her body sprang to life. Her head fell back as she gasped, feeling as if a river had rushed into her. Time was suspended. Her heartbeats seemed miles apart. She could count the beats, feel the air rushing in and out of her mouth. She realized she was listening to her body as each part worked to keep her alive. For the first time, she understood the complexity of the human body.

Had they kissed? Whatever had occurred was already forgotten and a pulse of panic seized her. With a glance, Dreiser instantly calmed her.

Joanne started to say something. This wasn't the time for words, she decided, placing her forehead against his as they gazed down at the floor. She found herself nodding in agreement to unspoken words. He was a good man, a very good man. Nothing inside him was evil or twisted. She had nothing to fear and much to experience. He might be wounded, but wounded she could handle.

She was wounded as well.

TWENTY-SIX

OFFICER ROGER Turnbill had just come on duty at the Ventura County jail when he saw an enormous man peering through the glass window. "Detective Marvin Brown," Eli said, holding up a phony ID encased in a leather holder similar to a wallet. "I need to see Tom Rubinsky."

The man was carrying a detective shield from the Ventura PD. Turnbill had never seen him before, yet the name sounded familiar. Brown was certainly not the type of person he would forget. "Put your ID in the bin," Turnbill said into the microphone.

Eli tossed the badge and ID into the bin, grunting in annoyance. "I don't have all night, my friend."

Turnbill studied the ID, then peered up at Eli again. The man's credentials appeared legitimate, but he still had a strange feeling. He'd been a correctional officer for seven years. Why had he never seen this man? "Are you new?"

"Transferred in from L.A. about five months ago," Eli said, stifling a yawn. "L.A. is the pits."

"You realize it's past lockdown, don't you?"

"This is an emergency," Eli told him. "You think I want to be here? I'd rather be at home with the missus. We've got a double homicide working, in case you haven't heard. Looks like Rubinsky's brother killed someone else today."

"I'll have to get permission from my watch commander," Turnbill said, recalling another officer mentioning a murder on the west side of town. "I'm not authorized to pull an inmate out of his cell after lockdown."

"Do whatever you have to do." Eli walked over and flopped down in a chair. Out of the corner of his eye, he watched the officer pick up the phone. He'd used the name of a Ventura PD detective he met several years ago. Unless the supervisor knew Marvin Brown personally and wanted to chat with him, there shouldn't be a problem. He stared at the large clock mounted on the wall. His timing was perfect. The evening watch was heading for home; the graveyard shift just reporting for duty. Turnbill would have trouble finding any supervisor during shift change, let alone finding one who was concerned enough to come down and shoot the breeze with a detective.

He saw Turnbill replace the phone in the cradle, then curl his finger at him.

"The only way I can let you see Rubinsky is in an interview room," Turnbill told him. "We're running on a skeleton crew tonight. Captain says we don't have the manpower to place a guard in the regular visiting area. You'll be locked inside with the inmate. There's a buzzer, of course, but . . ."

Dressed in tan slacks and a short-sleeve black sweater, Eli removed his parka and tied it around his waist. He stretched his arms over his head, then purposely flexed his biceps, watching as the officer behind the glass gawked in amazement. "I think I'll be fine, don't you?"

Turnbill instantly depressed the buzzer. Eli yanked open the door and stepped through. Piece of cake, he thought. Since weapons were not allowed inside a detention facility, he reached down and pulled out a Smith & Wesson .45 he had strapped near his left ankle, placing the gun and his jacket in a locker. Impersonating an officer was a serious offense, but Eli was an impatient man. He'd spent all day searching for Ian Decker's body in a muddy field near Magic Mountain. For all he knew, the body might be buried in someone's backyard. When he'd heard about the new killing over his police scanner, he'd decided to go straight to the source. Considering his operating expenses, twenty grand wasn't a great deal of money. Even if he put the Decker matter to bed within the next twenty-four hours and collected the remaining ten thousand from Dreiser, he'd still be in the hole financially. Money wasn't his primary concern, however. Gary and Tom Rubinsky had killed the wrong man. After going over Ian Decker's files, including the information his mother had provided regarding his disability, Eli was as outraged as Elizabeth Decker. For all practical purposes, the Rubinskys had murdered a kid. He didn't know much about the new victim, but he refused to allow Gary Rubinsky to take another life.

"I'll need to take a look at his property," Eli said, standing at the counter now.

Several of the phone lines were blinking, and Turnbill yelled to another officer in the back of the room, instructing him to handle the phones while he dealt with the detective. "Look," Turnbill said, "pulling a prisoner out past lockdown is one thing. Now you want us to find his property? Is this really that urgent a situation?"

"Sure is," Eli answered, seeing a gold wedding band on Turnbill's left hand. "Maybe the guy's brother is out there looking for his next victim. Is your wife home alone? Have you talked to her tonight?"

Turnbill stepped a few feet back from the counter. "Give me five minutes," he said. "I'll run down to the property room myself." He turned to the other officer. "Hold down the fort, Kip. Things get out of hand, give Captain Olson a call and he'll send someone to spot you."

"Here we go," Eli said, handing the plastic bag containing Tom Rubinsky's personal property back to Turnbill. "Thanks for being so cooperative."

"Anytime," Turnbill said. "You know where to go. They've already deposited Rubinsky in an interview room. Good luck catching his brother."

At the end of the corridor was another workstation, manned by a guard. Eli ducked into the men's room. He pulled out a piece of paper with a girl's name on it, which had been stuffed inside Tom Rubinsky's wallet, then dialed the number on his cell phone. A softly seductive voice came on the line. "Trudy?" Eli said, trying to mimic Tom Rubinsky's voice from the tape Joanne had given him from the preliminary hearing. "This is Tom, baby."

The sugary sweetness disappeared, and Trudy's voice took on a hard edge. "I heard that you were in jail, that the cops think you and Gary murdered Ian. Then tonight, they said on the news that someone had killed Willie. Where's Gary?"

"Gary's not here," Eli told her. "What were you doing with Ian? I thought you cared about me. Why would you have sex with my best friend?"

"All I wanted was some grass and a ride back to my apartment," Trudy told him. "Don't ever call here again!"

Eli heard the dial tone and slipped his phone into his hip pocket. His instincts had paid off, but now he had to make some adjustments. Fortunately he had brought his portable computer and enough equipment to do what he had in mind. Instead of continuing down the corridor, he returned to the front desk.

"That was quick," Turnbill said, scowling. "What did you do? Just look at the guy?"

"I haven't seen Rubinsky yet," Eli told him. "I have to get something out of my truck."

"What do you want us to do with the prisoner?"

"Keep him on ice," Eli answered, walking over and standing by the exit. Once he heard the clicking sound, he jerked the heavy door open and rushed out.

Approximately fifteen minutes later, a skinny dark-haired officer escorted Eli to the interview room where he'd already deposited Tom Rubinsky. "He was asleep," the officer said, finding the correct key and inserting it in the lock. "His jacket says he's dangerous. If he gives you any trouble, be sure to hit the buzzer more than once. Three of our men called in sick tonight. I'm pulling a double shift. There used to be a phone in this room linked to the front desk. Then some maniac tried to strangle a detective with the telephone cord. We tried to get an intercom installed but the county never approved it."

Eli walked into the interview room, taking a seat at a small table. Tom Rubinsky was slumped in the chair. "What do you want? And why are you here so late at night? It's hard enough to sleep in this place without someone waking you up and dragging you out of your cell."

"Detective Marvin Brown," Eli said, showing his fake ID. "Sorry I had to wake you, pal. When you hear what I've got to say, I think you'll be glad I did."

"How come I've never seen you before?" Tom asked. "I thought that other detective was handling my case."

"Well," Eli said slowly, "things change, Tommy."

"My name is Tom," the other man snapped. "I hate being called Tommy. It makes me sound stupid."

"Sounding stupid is the least of your problems," Eli told him. "Your brother just rolled over on you. He's in booking right now."

Tom bolted upright in his chair. "You're lying."

"Afraid not," Eli said, placing his massive hands on the table. "They picked him up about three o'clock this afternoon, not long after he shot and killed your mutual friend, Willie Crenshaw."

"Willie's dead?" Tom exclaimed, wrapping his arms around his chest. "Gary didn't do it. Willie was a dealer, you know? Anyone could have killed him. He's been on the skids for months. He even had a warrant out for dealing."

"Gary made a full confession," Eli said, flicking a piece of lint off his black T-shirt. "We caught him with that fancy decoy gun in his possession, his clothes covered with Crenshaw's blood. It's over, my man."

Tom remained silent, trying to assimilate what he'd heard. He was tired. Tired of being confined, tired of the regrets, tired of the whole disgusting mess. First Gary had shot Ian, a nightmare he would never forget. And Willie might have been a loser, but as far as Tom knew, he'd never intentionally hurt anyone. He was just your typical pothead. Like many drug users, Willie had started dealing to supply himself and his circle of friends. Then when his life had slowly drifted away, he'd had no choice but to sell drugs to survive. Even people addicted to hard stuff like coke, heroin, and crack could stay on a job longer than a pothead. The nature of the drug itself took away a person's incentive to work. It was like waking up every morning and taking a dozen sleeping pills. The only difference was that pot didn't put you to sleep. You could live in a rathole and be content. You could spend days without ever going outside, laughing your head off at some crazy old movie and munching out on anything that even vaguely resembled food. Gary could have easily become another Willie, except his brother had so much energy that he had to smoke three or four joints to get even slightly high. To get Gary to calm down, you had to practically hit him over the head with a sledgehammer. He looked over at Eli. "Willie's really dead? Are you certain?"

"He's spending the night in the morgue," Eli answered, tipping his chair back on its hind legs. "Not many people spend the night in the morgue unless they're dead, know what I mean?"

Tom scratched a patch of dry skin on his left forearm. "And Gary confessed? He told you he killed Willie?"

"Gary told us everything," Eli replied. "He told us how you insisted he go along with you the day you robbed the Quick-Mart. How you shot Ian, then stood and watched while he dug the grave. He claims you instructed him to kill Willie because you were afraid he'd sell out to the police."

"No way," Tom said, standing up and shoving the chair back to the table. "Everything you've told me is bullshit. Gary's a pathological lair. Ask anyone who knows him. He started lying while he was still in diapers. I think the first word out of his mouth was a damn lie."

"The ADA believes he's telling the truth," Eli continued. "She's already offered Gary a deal. He pleads guilty to second-degree murder, and the rest of the charges will be dismissed. All your brother has to do is tell the court what he told us this afternoon, and he'll be back on the street in six years. You'll go down for murder one, the jury will rule that special circumstances existed, and maybe after twelve years and dozens of appeals, you'll get your last meal and your lethal injection."

Tom's face flushed with rage. He swung around and punched the wall with his fists. The wall was solid concrete. His knuckles were bleeding, but he was so angry, he didn't appear to notice. "It's that Kuhlman broad, isn't it? She tried to trick me into believing Gary was going to testify against me the day they arrested me."

"Have you talked to your brother?" Eli asked quietly.

"The morning after I was arrested," Tom told him. "Gary said he called the jail to see how much money he needed to get me out. When they read off the charges and told him I was being held without bail, he told me he'd decided to turn himself in and tell the cops he was responsible for everything." Tom suddenly halted and leveled a finger at the detective. "That's the real story, not this crock of shit you've been feeding me."

"You planned the Quick-Mart robbery," Eli told him. "In order to keep Ian in line, Gary said you repeatedly beat him."

Tom leaned against the wall on the far side of the room. "You're just making this stuff up."

"Ian went to the emergency room for a cut on his head the day after the robbery."

"We didn't hit him," Tom said. "He got wasted on sloe gin and passed out the next day, banging his head against the car window."

"That's not how Gary tells it," Eli said, a hint of a smile on his face. He was going to score big. His veins were pumping with adrenaline, making it hard to maintain his composure. After looking at Ian's mug shot and seeing the injury over his left eye, Eli had checked all the hospitals in Ventura. He'd finally learned that Methodist Hospital had treated Ian the day after the robbery. Ian, however, had told the emergency-room physician that the injury had occurred the day of the robbery. The DA's office had made a mistake by not following through on this injury themselves, yet it wasn't uncommon for defendants to have cuts and scrapes when they were arrested, particularly low-class thugs like the Rubinsky brothers. Ian, by association, fell into the same category.

"Gary says you kept Ian a prisoner," Eli continued. "You knew you had to keep him away from Elizabeth for fear she might talk some sense into him. You also knew Ian would break down on the witness stand. That's why you decided to kill him."

"I don't have to talk to you," Tom said, a trickle of saliva running down his chin. "You didn't even read me my Miranda rights."

"You're already in custody," Eli told him, although Rubinsky still had the right to refuse to speak to an officer outside the presence of his attorney.

Tom narrowed his eyes. "What else did Gary tell you?"

"That you told him he had to kill Willie. Gary said you spilled your guts to Willie when you ran into him at the Sunny Day car wash. This was after you'd transported Ian's body in the Chrysler. You went to the car wash to clean the car of any evidence. That's almost impossible, by the way. With the kind of technology we have today, anyone who transports a corpse in a vehicle is dead in the water."

Eli stopped speaking, wanting to see Tom's reaction. On his way to the jail, he'd driven by Willie's Crenshaw apartment building, noticing the Sunny Day car wash on the corner of Lewis and West Main Street. As soon as he'd heard the news about Crenshaw's death, Eli'd pegged him as the anonymous caller. Under the guise of Detective Brown, he'd placed a call to the crime lab. They confirmed that a receipt from the Sunny Day car wash had been found on the floorboard of the Chrysler. Unless there was more going on than Eli was aware of, perhaps something related to the decoy gun, Gary Rubinsky would be a fool to risk stealing a hubcap, let alone committing a murder. Eli's primary goal wasn't to trick Tom into confessing. Since he'd falsely represented himself as an officer, nothing Tom said would be admissible in court. Eli's only interest was to get Tom to tell him the precise location of Ian Decker's grave. Once the police recovered the body, the rest of the case would fall in place. By then, Eli would be on his way to Bali.

"Call the guard," Tom demanded. "I want to go back to my cell."

Eli decided it was time to bring out the fireworks. Shortly after four that afternoon, he'd stopped searching and returned to the *Nightwatch*. Joanne had given him both a transcript and a tape recording from the preliminary hearing of the Quick-Mart robbery, which allowed Eli to compile a fairly extensive vocabulary of words and phrases spoken by Gary Rubinsky. Once he'd input Gary's speech patterns and frequently used words into his computer, his voice synthesizer could then mimic anything Eli typed. Interspersing Gary's real voice with the computer-generated Dalek, he'd recorded his version of Gary Rubinsky's confession. The fact that the recording was spliced gave it a ring of authenticity. Rubinsky was allegedly confessing to two homicides, so the starts and stops in his speech would be expected.

Finding out about Trudy had been a lucky break, Eli told himself. Since he'd brought his computer, he'd been able to insert new material into the phony confession. Reaching into his pocket, Eli removed a microcassette player and placed it in the center of the table, then rubbed his hands together in anticipation.

"Put that thing away," Tom barked. "I'm through talking to you. Didn't you hear me? Go see my attorney. Let her answer your questions."

Eli hit the play button and Gary Rubinsky's voice echoed out over the room. Tom appeared stunned, then returned to his seat at the table.

"Tom had a thing for this girl named Trudy," Gary's voice said. *"When he found out Ian had slept with her, he was furious. He shot Ian in the parking lot of the Economy Inn. I didn't want any part of it. What could I do? My brother was holding a gun on me."*

"That lousy son of a bitch," Tom shouted, a line of perspiration popping out on his forehead. Eli stopped the tape. "Gary shot Ian. And he didn't shoot him in the parking lot of the Economy Inn."

Eli depressed the play button again. *"We put Ian's body in the trunk of the Chrysler,"* Gary's voice said. *"I wanted to dump him along the side of the road somewhere, but Tom wouldn't let me. He said we had to bury him. . . . That way, the police might never find him."*

"Where did you bury him?"

"Is that your voice on the tape?" Tom had his arms wrapped around his chest and was rocking back and forth in his chair.

"Yes," Eli said, pausing the tape again. "I'm in charge of the Crenshaw homicide."

"Gary's out of his mind," Tom said. "I begged him not to kill Ian. And Trudy didn't have anything to do with Ian's killing. She dated Gary for a few months because he told her he could get her a part in a movie. She dumped him about six months ago. She got stranded one night and didn't know who else to call for a ride back to Los Angeles. In exchange for keeping Ian occupied, Gary gave her some pot and promised to give her a ride home the next morning."

"Why did Gary need to keep Ian occupied?"

"Because Gary wanted to hit the Quick-Mart that night," Tom said. "We'd made a copy of Ian's car keys, but we knew he wouldn't let us take the car out by ourselves. Ian's mother was calling him all the time. Gary knew the situation with Ian was about to blow up. He didn't want to steal a car, though. Using a stolen car in a holdup is a sure way to get caught, unless you ditch the car a few blocks away."

"Why don't you tell me what really happened the night Ian died?" Eli reached over and removed the tape recorder from the table. "The recorder is gone. Whatever we say from this point on is off the record."

Gary looked confused. "Why? Why would you want to talk to me off the record? You're a detective."

Eli glanced furtively at the door to make it appear that he didn't want anyone to hear what he was about to say. "I suspected Gary was trying to railroad you from the beginning," he whispered. "Gary was too strong. He overpowered you just like he did Ian. You cared about Ian, didn't you? You were horrified when Gary killed him."

Tom placed his head down on the table, his shoulders shaking as he sobbed. He lifted his head, a dazed look in his red-rimmed eyes. "It all started with my mom. She started ragging on Gary about getting a job. He went nuts and hit her. He'd hit her once before when we were younger, but this time was worse. She fell down and broke her arm. I'm surprised my old man didn't beat Gary senseless.

"Just before we hooked up with Ian again," Tom said, a lifetime of memories playing over in his mind, "my dad threw both of us out of the house. I didn't hurt my mother, but I still got punished. It was always that way. I sometimes imagined that Gary and I were the same person, that we just had different faces. Being out on your own is hard. I was only eighteen. I tried to get a job, but I didn't have any experience. I finally got a job as a busboy at an Italian restaurant. We rented a cheap apartment. Gary took the bedroom, and I slept on the sofa. Gary thought he could get unemployment benefits so he wouldn't have to work. The people at the unemployment office made him take a job as a laborer, though, cleaning up on construction sites. Gary was lazy. He'd lift weights at the YMCA for hours, but he hated to work. He'd rock along for a month or so, then he'd start calling in sick. First, it was a few days every month. Then he wouldn't show up for weeks. Eventually the company figured out he wasn't sick and fired him. Gary planned it that way so he could collect unemployment."

"When did you start committing crimes?"

"Maybe a year ago," Tom said, sniffing. "We were partying so much, everything is kind of a blur. Willie was another guy from the old neighborhood. He was closer to Ian's age than mine. We all four hung out together when we were kids. My brother did some dealing himself now and then, so Willie was always hanging around for one reason or the other. I was still bussing tables at Giovanni's, but Gary grabbed whatever money I brought home. When the restaurant went out of business, I took it really hard. One of the waiters had told me he was leaving, and I was hoping I'd get his job. Giovanni's was a classy place. If they'd made me a waiter, I would have been able to afford my own apartment. Drugs weren't a big deal for me. I always thought I could get away from Gary, get my act together." He stopped and linked gazes with Eli. "Things got out of hand. After the first robbery, I knew it was only a matter of time before we got busted." He made a circular motion with his hand. "All of this: the jail, the courtroom, sitting here talking to you. It's like I've already been here, you know, like it was gonna happen no matter what I did. I decided to live one day at a time, try to have as much fun as I could and forget about the consequences. I was an idiot. Everything you do has a consequence. As soon as you stop paying attention to what you're doing, you're screwed."

Eli had placed the tape recorder in his lap. Without Tom noticing, he'd inserted a new tape to record their conversation. "Tell me about the crimes."

"The first three robberies we pulled off with a toy gun," Tom told him, the excitement of those days showing on his face. "Gary was jazzed. He loved the thrill that we might get caught, the piles of cash. He used to joke about it. He had to open a bank account when he had a job so he could cash his payroll checks. He was always bouncing checks. After we started pulling off the robberies, Gary would laugh and say sticking up a store was easier than managing a bank account. When we were around other people, our code name for a robbery was the instant-teller machine."

Eli thought he'd heard it all, but this was a new one. "Can you give me an example of what you mean by that statement?"

"Okay," Tom said, leaning forward. "We're in a nightclub, see, and Gary opens his wallet. He realizes we're getting low on cash. Maybe we're with a couple of good-looking chicks. So Gary tells them we'll be right back, that we have to go find an instant-teller machine. It really was a kick," he said, chuckling. "We never planned anything ahead of time. Our only rule was that the store had to be part of a chain. Once we hit one store, we'd move on to another chain. The take was usually around five hundred bucks, a drop in the bucket compared to the kind of money these big corporations pull in every day."

Understanding the criminal mind was fascinating, Eli thought. What made perfect sense to the criminal would seem like insanity to the average person. "Why only target chain stores? The larger companies usually have more sophisticated security systems."

"We didn't want to hit mom-and-pop stores," Tom said, a look of pride on his face. "Those people work hard for their money. Not only that, what with insurance, those chains we hit probably made money off us. We might have been crooks but we weren't scum. We didn't hurt anyone. It wasn't like we were robbing old ladies."

Eli started to say something and then stopped. The fewer questions he asked, the more Rubinsky would tell him. He'd seen criminals in this state of mind before. Tom's demeanor had changed completely. Instead of being guarded and hostile as he'd been at the beginning of the interview, he seemed relaxed and eager to talk. Eli waited for him to pick up where he'd left off. After some time had passed, and Tom's eyelids seemed to get heavy, Eli changed his mind. He had to be aggressive, or his subject would fall asleep. The most important question had yet to be answered. "How many robberies do you think you and your brother committed?" Eli held up a palm. "You don't have to tell me. I'm just trying to put everything into perspective. To challenge your brother's statement, we need as many facts as possible."

Tom sucked in a deep breath, then slowly exhaled. "Around fifteen," he told him. "Like I said before, things were moving pretty fast. It might have been less, and then it might have been more. These are the type of things you'd rather not remember, know what I mean?"

"Was Ian involved in all of the crimes?"

"No," Tom told him, shaking his head. "Only the last three. Ian was our driver. As soon as we saw him at the mall that day, Gary jumped on him right away. We needed a fast car, and Ian's Firebird had a big engine. Gary traded our Jeep for that gun that looked like a cell phone. He had this big idea that we could sell it to a gunsmith who had friends in the mob. He thought the mob would pay us a fortune for it because no one had ever seen a gun like that. Then they would manufacture the gun and sell it on the street."

"Where is the gun?" Eli asked. "Does Gary have it?"

"I certainly don't have it," Tom said, crackling his knuckles.

Tom suddenly became agitated, fidgeting in his seat. "This is when I started getting spooked. We'd never used a gun before. As soon as Gary put his hands on that gun, I knew something terrible was going to happen. I never thought he'd shoot Ian, though. I thought it would be a clerk in one of the stores. Ian was my friend. We played together when we were kids. He wasn't smart, but he was one of the nicest guys I ever knew. He'd give you the shirt off his back. God!" Tom exclaimed, covering his face with his hands. "How did this happen?" He collected himself, then continued, "Don't you see? It doesn't matter if they send me to prison. They can even execute me. I'm going straight to hell. No court, no fancy lawyer, no one on earth can save me. You want to know the truth? I'll tell you the truth. I'm already in hell. They don't have to kill me. Hell isn't someplace you go to after you die. Hell is waking up every morning and remembering all the awful things you've done."

"Tell me about the night Ian died," Eli said, watching as tears streamed down Tom's face. "Help us put the real killer behind bars. Forget that Gary is your brother. From this moment on, Ian Decker is your brother. Gary would let you rot in prison to save his own neck. Ian would walk on water to help you. The only thing that will defeat Gary is the truth. Tell me everything you can remember about the night Ian died. Then draw me a map to Ian's grave. This is your chance for redemption, Tom."

Tom's face froze like a statue, his eyes open but unseeing. Eli glanced at his watch and saw that it was after midnight. He had already stayed longer than he'd intended. The longer he stayed, the greater the risk. Tom's confession wouldn't be admissible in court, but Eli could drop the recording in the mail to the Ventura PD, then pull anchor on the *Nightwatch* and disappear. When Tom didn't snap out of it, Eli waved his hand in front of him. Nothing, not even a blink. The man was doing more than remembering.

Tom Rubinsky was reliving the murder.

Eli had no choice but to wait. The prize at the bottom of this Cracker Jack box was far from a trinket. If he just sat tight, he told himself, he'd walk away with a gold medal—a full confession and a map to Ian Decker's grave.

TWENTY-SEVEN

"WE'VE GOT to take the stuff out of the locker," Tom told his brother. They were standing on the landing in front of their motel room at the Economy Inn. Gary flicked his cigarette ashes over the side of the railing.

"Why?"

"Because the last time I went over there," Tom said, "the manager stopped me on the way out. I think he's afraid I'm a child molester. He said he'd seen me at the rink several times, but he'd never seen me skate."

Gary dropped the cigarette on the concrete walkway, then snuffed it out with his boot. "What did you tell him?"

"I told him my sister skates," Tom said, running his hands through his hair. "And that I usually come and pick her up. Then he asked me who my sister was, and I pointed at some girl on the floor. The manager gave me a suspicious look and walked away. The rink is open until nine tonight. I still have time to clean out the locker."

"Do it," Gary said. "I'll keep my eye on Ian."

Tom started to go inside for the car keys, but Gary stopped him. "Don't leave the sack in the trunk. We'll have to keep it with us now."

"What are we going to do while we're in court?" Tom said, exasperated. "We can't carry a gun into the courthouse. We'll never get past the metal detector."

"When the time comes, we'll figure it out. We can always bury the gun somewhere. We've spent most of the money. The bills weren't marked, so carrying what's left of the cash with us won't be a problem."

Tom returned approximately thirty minutes later, the brown sack containing the money and the gun stuffed inside his leather jacket. "Hey, Ian," he said, "there's a rerun of *Saturday Night Live* on at ten. Go take your shower, and we'll watch it together."

Depressed and restless, Ian was getting bolder every day. "You guys are the ones who need to take a shower."

Tom had to find a way to get Ian out of the room, or at the very least, distract him in some way. The only place he could think to hide the gun was between the mattress and box spring. Gary was stoned. Sitting on the floor next to Ian, both of them were leaning back against the foot of the bed. Tom saw the remains of three joints in the ashtray. Gary was tossing handfuls of peanut M&M's into his mouth while he watched TV. "We're watching *Liar Liar* with Jim Carrey," Gary said, glancing over his shoulder at his brother. "I liked him better in *Ace Ventura: Pet Detective,* but this is pretty good."

"You stink," Ian said. "Either take a shower or sit somewhere else."

Gary was so drugged out, all he did was laugh. "I stink because I'm a man," he said, lifting his arm and shoving his armpit into Ian's face. "Bet you never smelled a real man before, huh?"

"Get away from me," Ian said, swatting at him.

Gary was in one of his unpredictable moods. Tom had seen him like that before. One minute he was the life of the party, then someone would say something and he'd flip out. He watched as Gary pinned Ian on the floor. "Want to smell my crotch, asshole?" he said, laughing manically. "I know why you were pissed off about Trudy. You're into guys, aren't you?"

Ian wrenched one of his hands free and tried to gouge Gary's eye with his finger. He missed Gary's eye, but managed to rake his nails across his face. "You little punk," Gary shouted, touching his cheek and seeing the blood on his fingers.

Tom saw his brother pull back his fist just as he was folding the gun and cash inside his jacket to place it between the mattress. He rushed over to break up the fight. Gary was too quick, though, and had already punched Ian in the mouth, breaking off one of his front teeth. Tom grabbed his brother around the waist, but Gary threw him off. While the brothers wrestled, Ian rolled across the floor. He saw Tom's leather jacket and the stack of bills, along with what appeared to be a cell phone. Ian seized the phone, pushing himself to his feet. Tom saw him out of the corner of his eye. "Get off me, Gary," he shouted. "Ian's got the gun!"

Ian was about to depress one of the keys when Gary sprang to his feet. "Give me that right now."

"No," Ian said, clasping the decoy gun to his chest. "You never told me you had a cell phone. I want to call my mother. I'm sick of both of you."

Gary and Tom knew they had to act fast. "It's a gun," Tom blurted out. "They made it to look like a cell phone."

Gary marched over and tried to pry Ian's fingers off the decoy gun, but Ian jerked away and shoved the gun into his left pocket.

"Leave him alone," Tom shouted. "Let me handle it."

Gary slouched in a chair, one leg thrown over the armrest. Tom cautiously approached Ian. "We weren't pulling your leg, Ian. It's not a cell phone, it's a gun. You don't want to shoot your leg off, do you?"

"No," Ian said, pouting. "I want to go home."

Tom held his hand out. "Give me the gun, and we'll take you home. Deal?"

"No," Ian said, shaking his head. "I don't believe you."

"That's it," Gary said. He walked over and twisted Ian's left arm behind his back, then he reached in Ian's pocket and yanked the gun out. Ian spun around and slugged Gary in the face. Gary pointed the gun at Ian just as Tom jumped in between them.

"You're making a mistake," Tom told his brother. "Let it be for right now."

"That's the gun they were talking about in the courtroom," Ian said, his face flushed with rage. "Everything you said about the robbery was a lie. There weren't two other men. You and Gary robbed the Quick-Mart. You thought I was so stupid I wouldn't know the difference."

"Calm down," Tom said, seeing the sinister look in his brother's eyes. "Let's go outside and get some fresh air. I'll explain everything. We have to stop making so much noise or someone will call the police."

Gary tucked his shirt back into his jeans. "Maybe it's time to take a drive."

Ian started inching his way toward the door. "I want to go home. Take me to my mother's house. I promise I won't tell anyone about the gun. Please, let me go home."

"Come on now," Gary said, smiling as he walked over and draped his arm around Ian's shoulders. "We're buddies. Friends have spats every now and then. You don't want to go running home to your momma like a baby. Just because we have a gun doesn't mean we robbed the Quick-Mart. Maybe the gun belonged to the robbers, and we just happened to find it."

Ian reached for the door handle. Gary body slammed him against the door. "You're either with us or you're not, understand?"

"Why can't you ever tell the truth?" Ian asked. "You didn't find the gun. You robbed that store."

"Hey," Gary said. "You leave, and we'll tell the police you skipped town, that you were the one who robbed the Quick-Mart. Then every cop in the world will be looking for you. Stick with us, and we'll beat this thing. Dreiser doesn't think the DA has enough evidence to prove the case." He flicked his finger against Ian's forehead. "Think. Use your brain for a change. You're not that thickheaded. Without us, you ain't got nothing."

Ian felt a throbbing inside his mouth. When he touched his front tooth, he winced in pain. All that was left of his tooth were a few jagged fragments protruding from the gum line. "You broke my tooth off," he told Gary. "It hurts like a bitch. I should break your tooth."

"Gary was wrong to hit you," Tom told him, wedging his body between the two men again. "You were wrong too, Ian. You shouldn't have insulted Gary by telling him he smelled."

Ian sulked a few moments, then spoke out again, "Why didn't you tell me about the gun?"

"We were trying to protect you," Tom said. "We were afraid you'd panic. Another reason we didn't tell you the truth was so you wouldn't have to lie on the witness stand. That's called perjury. Perjury is a serious crime."

"Robbery is worse," Ian argued. "I'd rather go to jail for perjury than for robbery."

"A witness saw you in the parking lot of the market," Tom reminded him. "No one will believe you didn't know what was going on. Maybe we did rob the Quick-Mart. We need money to live. Gary and I don't get checks from the government like you. Forget about what happened. We're still your friends."

"You're not my friends," Ian said, scowling. "You've never been my friends. I want to sleep in my own bed. I want to see my family, listen to my music, eat a home-cooked meal. I'm sick of this disgusting motel room. I can't breathe half the time because of the marijuana smoke. No one treats their friends the way you treat me. You act like I'm your slave."

"You want to go home?" Gary said, hissing the words through clenched teeth.

"Are you deaf?" Ian said defiantly. "I've been telling you I want to for weeks."

"Fine," Gary said. "Then we're going to take you home."

Ian's face brightened. "Are you serious?"

"Yeah," Gary said. "Get your things."

While Ian was stuffing his belongings into a pillowcase, Gary and Tom spoke privately on the other side of the room. "How can we take him home?" Tom asked. "You know how he is. He never lies. I don't think he *can* lie. Lying is beyond his capability. You have to have a good memory to lie, especially under pressure."

"'Lying is beyond his capability,'" Gary repeated, making fun of Tom. "What in the hell is that all about? Are you studying to be a shrink? Did you think I was serious when I said we were going to take him to his mother's house? You've got a screw loose, man."

Tom's face blanched. He grabbed his brother's arm. "You're not going to do what I think you're going to do!" he said. "Give me your word you won't hurt Ian. I can't let you hurt him, Gary. You've already ruined my life. I'm not going to stand by and watch you kill someone."

"I've ruined your life, huh?" Gary said, twisting away in fury. "I didn't hold a gun on you and force you to rob those stores. Take whatever stuff you want to keep. Right now, I haven't decided what I'm going to do about Ian. I do know one thing. We're not coming back to this room."

* * *

Tom was behind the wheel of the Chrysler, Gary was in the passenger seat. Ian was riding in the backseat behind Gary. "You have to take the car back," Ian told them. "That was the deal. You said you were only borrowing it, remember?"

"Excuse me," Gary said, jerking his head around. "How can we take you home without a car?"

"I can walk home from the lot," Ian said. "You guys will have to call a taxi. There's a pay phone on the corner. My mom is responsible for this car. You have to take it back, or I'll call the police and tell them that you have that gun. Then they'll know you robbed the Quick-Mart."

Tom slammed on the brakes in the middle of the street. A car behind them screeched to a halt, the driver blasting his horn. Didn't Ian realize what he was saying? Now wasn't the time to butt heads with Gary. "We don't have that much money left, Ian. It might have looked like a lot, but most of those bills are fives and ones. We can't rent a car. We don't have a credit card."

"Stop all the baloney," Gary barked. "The kid wants us to take the car back. We'll call Willie. He'll come and pick us up. Drive us to ABC Towing and Storage. I can't stand listening to Ian whining."

Tom made an illegal U-turn and steered the Chrysler in the direction of the storage lot. Gary sounded rational, but there was enough tension inside the car to cause an explosion.

They pulled up to the back gate to the ABC Towing and Storage lot. Ian got out and unlocked the gate with the key he'd stolen from his mother. He pushed the gate open and then motioned for Tom to drive the Chrysler into the lot. Tom felt the hairs prick on the back of his neck. Now that Ian was safely out of the car, he moved his foot from the brake to the gas pedal and slipped the gearshift into reverse.

"Drive into the lot," Gary told him, the nose of the decoy gun pressed into Tom's ribs. "Once we're inside, do exactly what I tell you. Brother or not, you're a breath away from a bullet."

Ian walked up to the driver's window. Tom asked him where he wanted them to leave the car.

"Over there," Ian said, pointing to an empty parking spot. "I think that's where it was parked when we took it."

The three men parked and exited the Chrysler.

"Look over there, Ian," Gary shouted. "There's a light burning inside the office. It might be your uncle."

Ian was approximately five feet away. As soon as he turned around, Gary shot him in the back. Tom didn't move or speak. His feet felt as if they were nailed to the ground. He watched as Gary shoved the decoy gun back inside the waistband of his jeans. He picked up one of Ian's lifeless hands and began dragging him toward the Chrysler.

"Here," Gary said, tossing something to Tom. "That's the key to the office. Find us another car. Make sure it has a current license plate."

Tom held up his palms, his whole body trembling. "No way," he said, watching as the key struck the ground. "I'm not going to leave my fingerprints inside the office. Robbing stores is one thing. Ian didn't deserve to die. You threatened to shoot me too. As far as I'm concerned, I don't have a brother."

Tom turned and headed toward the back gate.

"Get your ass back here," Gary yelled. "Don't make me shoot you. I had to kill Ian. You don't want to go to prison any more than I do. Because you're such a wimp, I always end up doing the dirty work."

Tom dropped his head and broke into a run. He heard the gunshot, then dropped to the ground, covering his head with his hands. "Please, God, help me," he prayed. "I'll never do anything wrong again." He heard the roar of an engine. A cloud of dirt struck his face. When he looked up, he saw Gary in the driver's seat of the Chrysler.

"Get in the car," his brother said, pointing the decoy gun at him. "I had to lift Ian myself. I should kill you just for that."

Tom had no choice. He either did what his brother said, or Gary would shoot him. He walked over and climbed into the passenger seat. He looked in the backseat, then realized Ian's body must be in the trunk. He was numb. Gary had killed Ian. Now they were murderers. He was shocked at how calm his brother was, as if he shot people every day. "What are we going to do if the police stop us?"

Gary had already sped out of the storage lot and was driving in the direction of the freeway. "We don't have any drugs on us," he said. "I smoked what was left of the pot last night. The police can't look in the trunk without a search warrant. After we dump Ian, we'll come back and get a clean car."

Tom was nauseous. He stuck his head out the window, hoping the fresh air would help. He noticed that they were on the 101 Freeway on the outskirts of Los Angeles. He had no idea where Gary was going. Suddenly he heard a banging noise. "There's something wrong with the car," he told his brother, settling back into his seat. "Listen, don't you hear it?"

"I hear it," Gary said, steering the Chrysler toward the nearest exit.

Ian's eyes sprang open. All he could see was a sliver of light. His body was wracked with pain, crammed into a tight space. The last thing he remembered was Gary yelling at him, something about his uncle and the office. He gasped for air, certain he was in a coffin. He frantically kicked out with his feet, connecting with a solid surface. His ankles ached. He cried for his mother. She'd always known when he was in trouble. He opened his mouth to call out her name, but nothing came out but a raspy whisper.

They couldn't have buried him yet, Ian reasoned, or there would be no light whatsoever. He prepared himself to die. Another dagger of pain entered his lower back, and his body contracted in a spasm. He touched the area with his hand. His clothes were soaked with warm liquid. Blood . . . it had to be blood. He recalled a loud noise before he lost consciousness. Either Gary or Tom must have shot him. He placed his palms against the top of the trunk and pushed with all his might. He was too weak. He had to preserve whatever air was left. Once they buried him, it would be over.

Trudy's lovely face appeared in front of him. He smelled her perfume. The panic was replaced with a feeling of euphoria. Trudy extended her hand to him, smiling just before she led him into the bedroom. He was transported back to the night they had made love. The searing pain was made bearable by memories of their lovemaking. She was there with him, snuggling up beside him on his bed. Just as he reached out to touch her beautiful hair, he felt himself being sucked into a dark tunnel.

"It's okay, Ian," Trudy said, the softness of her voice reassuring him. "I'm just going to the bathroom. I'll be back before you can count to ten."

TWENTY-EIGHT

Saturday, February 17, 2001, 1:05 A.M.

JOANNE BOLTED upright in bed. Leah was calling for her. Tossing on her robe, she hurried down the narrow hallway to her daughter's bedroom. The room was dark and she could barely see the outline of Leah's body under the covers. "Did you have a bad dream, sweetheart?"

"No," Leah said, clasping her mother's hand, "something's wrong."

Leah's hand was clammy and cold. Joanne turned on the lamp. Her daughter had thrown the covers off. The bedding beneath her was soaked in blood. Leah's skin was pasty white, and her eyelids fluttered. "Oh my God!" Joanne exclaimed, cupping her hand over her mouth. "My poor baby."

Leah tried to sit up, then fell back on the pillow. "I started my period last night. The cramps were really bad. I took some Tylenol. The pain kept getting worse. I bled through all the pads." She managed to hold her head up long enough to see the bloodstained sheets. "I changed the sheets about an hour ago. What's happening? Why am I bleeding so much? Am I going to die?"

"You'll be fine," Joanne told her, trying to remain calm. "I think you're hemorrhaging, though. You need to go to the hospital."

"Mother," the girl whispered. "I have to tell you something."

Joanne sat down on the edge of the bed, tenderly brushing Leah's hair off her forehead. "We can talk later," she told her. "I need to call an ambulance. You're losing too much blood." She was reaching for the phone next to the bed when Leah tugged on the sleeve of her robe.

"Please," Leah said, "don't call yet. I'm pregnant. I was going to have an abortion."

"Did you do something to yourself?" Joanne asked, even more horrified than before. Disregarding Leah's plea, she dialed 911 for an ambulance. Turning back to her daughter, she said, "Were you trying to get rid of the baby? Whatever you did, I have to know. This is serious, Leah."

"I didn't do anything," Leah told her. "I even went to a doctor yesterday. That's why I was late coming home. I wanted to make certain I was really pregnant."

Joanne was shattered. No wonder Leah had been acting strangely. "Why didn't you come to me, tell me? I'm your mother. No matter what the problem is, I'm here to help you."

"I didn't want you to know," Leah said, her breath catching in her throat. "I know you think I'm like Dad, that I tell lies and do bad things. I want to be perfect like you. I try, but I keep messing up. I want you to love me. Dad used to love me."

Joanne cradled her in her arms. "I love you more than anything in the world," she told her. "How could you possibly believe I don't care for you, that I look down on you? I've been hurting too, Leah. Every time I try to get close to you, you push me away."

"Dad said you didn't want us," Leah said. "Were you really in love with another man?"

"No," Joanne said. "Even if I had been in love with another man, I would have never abandoned you. All I've ever asked is that you believe me. The two years you were gone were the worst years of my life. I cried myself to sleep every night. I didn't know for sure that you were with your father. You could have been dead. What your father did to me was cruel, Leah."

"I still love my dad," Leah told her. "I know he broke the law. He was always good to me, though. Maybe that's why I wanted a boyfriend. I wanted someone to pay attention to me, hold me, tell me that I'm special."

"You are special," Joanne said. "You're beautiful, bright, sensitive." She stopped and wiped a tear from her eye. "I'm far from perfect, Leah. I make mistakes every day of my life. I guess I was wrong not taking you to see your father in jail. As soon as you're better, I'll make arrangements for you and Mike to visit him."

Joanne helped Leah walk to the bathroom. Dampening a washcloth with warm water, Joanne wiped the blood off the lower half of her daughter's body before she dressed her in a clean nightgown. Leah was shivering and looked down at her feet and saw another pool of blood. "Why am I bleeding so much?"

"You must be having a miscarriage," Joanne told her. "How far along were you?"

"The doctor said ten weeks," Leah said. "I promise, Mom, I've never had sex before. This was the first time."

"It doesn't matter, honey," Joanne said, holding her in her arms. "The ambulance should be here any minute." She picked up the blanket from the floor and wrapped it around Leah. "I had a miscarriage once. You're going to be fine."

"When did you have a miscarriage?" Leah asked. "You never mentioned anything like that."

"You were nine months old," Joanne told her, finding it hard to believe that the chubby little baby she pictured in her mind was now old enough to engage in such a conversation. "You never told me you had a boyfriend. Is it Nathan?"

"Nathan is one of the most popular boys at school. I thought if I could get him to have sex with me, then he'd make me his steady girlfriend. I drank a bunch of booze at this party and pushed myself on him."

"What party?"

"The night I told you I was spending the night with Gabby," Leah said, pulling the blanket tighter around her chest. "After her parents went to sleep, Gabby and I snuck out and went to this party at Trent's house. Trent goes to my school. Every time his parents leave town, he throws a party. His dad's a big boozer. He drinks vodka and buys it by the case. Trent pours out half of two bottles of vodka and mixes it with juice in this big punch bowl. Then he fills his dad's vodka bottles back up with water. Trent says his dad doesn't know the difference. He says he's doing his dad a favor because he's keeping him from becoming an alcoholic."

"All this deception," Joanne said, wondering how many other things her daughter had done that she didn't know about. Her mind raced back in time to her own childhood. She remembered throwing rolls of toilet paper at people's houses, smoking her father's cigarettes in the bathroom, making out in the backseat of a car with a boy she had just met. She'd also slipped out of her parents' house on numerous occasions. Funny, she thought, how age made a person forget.

"I wanted someone to love me," Leah told her, "to make me feel special the way Dad did. A lot of the girls at my school have sex with their boyfriends. Some of them are younger than me. The guys buy them presents, call them all the time, do whatever they want." She paused, her face twisted in pain. "Nathan is a nice guy. He would have never done anything to hurt me. I encouraged him. I asked him to come into the bedroom with me. I took off my clothes. I got on top of him. He had sex with me because he thought that's what I wanted."

Joanne pulled up a chair from Leah's desk. "When a person does something nice in exchange for sex or any other type of favor," she explained, "their affections are not genuine. What you're doing is buying their love or attention, not with money but with something even more valuable—your dignity. This kind of relationship might make you feel good in the beginning, but in time, you'll end up with nothing but regrets."

"I understand," Leah said, bending over at the waist. "Believe me, I'll never have sex again."

"You'll have sex again," her mother said, stroking her arm. "I'd like to believe that you'll wait until you're older, though—and that the next time you're intimate with someone, you'll be in a committed relationship. Love is what makes sex wonderful. The night this happened, what did you feel?"

"Nothing," Leah said. "I don't even remember it."

"Well," her mother said, "that's the way it usually is when you have sex with a person you don't love."

Joanne heard the doorbell ring and stood up. When she'd called, she had instructed the ambulance to turn off the siren once they passed through the security gates. She didn't want her neighbors to start asking questions. With the amount of time the ambulance had taken to get there, Joanne thought, she could have driven Leah to the hospital herself. She started walking toward the door, then stopped and turned back around. "Remember," she said, "no matter what kind of problem you have, I'm your best friend as well as your mother. I was wrong by keeping you from seeing your father. But please believe me, no one will ever care more for you."

Leah pushed herself to her feet, pulling on the terry-cloth robe her mother had placed on the back of the chair. "What are we going to do about Mike?"

Joanne rubbed her forehead. She'd been so overwhelmed that she'd forgotten all about her son. It was fine for Leah to go to the hospital in her gown and robe, but Joanne would have to get dressed. "Mike and I will follow you in the car. I can't leave him here alone. I'll tell him you're having female trouble. Perhaps he shouldn't know the truth. Of course, that's your decision not mine."

Leah looked her mother squarely in the eye. "Tell him the truth," she said, her voice no longer that of a teenager. "I'm tired of lying." In less than twenty-four hours, Leah had left her childhood behind.

TWENTY-NINE

ELI LEFT the jail at one forty-five that morning. After driving to the marina where the dinghy was stored, he rowed back to the *Nightwatch*. He'd been fortunate that the sea was calm, as he was physically and mentally exhausted. Listening to Tom Rubinsky talk for two and a half hours had been draining.

Eli wondered how the police would handle the case. Although risky as well as illegal, Eli was tempted to carry forth the subterfuge and have the real Detective Brown claim he was Tom Rubinsky's late-night visitor at the jail. He'd selected that particular officer for two reasons. Marvin Brown was an African-American, and he was almost the same height and weight as Eli.

Eli placed himself inside the mind of the younger Rubinsky. Before the guard had come to get him, he'd been asleep in his cell. Once Eli played the phony tape of his brother confessing, Rubinsky probably didn't remember anything outside of what he'd heard. In addition, it would be the word of a police officer against that of a man charged with first-degree murder. Eli doubted if the police would proceed in that direction, however. If Tom Rubinsky figured out the officer who'd come to the jail the previous evening was an imposter, the entire case could go down the toilet.

When he finally reached the *Nightwatch*, Eli collapsed in his bunk for two hours, then got up and consumed a pot of coffee and a stale doughnut before he once again boarded the dinghy. The crisp morning air was invigorating. He tried to relax as he glided over the dark waters. The only sound was the swishing of his paddles. In his stainless-steel briefcase, Eli had Tom Rubinsky's taped confession. He'd placed it inside an envelope addressed to the Ventura Police Department's homicide division. He had no intention of mailing the tape and taking a chance of it getting lost. As soon as he recovered Decker's body, he would stop by the police department and hand the package to the officer at the front desk. The officer would not remember him, outside of the color of his skin and his size. He wouldn't notice that Eli had a mole above his lip, nor would he remember the scar near his left ear.

Eli had never understood why black men were constantly misidentified. And it wasn't only Caucasians who seemed unable to distinguish one African-American from another. Even men and women of his own race were guilty.

The sun burst through the clouds, vanquishing the chill in the air. He broke out in a sweat as the muscles in his arms strained to propel the rubber boat through the water. People were always asking him why he didn't install a motor, even if only as an emergency precaution. Rowing the dinghy was his primary form of exercise. He kept a few weights on board the *Nightwatch*, but he seldom used them.

The professional fishermen had already set out to sea. Eli was relieved that he didn't have to navigate through their wakes. Once when the winds had been particularly strong, the dinghy had capsized in the choppy wake of a large fishing vessel.

Eli checked to make certain he had all the proper equipment in his large canvas bag, then slung it over his shoulder as he walked to his Toyota truck in the parking lot. "Such a stupid mistake," he said angrily, pulling out a computer-generated map and glancing at the circle he'd drawn. "If Gary Rubinsky hadn't killed you," he said, referring to Willie Crenshaw, "I might be tempted to shoot you myself."

Overall, however, Crenshaw had been a lightweight compared to the Rubinskys. As far as he knew, the man had never committed an act of violence. He also deserved credit for placing his neck on the line by calling Elizabeth, even if he had provided her with the wrong information. He suspected that the phone call had cost Crenshaw his life. But years of smoking pot had fried the man's brain. In the end, he'd died for nothing.

Placing the map on the dashboard of his truck, Eli removed his sunglasses from his pocket and slipped them on, cranking the engine and roaring out of the parking lot. Now that he had the correct coordinates, he had no doubt that he would find Ian Decker's grave.

Elizabeth and her daughter, Pauline, exited the Chevy Blazer around six o'clock Saturday morning at the edge of a field. At twenty-four, Pauline was a pretty woman, her curly dark hair cut just below her ears. Like her mother, she had fair skin, hazel eyes, and a willowy frame. Before her illness and her son's disappearance, Elizabeth had been extremely attractive. No one understood why she hadn't remarried. Pauline understood. Her mother had never remarried because of her brother. A hodgepodge of events were clustered within a few years after Ian's birth. Pauline's father had died, leaving the family in financial straits. Her uncle Carl lost his leg in a boating accident. Pauline had slipped on one of Ian's toys and fallen down the stairs, dislocating her collarbone. The following year, she had been hospitalized with pneumonia. It was as if her brother's entrance into the world had created some type of cosmic event. No matter what was going on in Pauline's life, her mother's attention was always focused on Ian. Pauline had felt like an outsider. She'd moved back into the house to look after her mother following Elizabeth's transplant, but her decision was also based on the fact that her brother was no longer around.

Ian had once again stepped into the spotlight, and Pauline was more annoyed than concerned. Ian wasn't dead, she told herself. She knew the Rubinsky brothers, and she'd heard rumors about Ian's activities. He'd been hanging out at bars, living the wild life. Because Elizabeth had always babied him, Ian couldn't face the reality that he might go to prison. As far as Pauline was concerned, Ian had most likely skipped out. What bothered her the most was the fact that her mother could lose her home if her brother didn't show up in court. Ian had even stolen two cars from her mother and uncle's business. Elizabeth preferred to blame the crime on the Rubinsky brothers, but the person who'd stolen the cars had possessed a key to the lot. Everything came down to one simple fact, a fact her mother simply refused to accept. Ian was a criminal.

Pauline was turning around to retrieve a bottle of water from the backseat when she saw Joanne's Lexus pull up behind them. "I have no idea why you wanted that woman to come today," she said. "This is turning into a circus."

"Mrs. Kuhlman offered to help," Elizabeth told her. "We can use all the help we can get. Besides, we're not looking for Ian. We're looking for Ian's grave. You're a nurse, Pauline. Has your work made you this callous? This is your brother, for God's sake."

"Ian's hiding out somewhere," Pauline told her, taking a long drink of water. "I've told you that a dozen times. You're making yourself sick coming out here every day. You never made Ian take responsibility for his actions. He doesn't care if we lose the house. You warned him repeatedly about the Rubinsky brothers. He thumbed his nose at you. That's why he hasn't called. He knows he's in serious trouble. When he was a kid, he used to hide in the garage when he did something wrong."

Pauline got out of the car, slamming the door behind her. Joanne walked over to introduce herself, but Pauline ignored her, staring out over the open field. "Why are we searching here?" she asked her mother, clutching her cell phone in her hand. "The rest stop back there doesn't have a McDonald's. I thought the man who called you said they buried Ian near a McDonald's restaurant."

"I've looked everywhere else," Elizabeth explained, removing the stakes and other tools from the back of the Blazer. "There's a Carl's Junior. Maybe the man who called got the two restaurants confused. He said Ian was buried near Magic Mountain. Look," she continued, pointing at something off in the distance. "I think that's the top of the roller coaster. We've been searching on the other side of the park."

Elizabeth shoved the wooden section of a rake into her daughter's hands, then handed her twenty stakes and a hammer.

"I can't carry all this stuff," Pauline told her. "You said I had to bring my phone. I've got a bad back, remember? I lift sick people every day. You should have reminded me to wear pants with pockets."

Elizabeth pulled a trash bag out of the trunk. "Put everything in here," she said. "That way you can drag it instead of having to carry it. Every time we have to make a trip back to the car, we waste time. When you find something, don't touch it. Call me and then we'll make a decision as to whether or not we should notify the police." She turned to Joanne. "Mrs. Kuhlman knows how to preserve a crime scene. We should be grateful that she offered to help us."

Joanne was dressed in jeans and a blue sweater. The day was clear and sunny, the temperature in the mid-sixties. She asked Elizabeth, "What would you like me to do?"

"We're going to set up a grid," the woman said. "That way, we don't cover the same ground twice." She reached into the back of the Blazer again and handed Joanne some stakes and a hammer. The prosecutor already had her cell phone clipped to her belt. "Write down my number."

"I already programmed it into my phone," Joanne said, waiting for the woman to tell her which area she wanted her to search. "My daughter became ill last night. She's resting now, but I don't think I should stay past noon. I'm sorry."

"You can leave now if you want," Elizabeth told her. "Your child should be your first priority."

"I want to help," Joanne said. "Leah will be fine. Her brother is with her, and my neighbor is bringing over some food. She can always call me if she needs anything."

Elizabeth gave the prosecutor a hug. "You were very kind to come."

"I hope I can help," Joanne said. "Tell me what to do."

"Oh," Elizabeth said, reaching into the back of the Blazer again, "we poke the ground with these poles. Today is our best shot. The ground is still soft from the storm we had last week. By tomorrow, it will be hard again. It's good that's there's three of us, even if you can't stay all day. Pauline, start from here and walk straight for a hundred feet, then make a right turn and keep going. I'll leave the car unlocked. When either of you run out of stakes, just come back for more." She turned back to Joanne. "I'd like you to start in the opposite direction from Pauline. After a hundred feet, turn left. Every fifty feet, stop and place one of the stakes in the ground. You'll save yourself some aches and pains if you use the hammer rather than trying to push the stake in with your hands." She glanced at Joanne's hands. "I should have told you to bring gloves."

"Don't worry about it," Joanne said, touched by Elizabeth's stoic and organized approach to finding her son. This frail woman, with the withered face and thinning hair, possessed an immense inner beauty. Every movement and every word seemed to have a purpose. Due to the situation with Leah, Joanne had planned on calling and bowing out. Leah had insisted she go, reassuring her mother that she would be fine. Because the girl had miscarried so early in the pregnancy, the doctor had sent her home with medication to stop the bleeding and muscle relaxants for the cramping. He suggested they make an appointment to see their gynecologist, however, to make certain that there wasn't any remaining tissue. Leah said all she wanted to do was sleep. Mike had promised his mother he wouldn't leave the house until she returned.

Outside of a few straggly trees, the ground they were searching was flat. They didn't really need the phones, Joanne thought, as they could maintain visual contact with each other as they set up the outer perimeters of the grid. They'd only been searching for approximately twenty minutes when they heard Elizabeth screaming. Pauline and Joanne both started running toward her, knowing she must have found the body.

Elizabeth was on her knees. A hand protruded from the dirt. Attached to the skin of one of the fingers was a small green remnant of cloth. Portions of the flesh had been eaten away. Pauline had to turn away, fearful she was going to vomit.

"It's okay, Ian," Elizabeth said, scooping out the dirt around the hand with her small shovel. "Mother is here. We're going to take you home now. You're not alone anymore."

Joanne placed a hand on Elizabeth's shoulder. "Perhaps you should wait until the police arrive," she said. "You might be destroying valuable evidence."

"I've waited long enough," Elizabeth said, a fanatical fire in her eyes.

Joanne walked a few feet away and called the Valencia Sheriff's Department, notifying them that they'd found what appeared to be Ian Decker's body.

"For Christ's sake," Elizabeth cried, "can't one of you help me?"

Tears were streaming down Pauline's face. Joanne walked over and put her arm around her. "What should we do?" Pauline asked. "I didn't believe Ian was dead. I was concerned about my mother's health, don't you understand? I love my brother."

"Please," Elizabeth shouted, having uncovered an entire arm. "For the love of God, get the shovels and help me. He's been in the ground too long. We can't wait for the police."

The emotion of the moment overtook Joanne's reason. She dropped to her knees and began digging, tossing the earth over her shoulder. The crime lab could take all the dirt and put it through their sifter, she told herself. There was no way to exhume a body without disturbing the crime scene.

Pauline stood with her arms wrapped around her chest. A few moments later, she got down on her knees beside her mother and began digging. "If you see any kind of object," Joanne said, panting, "try not to touch it. Scoop it up with the shovel and place it a few feet away, then put one of those yellow stakes beside it so we'll know where it is when the police get here."

The three women worked in silence. Another arm was uncovered, then a shoulder. Finally, they saw strands of hair caked with dirt and both Joanne and Pauline laid down their shovels. Elizabeth used her bare hands, sweeping away the dirt until she had exposed the top portion of the face. She leaned forward and tenderly kissed his forehead, then rocked back on her legs, staring up at the sky. Joanne and Pauline exchanged questioning looks, yet neither woman spoke. Elizabeth was obviously praying, Joanne told herself. The woman's eyes were closed and her mouth was moving, although she couldn't make out what she was saying. Joanne bowed her head in respect, but she didn't know what kind of prayer she was supposed to say. Ian Decker hadn't deserved to die. She had a bitter taste in her mouth, not just from the smell of rotting flesh. She wanted to shake her fist at the heavens, shout at the top of her lungs, demand that God put an end to the violence, the senseless deaths. She didn't mind fighting the battle. She was just tired of losing. When would good finally triumph over evil? Would she ever see such a thing in her lifetime? With her own hand, Joanne swept the earth off the corpse's abdomen, making certain she didn't touch anything that resembled a wound. She suddenly heard a voice inside her head. Her own thoughts, she assumed.

Elizabeth opened her eyes and stared out over the field. Pauline and Joanne continued digging around the lower half of the body. Between Crenshaw's murder, her daughter's miscarriage, and now this, Joanne was afraid she might faint. Elizabeth brushed more dirt off the face, then pushed herself to her feet.

"This is not my son!"

"What?" Joanne said, her jaw dropping.

Pauline leaned over and stared hard at the face. "She's right," Pauline said. "This isn't my brother."

"Are you certain?" Joanne asked, repositioning herself so she could get a better look at the body. The features looked familiar, but she had to agree with the other women. Ian Decker's face was more elongated. And his eyes were set farther apart. "I think I know who this is," Joanne said, picking up the man's arm and looking at his ring finger. "It's Gary

Rubinsky. I recognize the ring." She tried to remove the ring to get a better look at the insignia. When she realized the finger might detach from the joint, she spat on the edge of her shirt and wiped the ring clean. "See," she said, motioning for Pauline and Elizabeth to come closer, "Gary Rubinsky graduated from Ventura High School. This is his senior ring."

Elizabeth made the sign of the cross, certain her prayers had been answered. "It's a miracle, don't you see? They couldn't kill my son. God wouldn't let them. Instead, God took the life of this terrible man. This is divine justice."

Joanne felt lightheaded, caught up in a swirl of emotion and confusion. "Where is Ian, then?"

"Alive!" Pauline said, walking back toward the car. "I told you all along he wasn't dead. No one ever listens to me."

THIRTY

ELI WAS shocked when he saw Joanne's Lexus parked behind a Chevy Blazer on a farm road three miles from the Interstate 5 exit. A slender brunette was leaning against the side panel of the Blazer, her face smudged with dirt. "Don't tell me the sheriff only sent one guy out here," Pauline said, squinting at the big man over the top of her sunglasses. "What are you going to do? Throw the body into the back of your pickup truck?"

"Daniel Stewart," Eli said, thinking the woman was a Ventura detective. "Is Joanne Kuhlman here?" He didn't want to make a mistake and try to pass himself off as Marvin Brown. Daniel Stewart was another of his aliases. Once he left town, the Connors name would drop to the bottom of the list. He would never be able to use his real name again. "You mentioned a body. . . ."

"My name is Pauline," she said. "Ian Decker is my brother. We found a man buried out there, but it isn't Ian. We're almost positive it's Gary Rubinsky. Are you a police officer?"

"No," Eli said, experiencing an uncomfortable sensation in the pit of his stomach. He'd been so certain he would find Ian's body, he'd even placed a call to Arnold Dreiser, arranging to meet him later that evening at the Cliff House restaurant to collect the rest of his money. Rubinsky was either one hell of an actor, or a far more sophisticated criminal than they realized. Why would Tom direct him to his brother's grave? He could understand Tom being angry that Gary had betrayed him. Nonetheless, how could he have arranged for someone on the outside to kill Gary and bury him in only a matter of hours? Even if such were true, why would he want Eli to find him? Had Tom killed both Ian and Gary? Tom was already in custody at the time of the Crenshaw homicide, and from what Eli understood, Gary was the prime suspect. The situation was mind-boggling. With Gary in the ground, Tom in the county jail, and Willie Crenshaw in the morgue, the only remaining suspect was Ian Decker. "Who identified the body as Gary Rubinsky?"

"I've known Gary for years," Pauline said. "One of my girlfriends even dated him. I mean, he isn't in the best condition, but he looks like Gary and he's wearing a high school ring from the school Gary attended."

"Have you heard any news about your brother?"

"No," Pauline said. "He'll turn up eventually."

Eli's gut instinct told him to turn tail and run. He'd been in the wrong place at the wrong time before, and the results had been disastrous. For all he knew, Tom Rubinsky could have led him into a trap. He should have never taken Arnold Dreiser to the *Nightwatch*, even though most of the weapons he had on board were kept hidden. Dreiser was both smart and curious, a dangerous combination for a man with Eli's history.

Pauline walked to the other side of the car to make a phone call. Eli could see Elizabeth and Joanne off in the distance. Regardless who was buried out there, how had the three women managed to find the grave before him? They were at least fifteen miles away from the area where the original search had been concentrated. His mind hurled him back in time, to that hot summer night in Washington that had forever changed his life.

Tuesday, August 24, 1994, 10:14 P.M.

Eli was in his apartment, stretched out in his recliner watching television. His wife, Abby, an elementary schoolteacher, was grading papers in the spare bedroom they used as an office. They'd been married for three years. As soon as the agency assured him his post with the Washington bureau was permanent, the couple intended to buy a house in the suburbs and start a family. The phone rang, but Eli ignored it, thinking it was Abby's younger sister, Martha. They spoke on the phone almost every night.

Abby appeared in the doorway. "It's for you," she said, her brows furrowed with concern. At thirty-two, she was a statuesque woman with large, expressive eyes and gorgeous skin. She had tried to talk her husband into leaving the agency, terrified that something was going to happen to him. With his technical skills, he could have easily obtained a job in the private sector, but things were looking good for him. His last performance review had been excellent, and his supervisor had all but promised him a promotion. The agency provided excellent benefits, and Eli enjoyed his work.

Eli picked up the portable phone. "Loyd Berman," a familiar voice said. "You've been assigned to deliver a document for the attorney general's signature."

"Where's the document now?" Eli picked up a pen and a notepad off the coffee table. He knew better than to complain, just as he knew not to question the nature of the document. CIA agents weren't used as messengers unless the material was classified and the principals involved were high-level government officials.

"At Senator Weinberg's house," Berman said, rattling off an address. "Milhouser attended a state dinner tonight. He'll be waiting for you in his office at eleven. Once he signs the document, deliver it to the guard shack at the Hall of Justice. They've also been notified. Bring a signed receipt when you come to work in the morning."

Eli disconnected, stepping into his shoes and heading to the bedroom to strap on his service revolver and pick up his wallet and identification. Abby came out of the bathroom in her nightgown, her hair in a ponytail on the top of her head, her face void of makeup. "How long are you going to be gone?" she asked. "Should I wait up for you?"

"I'll be back before midnight," Eli told her, walking over and pulling her into his arms. He kissed her on the lips, then playfully patted her on the buttocks. "Even if you go to sleep, I might have to wake you."

"I'll wait up," Abby told him, smiling seductively.

As he rode down in the elevator to the underground parking garage, Eli didn't anticipate any problems. Senator Weinberg's town house was only a few blocks away. Overall, the capital was a small town, a small town crammed full of monuments, politicians, and people whose jobs were either to protect them or to serve them.

The senator's housekeeper met Eli at the door. Weinberg came down the stairs in his bathrobe and personally handed Eli the package. "Sorry about this," he said, a stout man in his late sixties. "I got tied up on another matter."

Eager to get home to his wife, Eli had arrived at the Department of Justice thirty minutes early. The outer door to the attorney general's office was standing open, but the door to his private office was closed.

Eli took a seat, assuming the senator hadn't returned from his dinner. A few moments later, he heard a gunshot. Yanking his service revolver out of his shoulder holster, he'd kicked open the door to Roland Milhouser's office, finding two men standing over the attorney general's body. The men flashed Secret Service badges and ordered Eli to leave immediately, informing him that the attorney general had just committed suicide. One agent stood guard over the body while the other escorted Eli out of the building.

Eli called Loyd Berman from his cell phone and told him what had transpired. Berman told him to keep his mouth shut and bring the unsigned document to the office the following day. Eli heard news of the attorney general's death on television the next morning. The newscast said Roland Milhouser had shot himself in his study at his home in Georgetown.

Eli was certain that Milhouser had been murdered. Milhouser had not shot himself in his study in Georgetown, and this fact alone should have been enough to launch a major investigation. Fearful Berman might be involved, he'd gone straight to the head of the agency. The murder or cover-up, whichever it turned out to be, had been expertly executed. Security records at the Department of Justice listed no record of Eli signing in to enter the building, nor had Milhouser been logged in when he allegedly returned from the state dinner.

The weeks that followed were a nightmare. The agency placed Eli on sick leave, insisting he undergo counseling sessions with the agency's staff psychologist. With the help of a friend in the Secret Service, Eli spent weeks sorting through photographs of every Secret Service agent, both active and inactive. His conclusion was the men he had seen in Milhouser's office were imposters. He doubted if Milhouser would have killed himself in front of two Secret Service agents, and Eli had been present in the outer office when he'd heard the gunshot. The men Eli had seen had been the killers.

Senator Weinberg resigned his position and returned to his home in West Virginia. A new attorney general took office. Eli's friends in the agency told him to forget it, that whatever had happened was over his head. As Eli had told Joanne, Washington was a dangerous town.

Three months after the incident, Eli took his story to the *Washington Post*. After extensive research, the newspaper refused to print it, claiming they could find nothing to substantiate Eli's claim that Roland Milhouser had been murdered. Although they had no proof, the paper believed Milhouser had been having an affair with a younger woman. He'd also been seeing a psychiatrist and had been placed on antidepressant medication. All evidence pointed to suicide.

The next day, Eli received his first threat, a computer-generated letter telling him to stop prying into the death of Roland Milhouser or his wife would be killed. Eli presented the letter to his superiors at the agency. They examined it and found no fingerprints or other identifying information. The head of the agency suggested that Eli be placed on disability due to mental problems, ending his career in law enforcement. When Eli continued the investigation into Milhouser's death on his own, an unknown person fired at Abby as she exited her car at a shopping mall.

Eli cashed in his retirement, leaving the rest of the money in the savings account for his wife. He kissed Abby goodbye one morning and told her he was going out to look for a new job. He never went home again.

Why had the attorney general of the United States been murdered? Because he had been having an affair with the First Lady long before her husband had been elected president. It had taken Eli years to uncover the truth, but his sources were irrefutable. It had broken his heart to leave Abby behind, but he refused to allow the woman he loved to live on the run as he had done for the past seven years. Eli had been declared legally dead, and his wife had remarried. Although he'd finally learned the reason Milhouser had been murdered, he had never been able to identify the men who had killed him. The people responsible for Milhouser's death would not forget about Eli. Even today, he suspected they still had people attempting to find him.

Eli heard the shrill of a siren, and was jarred back to the present. He saw a string of emergency vehicles approaching. "I have to go."

Pauline asked, "What do you want me to tell Joanne?"

"Nothing." Eli rushed back to his truck and took off. As soon as he reached the freeway, he called Joanne on her cell phone.

"Pauline said someone was here asking for me," she said. "From the description she gave, I assumed it was you. Why didn't you stay? How did you know where to find me?"

"I was searching for Decker's body," Eli told her. "In case you've forgotten, that's what I was hired to do. I saw your car and stopped. How did you figure out where the grave was?"

"I didn't," she said. "Elizabeth told me to meet her here this morning. I offered to help out. She said they'd searched on the other side of the amusement park and found nothing. This morning she woke up and decided that the man who called her could have confused a McDonald's restaurant with a Carl's Junior, which meant we were searching in the wrong area. There's no doubt the body we found is Gary Rubinsky, and from the lack of decomposition, he hasn't been dead more than a day or two."

"Be careful, Joanne," Eli said. "We don't know who we're dealing with right now."

"You can say that again," she answered, completely baffled. "What happened to Ian Decker is the big question. We can't discount that he might have killed both Gary Rubinsky and Willie Crenshaw."

"Let the police do their job," Eli advised. "If Ian killed those two men, they probably deserved it. I talked to Tom at the jail last night. He swore Gary shot Ian in the parking lot of ABC Towing. I'm fairly certain Willie made the anonymous call to Elizabeth. From what Tom said, Willie drove them to that field to test fire the decoy gun. Willie's primary source for marijuana owns a small farm around there, so both Tom and Gary were familiar with this area. They must have thought it was a good place to bury a body."

"But Tom is in jail," Joanne argued, "and Gary is dead. Tom could have killed Gary, but he was in jail at the time of Crenshaw's murder. The only person who has been out of pocket the entire time is Ian Decker."

"Off the top of my head," Eli said, "I can only think of one possibility."

"Tell me."

"Gary could have run out of money," he said. "Maybe he tried to cut a deal with the mafia for the decoy gun. Instead of paying him, they killed him and took the gun. Stay in the courthouse where you belong. Everything about this case stinks. When I tell you goodbye, it'd be nice if you were alive."

"Are you leaving town?"

"Soon," Eli said, wishing he was already at sea. "I'm going to check one more lead. Unless it looks promising, I'm heading out."

"What about Ian? Arnold paid you to find him."

"Not every story has a happy ending." Eli said, a statement he knew all too well. "Let me go now. Page me if you need me. Don't worry, I'll see you before I leave town."

THIRTY-ONE

B Y SUNDAY morning, Leah was feeling fine. Mike had wanted to go to a friend's house after lunch, but Joanne told him that she had something she needed to discuss with both of them.

Joanne sat her children down in the family room. "Visiting hours are from seven to nine tonight at the jail," she told them, clearing her throat. "If you'd like to see your father, I'm willing to drive you."

The children were caught off guard. "Maybe we should go another time," Mike said, his face flushing. "Leah was, you know, sick yesterday and all."

"I'm all right," the girl said. "I want to see Dad." She turned to her brother. "Don't you want to see him, Mike?"

Joanne's son was silent, brooding. "I don't know," he said. "Dad never said he was sorry. When he calls, he still acts like he's some kind of big shot, like he's only in jail because someone else made a mistake. Mom's been through a lot. And he hurt me too. For two years, I thought my mother didn't love me. He's still never admitted that the awful things he told us weren't true."

Leah leaned over and touched her brother's arm. "Please go, Mike," she pleaded. "Dad loves you. The prison they send him to may be far away. We may not have a chance to see him again for a long time."

Leah leaned back in the chair, tossing her feet up on the ottoman. "What Dad did doesn't change the fact that he's our father. He changed our diapers, told us bedtime stories. He put together our toys at Christmas, taught us how to ride a bicycle. By not seeing him, we're erasing half of our life. Mom should see him as well. He's not an axe murderer."

"I agreed to drive you," Joanne said, shaking her head. "I admit you and Mike should see your father, but I have nothing to say to him."

Leah's eyes sparked with emotion. "I bet you have a lot to say to him," the girl argued. "You're mad as hell because of what he did. Why shouldn't you confront him? Why keep it bottled up inside? Maybe that's why you and I have trouble getting along sometimes. You associate me with Dad. Because I refuse to hate him, it's like I'm taking his side. And you're the one who told me it wasn't right to hate anyone."

"Some of what you said is true," Joanne said, looking down at her hands. "I guess I do see you as taking his side sometimes. I'll try to be more understanding in the future. I loved him. I tried to be a good wife to him. I never wanted our marriage to end. Seeing him would open up too many old wounds. I'm not emotionally prepared to deal with that just yet."

"Remember that book you used to read to me when I was a little girl?"

"I read you a lot of books," Joanne said, recalling the days when they were all together and happy.

"*Alice in Wonderland*," Leah told her. "Where the girl falls down the hole and finds herself in another world. Well, that's what happened to Dad. I don't know why he fell into that hole, why he started gambling and got himself in so much trouble. But that's the way I see it. He fell into a hole, and he couldn't get out."

Joanne bristled. "*Alice in Wonderland* is a children's book. Your father isn't a child."

"No," Leah corrected her. "That book was political satire. We studied it in school last semester. I was just trying to make a point, and like always, you don't want to listen."

"I am listening," her mother said. "I just don't agree with you."

"You have to do more than listen, Mother. You have to understand. Most of the time when I talk about Dad, you just clam up and walk away." She paused, and then proceeded. "I used to talk to Dad all the time. He told me the people at his work didn't appreciate him, that guys with a lot less experience than him were being promoted. He wanted to prove that he was smart, that he knew more than anyone realized. And he finally did it, didn't he? He invented that computer program. All these big companies wanted to buy it."

"Before your father invented this computer security program," Joanne told her, "he'd already started gambling and stealing money from his employer. All the money he made off the sale of his computer program is going to be lost. You know why? Because he built a house of lies. A house of lies always collapses."

Mike had been pondering the statements of his mother and sister. "I'll go," he suddenly said. "What time do we have to leave?"

"We should leave here by four," his mother told him. "We'll stop somewhere in L.A. and have dinner before we go to the jail."

Leah jumped up and hugged Mike, then walked over and embraced her mother. "I'm going to rest until it's time to go," she said, heading to her room.

The resiliency of youth was incredible, Joanne thought. The night before she had found her daughter in a blood-soaked bed. A day later, Leah was as perky as a cheerleader. Losing the baby had solved her problem, Joanne realized. She hoped Leah would keep her promise and not risk getting pregnant again.

The day was clear and sunny. Eli was huddled on the lower deck of the *Nightwatch* staring at a computer screen, the scrap of paper with Trudy's phone number on it beside his console. This was his last lead. He certainly couldn't take a chance and visit Tom Rubinsky at the jail again. He'd already taken too many chances.

He was still suspicious about how Elizabeth Decker had managed to find the grave. Eli didn't put a lot of stock in intuition or luck. Outside of the organized-crime scenario, he wondered if it was possible that Ian had murdered Gary, then called and told his mother where he'd buried the body. That Ian would want to get something as serious as a murder off his chest was compatible with his psychological profile. Attempting to extract information from Ian's mother would be an exercise in futility. Elizabeth would protect her son at all costs.

Eli tried calling Trudy's phone number, but there was no answer, not even a recording. Having a last name would have made things easier. The only way he could get her address was to hack into the phone company's database, which provided service to her area. After making a few calls, he'd discovered that the area of Los Angeles where she resided had previously been serviced by GTE, but several years ago GTE had merged and formed a company called Verizon. Hacking into a major communications company would be a time-consuming project. Eli searched the Internet, and found a dynamite program, far from legal yet precisely what he needed. By three o'clock Sunday afternoon, he had her full name and address. Her name was Trudy Gilbert, and the address was 555 Sheffield Drive, Unit 369.

Having no idea when his subject might return, Eli packed a cooler with soft drinks and sandwiches. Arnold Dreiser had paged him several times, but he had not replied. He couldn't demand payment of the remaining ten thousand since he had not yet recovered the body of Ian Decker. Additionally, Eli wasn't certain where Arnold Dreiser stood. The only person he felt certain he could trust was Joanne.

Dropping the dinghy into the water, for the first time Eli wished he had installed an outboard motor. He hadn't been sleeping well lately, and would have to expend an enormous amount of energy to get to shore. Because of the great weather falling on the heels of the heavy rains of week before, the sea was filled with boaters. He longed for the azure waters of Bali, stretching out on the beach and relaxing, far from the problems of the civilized world. Years ago, he'd discovered an isolated island, far from the luxury hotels and ports where all the cruise ships docked. Almost everyone in the small village were natives. He was ready to toss down rum and Cokes in the village bar, possibly wrap his arms around the smooth, warm skin of a beautiful, joy-filled woman. The farther away a person went from civilization, the closer they got to paradise.

Sunday, February 18, 2001, 1:30 P.M.

Eli was parked on Sheffield Drive, about to doze off. He'd already emptied the cooler, and the boredom of sitting and staring at an apartment complex was about to lull him to sleep. A Mustang convertible suddenly roared past him into the parking garage, driven by a strikingly pretty young woman with long, dark hair. Eli exited the Toyota and followed her through the maze of buildings that made up the Coronado apartment complex. He stood several feet away as the woman stopped in front of the door to apartment 369, reaching in her purse for her keys. Bingo, he thought, knowing he'd located Trudy Gilbert. Before she entered the apartment, Eli rushed up to her, flashing the phony ID he'd used at the jail. "Detective Brown," he said. "I need to see some identification."

"What did I do?" Trudy asked, reaching into her purse again for her license.

Once Eli had confirmed that he had the right person, he said, "We can talk inside if you'd like. I don't want to embarrass you in front of your neighbors."

"Fine," Trudy said, kicking open the door.

The apartment was lavishly furnished, with velvet sofas and marble tables. "I'm sorry," Trudy told him, smiling sweetly. "I have to go to the bathroom."

"No problem," Eli said, dropping down on one of the sofas. From the looks of the apartment, he assumed she was a working girl. He occupied himself by flipping through the pages of a magazine when he suddenly saw Trudy standing over him, a 9mm Ruger in her outstretched hands. "Don't move," she said. "Put your hands over your head."

Eli had made some poor decisions in his lifetime, but this might end up being the worst. He followed her instructions, raising his arms over his head. Trudy walked over and flipped open his jacket, snatching his .45 out of his shoulder holster and dropping it into one of the pockets of her white leather jacket.

"Now get out," she said, motioning toward the door with the gun.

"Wait a minute," Eli said, standing. "I just want to talk to you. I'm not here to arrest you."

"Out!" Trudy shouted. "Leave or I'll shoot you."

"No problem," Eli said, walking toward the door.

A male voice called to her from the other room, and Trudy was momentarily distracted. Eli lunged at her, twisting her arms behind her back and forcing her to the floor. He removed the 9mm from her hand, then reached into her pocket and retrieved his Smith & Wesson.

"Who's in the other room?" Eli said, releasing the safety on his revolver and pointing it at the bedroom door.

"You don't understand," Trudy cried. "They shot him. He would have died if it hadn't been for me. I didn't have a choice. Gary was going to kill me."

Eli yanked Trudy to a standing position, then shoved her toward the bedroom. Ian Decker was propped up in bed with several pillows behind his head. His skin was ashen, and there was no doubt he'd been seriously injured. After depositing Trudy in a chair, Eli went to check on Decker. "Who shot you?"

"Gary Rubinsky," Ian said. "Who are you?"

"I was hired by your attorney to find you," Eli told him. "Have you been treated at a hospital?"

"No," Ian said weakly. "Trudy put some medicine and bandages on my back. She said if I went to the hospital, the police would arrest both of us."

Eli sat down on the edge of the bed. Gently rolling Ian onto his side, he removed the bandages and examined the gunshot wound. The entrance wound was only a few inches to the left of his spine. "The bullet has to be removed," he told Trudy, placing his palm on Ian's forehead. "He's burning up with fever. He needs medical treatment immediately. He'll die if he doesn't go to the hospital."

Trudy hung her head and began sobbing. "I don't want him to die."

"She killed Gary in self-defense," Ian said, craning his neck around. "She did it for me. She's never done anything wrong. People think she's a prostitute, but she isn't. She's an actress. Her father pays her rent."

"Tell me how this happened," Eli said, gently rolling Ian over again and repositioning his pillows. "I can't be here when the ambulance comes. I need to know the truth in order to help you."

"I found the gun," Ian said. "That gun that looked like a cell phone."

"Where is the gun now?"

"I don't know about the gun Gary had," Ian said. "But Trudy's father gave her a gun a long time ago, right after she moved out on her own. He's a gun collector."

"What happened the night you were shot?"

"After I found the gun," Ian told him, "I knew Gary and Tom had robbed the Quick-Mart. Before then, I was stupid. They had convinced me two other men had pulled off the robbery, that they were just inside the store buying beer at the time. The night I got shot, Gary and I were fighting in the motel room. Tom pulled Gary off of me, and then they started going at each other. I saw the gun on the floor near a stack of money. Because I didn't know it was a gun, I was going to use it to call my mother. Gary and Tom both started shouting at me." He winced in pain. "They were afraid I was going to shoot them."

"Slow down," Eli said, handing him a glass of water. He picked up a bottle of pills off the nightstand, glancing over at Trudy. "What are these?"

"Codeine," she said. "The dentist gave them to me when I had my wisdom teeth extracted. I gave him a pill about four hours ago."

Eli opened the bottle and poured out two pills, handing them to Ian. "Take these, then keep talking."

"I put the gun in my pocket, but Gary got it away from me," Ian said, handing back the glass of water after he'd swallowed the pills. "We all three left in the Chrysler. Gary said they were going to take me home. I told them they had to take the car back to my mother's business. When we took it, they said we were only borrowing it. We drove into the lot and got out of the car. Gary said something to me. I think he said he saw my uncle Carl in the office. When I turned around to look, he shot me in the back."

"Then what happened?"

"I passed out," Ian said, reliving that awful night. "When I came to, I thought I was in a coffin. Then I must have been delusional or something because I imagined I was with Trudy at my apartment. I came to again because the car was bouncing around. That's when I realized I was in the trunk. I'm not sure exactly what happened, but the car suddenly stopped moving. I waited, thinking they were just going to leave me there and not come back. I finally found a tire tool and used it to pry open the trunk. As soon as I got out, I saw Gary and Tom inside the office. I closed the trunk and crawled several aisles over, hiding underneath another car."

"Didn't they see you?

"No," Ian said. "They were inside the office. When they came out, they started arguing again. Tom drove the Taurus over where the Chrysler was parked. When Gary opened the trunk and saw I was gone, he went nuts. Tom just left him there and drove off. I saw a police car pass by, but the officer didn't stop. Gary must have seen the cop car too. He got into the Chrysler and left."

"How did Trudy get involved?"

"I managed to walk to the office," Ian explained. "They had left the door unlocked when they went in to get the keys to the Taurus. I was afraid to call the police because I knew that Gary and Tom had robbed the Quick-Mart. Since they shot me, I had no idea what kind of crimes they might have committed. Gary and Tom told me no one would ever believe that I didn't know that they were committing crimes, and the court would send me to prison. I was afraid to call my mom because her phone might have been tapped. I didn't know who else to call, so I called Trudy."

Trudy spoke up, "As soon as I got to the storage lot, I wanted to call the police and an ambulance, but Ian refused. I helped him to the car and brought him to my apartment. The place where he was shot didn't look that bad, and the bleeding had almost stopped. I thought if I put antiseptic on it and took care of him, he'd be alright." She stopped speaking and coughed. "I think I'm getting sick. I don't feel well."

Eli was trying to put the pieces of the crime together in his mind. "I still don't understand how Gary Rubinsky got buried in Valencia."

"We heard on TV that the police thought Ian was dead and that they were searching over by Magic Mountain," Trudy said. "Then we heard that Tom had been arrested. Gary called Sunday night, wanting me to let him stay here. I couldn't let him stay here because of Ian."

Eli recalled the phone call he'd made to Trudy from the jail. "Why didn't you just hang up on him?"

"Gary knew where I lived," Trudy said, sucking in a deep breath. "I knew if I didn't do something, he'd show up on my doorstep. He sounded like he was high on drugs. He told me something had happened and he had to get out of town or find a place to hide where no one would find him. He tried to hit me up for money also. I agreed to meet him at a Denny's restaurant on the outskirts of L.A."

"Where exactly did you meet?"

"Near the 405 and the Interstate 5 Interchange," Trudy told him, wrapping her arms around her chest. "We never went inside the restaurant. Gary insisted that we talk in my car," she said. "He told me he'd traded the Chrysler for Willie's Jeep. I was confused because the Jeep used to belong to Gary and Tom. My radio was on and the news report said a man named William Crenshaw had been murdered that morning. I knew Gary had killed Willie. I could tell by the way he was acting. I told him to get out of my car." She paused and placed her hands over her face. A few moments later, she continued, "He pulled out this funny looking thing that looked like a cell phone. Ian had already told me about the decoy gun. I have a license to carry the Ruger. My dad didn't want anyone to hurt me. He wanted to make sure I was safe. I usually keep the gun in the side panel of my car. Since all this happened, I've been carrying it in my purse. I know how to use it because my dad used to take me to the firing range." She paused and gulped air. "I knew Gary was going to kill me. I was terrified. He told me to start driving. We got on the Interstate 5, and then he told me to get off on one of the exits on the other side of Magic Mountain. As soon as Gary told me to stop the car, I pulled out my gun and shot him in the chest. If I hadn't shot him, I'd be dead."

"And then you buried him?"

"Yes," Trudy said. "I knew the area we were in was close to where the police had been searching for Ian. I thought the police would find Gary and think Willie, Tom, or someone else had killed him. I pushed Gary out of the car, then I dragged him as far from the road as I could."

"You're not that big," Eli said, rubbing his chin. "Gary was a big man."

"Let me tell you something," Trudy said emphatically. "After you kill someone, you're wound up enough that you could carry a horse. Not only that, I'm stronger than you think. I lift weights at the gym. Besides, I didn't drag him that far. The ground was soft, so I just dug out a spot with my hands, then kicked a lot of dirt over him."

"I wanted to call my mother," Ian said, adjusting a pillow behind his neck. "Trudy didn't think we should take a chance. She said I should wait for things to calm down, particularly because my mother was so involved with the police."

"Incredible," Eli said, picking up the phone to call both the police and an ambulance. "You'll both be okay," he continued, once he had made the calls. "The hospital will remove the bullet, sew Ian up, pump him full of antibiotics and before you know it, he'll be as good as new."

"What about me?" Trudy said, pointing at her chest. "They're going to send me to prison, aren't they?"

"You killed Gary in self-defense," Eli said. "Not only that, you saved Ian's life. You may have to sweat it out for a few days. Burying the guy and not reporting the crime may cause you some problems. Eventually, you'll be cleared."

Trudy chewed on a fingernail. "How do you know that?"

"Because your story will match up with the facts," Eli said. "All you have to do is give the police the same statement you just told me. Your picture will be plastered in all the newspapers, and you'll probably end up starring in a TV series." He stopped and smiled at Ian. "Just don't forget about your friend."

Trudy walked over and stroked Ian's cheek. "I love Ian," she said. "He's the best thing that ever happened to me. We made a pact. If either of us has to serve time in jail, we'll wait for each other. All the other guys liked me for the way I look. Ian loves me for myself. Even if I got old and fat, Ian would still love me."

Ian Decker pulled Trudy's hand to his mouth and kissed it, his face glowing. "When this is all over, we're going to get married."

"Sounds like a plan," Eli said, ducking his head as he walked out of the bedroom and disappeared through the front door of the apartment.

THIRTY-TWO

Sunday, February 18, 2001, 3:15 P.M.

DREISER CALLED Joanne, wanting her to go to dinner with him. "I can't," she said. "I'm going to take Mike and Leah to see their father tonight."

"What brought you to this decision?"

"Because I think it's the right thing to do," Joanne said. "Come over now, if you can. We can go for a walk on the beach. It's a gorgeous day."

"I'm on my way."

Approximately thirty minutes later, Joanne and Arnold were strolling near the water's edge. Joanne had her jeans rolled up several inches, and was darting in and out of the surf, laughing and playing like a kid. Arnold squatted on the sand, smiling as he watched her. He'd never seen her this relaxed. She was more lovely than he had ever imagined. His cell phone rang. He was inclined to ignore it, but habit forced him to answer it.

"This is Eli," a deep voice said. "I hope you're not the kind of man who goes back on his word. You owe me ten grand, Dreiser."

"You found Ian Decker's body?"

"I've got even better news that," Eli boasted. "Ian is at Good Shepherd Hospital in Los Angeles. All they need to do is a little patch-up work and he'll be fine. He took a bullet in the back, but it doesn't look as if it did any serious damage. That decoy gun doesn't have a scope. It's hard to site a target."

"Ian is alive!" Dreiser shouted to Joanne. She rushed over and placed her head next to Dreiser's in order to listen in as Eli continued telling them what had transpired.

"The only outstanding issue is the decoy gun," Eli said. "The girl claims she doesn't have it. Everything she and Ian told me seemed to be the truth. Somewhere down the line, I guess the gun will surface."

"The police already recovered the gun," Joanne told him, taking the phone out of Dreiser's hands. "When this Gilbert girl buried Rubinsky, she must have buried the gun with him. Maybe it got caught up in the folds of his jacket. The crime lab also found a piece of green fabric from the motel room stuck on one of Gary's fingers. Since the curtain was ripped when they first searched the room, and the fabric has both Ian's and Gary's prints on it, they must have struggled over the gun. Both of their hands were probably sweaty. We'll know more once the lab completes the DNA testing."

"All that's left then is for us to settle up," Eli said after Joanne had handed the phone back to Dreiser. "I'm itching to get out of here."

"You've earned the money fair and square," Dreiser told him. "You'll have to wait until tomorrow if you want cash though."

"No problem," Eli said. "Oh, the police have already notified Elizabeth. When I called the hospital to get an update on Ian's condition, they told me his mother and sister were already there."

"Where do you want to meet tomorrow?" Dreiser was ecstatic. "Same place and time?"

"Always," Eli said, disconnecting.

Joanne wrapped her arms around Dreiser's neck. Seizing the opportunity, he clasped her tightly and kissed her. "When will you be home tonight?" he asked. "We might not be able to have dinner, but we could meet somewhere for a drink."

"Come now," she said, standing and taking his hand. "I want to introduce you to my children. I'll call you as soon as we get back from Los Angeles. We'll meet right here. I'll leave a note at the gate to let you in just in case I'm late. The moon will be out tonight. I'll bring a bottle of wine, and we'll celebrate."

Dreiser stopped walking, anxious about meeting her children. "I should go to the hospital now and see Elizabeth."

"All I'm asking for is ten minutes," Joanne said, falling serious. "This is a big thing for me, particularly since I'm taking Mike and Leah to see their father tonight. We're going to have to leave right away. I don't want to take a chance on getting stuck in traffic."

Dreiser thought he understood. She didn't want her children to develop false hopes that she might reconcile with their father. By bringing a man into their home, she would be making a strong statement. "I'm not the token boyfriend, I hope."

"No," Joanne said, her eyes sparkling in the sunlight, "you're the only boyfriend."

Joanne parked to the rear of the Los Angeles County jail, and Mike and Leah walked beside her to the visitors' entrance. No matter how old or new a detention facility was, there was always a depressing squalor to it. Leah stayed close to her mother, walking with her head down. Joanne saw Mike looking up at the barred windows.

Inside the building, they had to stand in a long line to register. Babies cried, toddlers squirmed in their mother's arms, rough-looking men and women slouched in the plastic chairs, waiting to visit friends or family members. The longer a person was incarcerated, Joanne speculated, the fewer visits they received from friends. Most of the people assembled in the visitors' waiting room had come to see fathers, sons, sisters, mothers, uncles, aunts. They had the weary look of obligation on their faces. After Mike and Leah had signed in, they found three chairs and sat down. "You'll have to go in separately," Joanne explained. "Your father will be behind the glass. There will be a phone . . ."

Mike cut her off. "We've seen it on TV, Mom. We know what to expect."

"Are you going to see Dad?" Leah asked anxiously.

"No," Joanne told her. "I didn't put my name on the list."

"I think you should," Leah continued. "I know you're not married to him anymore. And I'm not asking you to forgive him. Something about him must have been right. You married him. You had two children with him. It's not like you can forget about him completely."

Joanne felt as if she couldn't breathe. The room was too crowded, and there wasn't enough ventilation. She wondered if she was experiencing a panic attack. She stared at the clock on the wall, listening to the minutes tick off inside her head. Finally they called Leah's name. She looked over her shoulder at her mother as she walked to the door.

"She shouldn't have asked you to see him," Mike said, leaning forward over his knees. "Maybe you bringing that guy to the house today made her mad." He saw the perspiration on his mother's brow. "She upset you, didn't she?"

"I'm fine," Joanne lied. "Will you be okay if I step outside and get some air? I won't be long. Listen for your name."

"Go on, Mom," Mike said, patting her on the shoulder. "No one's going to hurt me inside the jail."

When Joanne stepped outside the door, she found herself in a group of smokers. She didn't want to get too far away. She decided she could breathe better inside. By the time she returned, Leah was already back. She must have been outside longer than she thought. Mike's name was called next, and he shuffled to the door.

"Dad looks pretty bad," Leah told her, pulling out a tissue and blowing her nose. "All he did was keep telling me how much he loved me. He said once this trial is over, he'll be moved to Ventura. Then we can visit him more often. I'm glad I didn't tell him about what happened last night."

Joanne rested her head against the wall. The events of the past two days were taking their toll. She doubted if she'd feel up to a romantic rendezvous with Arnold, but it was nice to know he would be waiting for her to call. There would be other days and other nights. "Are you feeling alright?"

"I'm still a little weak," Leah said, sighing. "I learned my lesson."

They waited in silence. Approximately fifteen minutes later, Mike came out and they left. The boy didn't mention anything he'd discussed with his father, and Leah reached over and turned on the radio when they got into the car. Halfway to their house, Joanne couldn't stand the oppressive atmosphere inside the car. "Turn the radio off," she told Leah.

"Is something wrong?" her daughter asked.

"No," Joanne said. "I just want to tell you something. Your father has been charged with a multitude of felonies. None of them involve violence, which falls in his favor. The prisons are overcrowded. Most of the judges tend to be fairly lenient with white-collar offenders, particularly if they have no previous criminal history. Because I love you, and you love your father, I'm going to speak to the district attorney in Ventura. What I'm trying to tell you is that I'm willing to withdraw my complaint on the child-stealing charges."

"Does that mean Dad won't go to jail?" Leah said excitedly.

"All it means is that he might be discharged on those particular charges," Joanne told her. "I'd appreciate it if you don't mention this conversation to your father. As long as a crime was committed, the state has the right to prosecute even if the victim withdraws their complaint."

"Why are you doing this?" Mike said from the backseat. "We had a great life and Dad ruined it. Both Leah and I believed the things he told us about you. How do you think I felt when Dad told me my own mother wanted to be with some guy more than she did her own kids? How do you think I felt when you never called, not even on my birthday? I used to lock myself in my room and cry. I thought I'd done something terrible and caused you to hate me. Tonight, for the first time, Dad admitted that none of that stuff was true."

"He told me the same thing," Leah said, giving her mother a sheepish look. "The fact that you would even consider helping Dad shows what a great person you are. I'm sorry for the way I've been acting since we came home. I know Dad spoiled me for a reason. The more he did for me, the less guilty he felt. By making a fuss over me and buying me everything I wanted, I thought he was the greatest father on Earth. He wasn't even doing those things for me. He was doing them for himself. Even if he hadn't been embezzling or gambling or whatever, I know now that a good parent doesn't raise their children that way. A person is never going to get everything they want in life. A kid needs to learn to handle disappointment as well as success."

Joanne felt tears forming in her eyes. Something remarkable had occurred during the past two days. She envisioned Elizabeth Decker at her son's bedside, a child she had been certain was dead. Arnold Dreiser, a handsome, intelligent, and appealing man seemed to genuinely care about her. But those things were external. The most important thing was her relationship with her children.

What Joanne had been fighting so hard to achieve had finally happened. Inside the small space of the car, there was an overwhelming infusion of love. And it wasn't just Joanne's love for her children. It was Mike's love for his mother, combined with his love for his sister. And it was Leah's love for her brother, as well as her love for her mother. Whatever disparaging comments the children had made regarding their father, Joanne didn't sense any bitterness. They had all reached another level of understanding and acceptance. Whatever Doug had taken away, Joanne was reclaiming. No matter how her relationship with Dreiser progressed—or how many years her former husband spent in prison—Joanne, Mike, and Leah had finally merged again as a family.

EPILOGUE

JOANNE, ARNOLD, Mike, and Leah had just finished packing the last box for the move. Eli was sitting on the front porch by himself finishing off a bottle of champagne.

Dressed in shorts and a tank top, Joanne flung open the screen door, then marched over and snatched the plastic glass out of his hand. "Don't get drunk," she said, her hands on her hips. "You'll set a bad example for the kids. Not only that, the party isn't supposed to start until seven. You bailed out on us two hours ago."

"Hey," Eli said, stretched out in the recliner with his arms over his head, "you invited me to a barbecue. No one said I had to work all day for a few hotdogs and some cheap champagne. Where did you buy this stuff? Kmart? I'm not even certain it's champagne. Why didn't you just buy a case of beer?"

Joanne blew her bangs off her forehead. "We're not having hotdogs," she said. "Arnold bought steaks." She took a sip out of his glass, then wrinkled her nose. "You're right," she told him. "This stuff is awful. Run down to the liquor store and pick up some beer. We're going to trade off taking showers. I'll make certain there's some hot water left if you hurry."

"I should have left for Bali two weeks ago," Eli grumbled, pushing himself to his feet. "After I spent two years tracking down your ex-husband, you talked the DA into dismissing the child-stealing charges."

"Doug received a fifteen-year-prison sentence," Joanne told him. "He's still facing charges in other jurisdictions. His attorney thinks the other cases will tack on another five or six years. I did it for Mike and Leah, Eli. You were wrong about the money, by the way."

"How so?"

"Jorge Baudelaire, the person responsible for the offshore account, turned out to be an honest man," she said, smiling. "We don't know how much will be left after the money Doug took or gambled away is reimbursed, but whatever is left will go into a trust for the children. That is, after we pay the taxes."

"Amazing," Eli said. "How did you manage that? Weren't you divorced when Doug made that deal with Forrest Hoyt Technologies?"

"Nope," Joanne said. "The divorce wasn't final until a few months ago."

"What about the Decker case?" Eli asked. "I stuck my neck on the line, and the guy wasn't even dead. When I passed myself off as an officer at the jail, I took a big chance."

"You got paid," Joanne said, uncertain if he was joking or serious. "I wish I had an extra twenty grand in my bank account right now. For all I know, that might be all that will be left of the fifty million. If you don't stop complaining, I'll report you to the IRS."

"You're something else," Eli said, tousling her hair. "I should send you a bill for watching your kids last week, let alone all the house hunting I did for you. That's a nice little place you bought. Living a few blocks away from Dreiser should get things rolling in the right direction. Maybe I'll see a wedding ring on your finger the next time I come back to the States."

Joanne threw her arms around his neck, kissing him on the cheek. "You're the best, Eli," she said. "Mike and Leah had a wonderful time last week. With the house torn apart for the move and the pressure of Tom Rubinsky's trial, not having to worry about the children was a lifesaver. Mike wants to be a detective now. Leah has been trying to talk Arnold into buying a boat. They loved spending their spring break on the *Nightwatch*."

"They're good kids," Eli said, a hint of sadness appearing in his dark eyes. "What's going to happen to Tom? In a way, I feel sorry for him."

"Eighteen robberies," Joanne said, arching an eyebrow. "I don't feel sorry for anyone who participates in that many crimes. Doug was a criminal, but he didn't commit crimes of violence. Kennedy might offer him a deal, but I doubt if he'll consider anything under fifteen years."

Eli started down the steps to go to the store. Joanne trailed after him.

"What's in Bali?" she asked. "Why don't you hang around, settle down? Arnold offered you a job with his law firm. You can't keep running forever."

Eli knew where Abby lived, that she no longer taught school. He knew her new husband was a dentist. He even knew their mortgage payment, that Abby drove a BMW and had learned how to play golf. In the first few years after he'd left Washington, he would dial her number from a pay phone from time to time just to hear her voice. Things were too sophisticated today. He couldn't afford to take such a risk. When his computer sleuthing had revealed his former wife was shopping on-line for baby furniture a few weeks back, Eli had been plunged into a paralyzing depression. For three days straight, he had remained in his bunk staring at the ceiling. He had told himself it was over. But in the back of his mind, there was always a glimmer of hope. Once he'd learned that Abby was expecting a child, he had to face reality. At his darkest moment, Joanne had paged him, pleading with him to take the children off her hands during the week they were out of school for spring break.

"You better get ready for your guests," Eli told her, opening the door to the Toyota.

"Elizabeth and Ian Decker cancelled," Joanne told him. "Ian's scheduled for an operation on his kidney tomorrow. They may have to remove it."

"Is he going to be all right?"

"The doctors assured Elizabeth he'll make a full recovery," Joanne said, leaning against the car. "I guess a person can get by fine with only one kidney. They couldn't operate until they cured the infection." She paused and then added. "Oh, before I forget, a single woman is coming to the party. I hope you brought some clean clothes."

"Now you're turning into a matchmaker," Eli said, scowling. "I'm leaving town next week."

"You said that two weeks ago, remember?" Joanne said, winking. "Anyway, I didn't have anything to do with it. Arnold bet me a thousand dollars that you'd cancel your trip because of this lady. She must be someone from his office."

"You folks are nuts," Eli said, backing out of the driveway. He suddenly heard a loud crunch. A silver Volvo had turned into Joanne's driveway as he was backing out. He got out of his car to survey the damage.

The other driver exited her car at the same time. Eli was dumbstruck, certain he was hallucinating. A tall, shapely woman, wearing a sarong dress and high heels, walked over and bent down to check out her front bumper. "It doesn't look that bad," she said, without turning around. "This is a rental car. I'm glad I decided to take out the insurance."

Eli felt woozy. It had to be the cheap champagne. Even her voice was the same. The woman turned around and smiled, two deep dimples in her cheeks. The headlights of the Volvo made it difficult for her to see Eli, but Eli could see her perfectly. "Abby," he said. "Tell me I'm not dreaming?"

"Elliot," the woman said, rushing over to him. "Is it really you?"

Eli folded her into his arms. "I thought you were dead," Abby said, pushing him away. "Where have you been? Why didn't you call me, at least let me know you were safe. My God, all these years . . ."

"I'll explain everything to you later," Eli told her. "They threatened to kill you because of what I saw. I loved you too much to let anything happen to you."

Abby began crying. "Why didn't you take me with you?"

"I've been living at sea all these years," Eli said. "Every six months, I have to change my name. I can't work at a regular job, open a bank account. I can't even vote. They killed an attorney general, Abby."

Eli reached over and tenderly wiped the tears off her face. "Where's your new husband?"

"We split up six months ago," Abby told him. "How did you know I got married?"

"Forget it," Eli said, his heart soaring. Then he remembered the baby furniture, and frowned. "But you're going to have his baby. Did the guy hurt you or something? If he did, I'll . . ."

Abby placed her palm on his chest. "Calm down," she said. "Randy didn't hurt me. What made you think I was pregnant?"

"I have your credit card number," Eli answered, still reeling with disbelief. He caught a whiff of her perfume, the same as always. "I can track almost everything you buy over the Internet. You ordered baby furniture two weeks ago."

"It was for my sister, Martha," Abby said, wrapping her arms around his waist. "I never stopped loving you, Elliot. I don't even know why I married that stupid jerk. All he wanted to do was play golf and drink martinis. I was hurt and lonely. I would have been better off alone. I don't think he loved me any more than I loved him."

"Why did he marry you?"

"Who knows," Abby said, looking down. "I think he just wanted someone to go to parties with him. He made me quit teaching, then he hardly ever came home."

The time for talk was over. Eli swept her up in his arms, carrying her around to the passenger seat of the Toyota. Abby began giggling. "Where are we going? An attorney named Arnold Dreiser paid for my airline ticket. I'm supposed to meet him here tonight. He represents an exclusive private school in Santa Barbara. He said they're looking for a new headmistress. I have my master's degree now."

Eli laughed with joy, depositing her into the seat. He'd create a new identity for Abby just as he had for himself. There was risk involved, but if Abby still loved him, somehow they would make it work. They'd go to the islands, Europe. People said New Zealand was a nice place. A lanky leg remained outside of the car. "Best legs in the universe," he said, stroking the smooth skin of her thigh. "Baby, you've got the only student you'll ever need."

"Oh, yeah," Abby said, grabbing hold of his shirt and pulling him closer. "And who is that, pray tell?"

"Me," Eli said, circling around to the other side of the car. When he realized Abby's rental car was blocking the driveway, he stepped on the gas and drove across the lawn.

Having already taken their showers and dressed, Dreiser and Mike were sitting shoulder to shoulder on the front steps. "Did you see that?" Mike yelped, placing his hands on top of his head. "Eli drove his truck across the lawn. Mom is going to have a cow. She said we had to leave everything in perfect condition."

Arnold draped his arm around the boy's shoulder. "Trust me," he said. "Eli will pay to take care of the yard. That was Abby, pal. You aren't going to see your friend Eli for the rest of the night. I think he and Abby are going to have their own party on the *Nightwatch*."

Mike's eyes lit up. "You mean we really did it?" he asked. "The lady in the pictures was the woman Eli left with?" When Dreiser nodded, the boy became tense. "You aren't going to tell him I went through his stuff, are you? I wasn't really snooping, I promise. I was just trying to find a deck of cards. When I found this drawer full of pictures and letters, I was curious. In the pictures, Eli looked so happy. I just thought if we could find his girlfriend, he might cheer up."

"You did good, Mike," Dreiser said, standing and stretching. "All we needed was her name and the city she lived in. Finding people these days isn't that difficult, and the picture of her standing in front of that school helped a lot. Now go get the sack of coals and the starter fluid. We've got to get this show on the road. There's some hungry people coming."

Leah walked out on the porch and twirled around in her new strapless dress. "How do I look?"

"Beautiful," Dreiser said. "Like a million bucks."

"Are you sure this dress doesn't make me look fat?"

"You look as skinny as a rail."

The girl disappeared back into the house. Joanne darted out in a low-cut pink top and a pair of white pedal pushers. "How do I look," she said, fingering her hair.

"Beautiful," Dreiser said, glancing over at Mike. "You look like an angel."

"Man," Mike said, dumping the coals into the barbecue pit, "you've got this girl stuff down pat."

Dreiser smiled, squirting starter fluid on the coals, striking a match, and watching as the flames leapt into the sky. He thought of Jake and wished his son could have been standing beside him. Then he reminded himself that Mike might be thinking the same thing about his father. Life didn't always work out the way a person expected, but at that very moment, life was good.

ACKNOWLEDGMENTS

I WOULD like to express my gratitude to the many people, angels, family members, doctors, and heaven-sent muses for providing me with the strength and inspiration to tell this particular story. Attaching names to all who have helped me would be impossible. The underlying issue in this novel—the plight of the mentally disabled within the criminal justice system—seemed to be of such great significance that the majority of this book was written in tremendous pain. I am now almost completely recovered, and eager to begin my next project.

To my agent, Peter Miller: Thank you for your friendship and support of my work since the publication of my first novel, *Mitigating Circumstances*. To my wonderful family here in California: Forrest Blake Skyrme; Jeannie Skyrme; Rachel Skyrme; William Taylor; Jean Taylor; Nick, Mark, and Ryan Taylor; Sharon and Jerry Ford; as well as my incredible mother, Ethel Laverne Taylor. To my Omaha family: Chessly Nesci, James Nesci, and Jimmy Nesci; Amy and Mike Hightree. To my Dallas family: Gerald Hoyt and Barbara Skyrme, as well as Remy Skryme. To my Colorado family: Linda and John Stewart. To my extended family in Santa Barbara: Pauline, Joann, Ann, Carol, and Virgil. For all the technical support and inspiration from John Paul Thomas and Jean Barnett of SDSI Business Systems, my partners in the *Fight to Write* enhanced CD-ROM and book soon to be released. To my former editor and friend,

Michaela Hamilton, in New York, as well as my present editor, Peternelle Van Arsdale. To my present and former assistants, Irene, Alex, Alexis, Mary, Chris, Geranamina, and all the others who have assisted me, I may not know your name, but I appreciate everything you have done on my behalf.